ChangelingPress.com

Beast/Hawk (Duet)

Harley Wylde

Beast/Hawk (Duet)

Harley Wylde

All rights reserved.
Copyright ©2021 Harley Wylde

ISBN: 9798471441798

Publisher:
Changeling Press LLC
315 N. Centre St.
Martinsburg, WV 25404
ChangelingPress.com

Printed in the U.S.A.

Editor: Crystal Esau
Cover Artist: Bryan Keller

The individual stories in this anthology have been previously released in E-Book format.

No part of this publication may be reproduced or shared by any electronic or mechanical means, including but not limited to reprinting, photocopying, or digital reproduction, without prior written permission from Changeling Press LLC.

This book contains sexually explicit scenes and adult language which some may find offensive and which is not appropriate for a young audience. Changeling Press books are for sale to adults, only, as defined by the laws of the country in which you made your purchase.

Table of Contents

Beast (Reckless Kings MC 1) 4
   Chapter One 5
   Chapter Two 18
   Chapter Three 33
   Chapter Four 48
   Chapter Five 58
   Chapter Six 70
   Chapter Seven 80
   Chapter Eight 92
   Chapter Nine 105
   Chapter Ten 116
   Chapter Eleven 124
   Epilogue 134
Hawk (Reckless Kings MC 2) 142
   Prologue 143
   Chapter One 148
   Chapter Two 164
   Chapter Three 180
   Chapter Four 193
   Chapter Five 207
   Chapter Six 223
   Chapter Seven 236
   Chapter Eight 255
   Chapter Nine 275
Harley Wylde 294
Changeling Press E-Books 295

Beast (Reckless Kings MC 1)
Harley Wylde

Lyssa -- I should have known I'd end up with a biker. Most of my friends sighed over men in suits. Not me. I always liked a bad boy in grease-stained jeans. Probably comes with being raised by a club President. My daddy didn't raise a fool, but my mother raised a dreamer. And if there's one thing I've dreamt about the last few years, it's Beast. He's big. All alpha. But more importantly, the first time I see him in person, the moment our lips touch, I know he's going to be mine. I might have been the princess of the Dixie Reapers, but I was meant to be his queen.

Beast -- A goddess walked into my clubhouse and turned my life upside down... in the best of ways. Just one problem. Well, two. The first is that my little pixie-sized honey isn't just any woman. Her daddy is the President of another club, and her grandfather is a world-renowned assassin. And secondly, trouble is on her heels. The punk who thinks he can take what's mine is easily dealt with, but going toe to toe with Torch and Casper VanHorne is enough to leave any man shaking in his boots.

Good thing I'm not just any man. I'm Beast. President of the Reckless Kings MC. And I'm the man who's going to claim Lyssa, even if I have to knock her up to do it.

Chapter One

Beast

Brick flashed his phone screen to me with a wide grin. "They look good, don't they?"

I nodded. What else was there to do? I wasn't so big an asshole I'd deny his sister any true happiness she could find. I'd wanted it to be with me, but after all she'd been through, she'd needed a clean break and a fresh start. Far the fuck from here.

"Kid looks cute."

"Yeah, she does. Charlotte keeps calling Jenna her miracle baby." Brick sighed. "I miss the hell out of her."

He wasn't the only one. I understood why Charlotte had left, even gave her my full support. Still hurt like a bitch, watching her taillights fade into the distance, knowing damn well she'd never set foot in this town, or even this state, ever again. She'd lost her baby, and the doctors had said she might not have another. She'd proved them wrong.

"How's what's-his-face?" I asked.

Brick snorted. "You don't like saying his name, do you?"

Nope. Not even a little. Every time Brick showed me pictures of Charlotte and her family, I thought about everything I'd lost the day she'd left. I'd been in love with her since long before I should have noticed her. Didn't matter. I wasn't what she needed. In the end, she'd settled in Alaska, found herself a nice, ordinary guy who worked for the National Park Service as a wildlife biologist. The guy made enough to take care of Charlotte and their daughter by legal means, and as much as I wanted to hate the man, he seemed like a decent sort.

Brick sighed. "Rob is doing fine. Got a promotion last week, in fact. Charlotte seemed excited."

Perfect. "Great! I'm sure Rob is the perfect husband for her, and the best dad ever."

"Look, brother. I'm sorry Charlotte left. I know you had feelings for her, but she's in a good place. Rob treats her like a queen, and she's far away from all the shit the club deals with. The only danger she might face is a fucking bear or wolf. And I mean the animal kind, not the humans we run across who are fucking rabid."

I knew he was right. Knew it, but didn't have to like it.

"Fine. She should have moved away from here, from the club. I'm glad she's safe and loved. I won't say I'm thrilled she's gone, but I'm happy for her."

It wasn't a complete lie. I really did want her to be happy, even if it wasn't with me. I could do without all the pictures of her new life. Brick liked showing off his sister and her kid, and I accepted it. Just didn't like it being shoved in my face every damn week.

"You ready for tomorrow?" Brick asked.

Not even close. "Did Torch say what the fuck he wanted?"

"You really haven't paid attention, have you? It wasn't Torch who called. It was Venom. The club needs a favor."

Of course, they did. Everyone wanted something. "What time are they arriving?"

"Any second. Something about wanting to rest tonight, then talk in the morning before they head out first thing."

"Guess I better drink up." I finished off my beer and got another. Didn't have anyone to blame for my shit mood except myself. If I'd made a move on

Charlotte sooner, she never would have gotten hurt. She'd have been mine, and I'd like to think we'd have been happy. Hindsight was a bitch.

It was unusual for a club to ask for a favor without giving any details. The Dixie Reapers were a good sort, so I wasn't worried they'd ask for more than I was willing to give. Even if it was a bit odd. They had clubs they were closer to, even tied to by blood. So why come here? For that matter, why not settle this shit over the phone? It wasn't exactly a short drive.

The clubhouse doors swung open and light spilled through the doorway, silhouetting a petite woman with curves in all the right fucking places. Hair black as pitch and skin white as snow. Fuck. I sat up a little straighter. Hadn't seen the likes of her around here before. Maybe today wasn't such a shit day after all.

She slowly turned her head, taking in the room. When she spotted Brick and me, she sauntered forward, the doors shutting behind her. My eyes adjusted to the dim interior again and I sucked in a breath. A tight black sweater clung to her like a second skin. Ripped denim molded to her shapely legs. The black boots on her feet were tiny but badass. She looked like a biker's wet dream.

"Dibs," I murmured, not taking my gaze off her.

Brick snorted. "Guess you're over Charlotte now."

If this angel gave me a chance? Possibly. I'd always have a place for Charlotte in my heart, but it didn't mean I planned to spend every night alone. I'd had my share of club whores since she'd left, but this woman... she wasn't the usual sort to stroll through our doors. She came closer, her jaw set and her stride purposeful. She was a woman on a mission.

When she stopped in front of me, I turned to face her fully. Her eyes were a dark blue, framed by thick sooty lashes. Put some red lipstick on her, and she'd look like Snow White. Perfection. My gaze skimmed over her before lifting to her face once more.

"You done?" she asked.

"Just getting started."

She snorted and folded her arms, pushing her breasts up. I wondered if she'd done it on purpose, or if she had no clue she'd just shoved them so high her sweater had dipped low enough to expose the black lacy bra she wore underneath.

"I'm starting to think it was a mistake to come here," she said.

The clubhouse doors opened again and the heavy tread of the men coming inside drew my attention. None wore cuts, but it didn't mean they weren't lethal. I could see they were each carrying multiple weapons, and the way the youngest was eyeing the woman in front of me said plenty. The little angel had brought trouble with her.

"Shit," she murmured. "I thought I had more time."

"More time for what?" I asked.

She sighed and focused on me. "I'm sorry. Please forgive me."

Before I could ask what she meant, she stepped between my legs and pressed tight against my chest. Her small hand wrapped around the back of my neck and she slammed her lips against mine. Fire licked along my nerve endings as she parted her lips and let me have a taste. Christ! I'd never have thought I'd like such a strong woman. Most flirted but didn't make such bold moves.

I wrapped an arm around her waist and held on

as I took over, dominating her mouth. She whimpered and moaned, her hold on me tightening. I heard the unmistakable click of a gun being cocked, but I didn't break the kiss right away. I enjoyed her a little more. When I pulled back, her lips were swollen, and her cheeks flushed. So fucking beautiful.

"What the fuck, Lyssa?" the younger one demanded.

She pressed her face against my chest before turning toward the men. I stood, keeping my hand at her waist. From the corner of my eye, I saw Brick had his gun trained on them, and the Prospect behind the bar had pulled out an AR-15. The others had their hands on their weapons. Every other brother in the room was on high alert. Whatever these assholes wanted with the woman -- Lyssa, he'd called her -- they couldn't have her. If they even tried to walk out of here with her, they'd die. It was clear she didn't want anything to do with them.

"I told you I wasn't available," she said. "You wouldn't listen. I don't play around with little boys, Tony."

His face turned purple and he snarled before lunging for the woman. I moved without thought, shoving her behind me. The man drew up short.

"I believe she's made it clear she's not interested. Run along, little boy."

The guy sneered at me. "Like she wants anything to do with an old man like you. You probably have saggy silver-haired balls and a shriveled-up dick."

I heard a slight snicker behind me, and then Lyssa was all out laughing. I glanced over my shoulder and saw a tear slip down her face, then another, as she tried to catch her breath. "Something funny?"

She struggled a moment but finally pulled

herself together. "Yeah. The fact he thinks he has anything I want. Besides, you aren't old. More like a well-aged bottle of scotch. All rugged and manly, sexy as hell, and just right for keeping me warm at night."

My eyebrows lifted and I fought not to smile. Yeah, I definitely liked this one. I turned back to the kid, who did his best to glower at her, even though he couldn't see much of her with the way I was standing. The fact the guy on his left still had a gun pointed at me didn't deter me. I knew even if he got a shot off, none of them would walk out of here alive. My club would make sure of it.

"Get the fuck out of my clubhouse, while you still can."

"I'm not scared of you," he muttered.

"Then you're stupid as fuck. I don't give a shit who you are. This is my place and I want you gone. You either listen and walk out on your own, or you can leave in pieces wrapped in plastic bags." I glanced at the man holding the gun. "And that's not a gun, youngster."

I nodded my head toward Kye, the Prospect behind the bar. "That is."

I could tell the punk wasn't sure if I was bluffing, but his gaze darted to Kye more than once. After a moment, he turned and left, his entourage following in his wake. I had a feeling he'd be back, but first, I needed to know what the fuck all that was about, and who the angel was who'd kissed me.

"All right, darlin'. Start talking."

"My name is Lyssa, like the asshat said, and I heard about your club from a friend. I know you helped Lilian when she ran from Dragon. Those guys have been hounding me for a while. I could have gone to my dad, but…" She shrugged a shoulder. "If I'd done that, he'd have locked me in my room and never let me leave."

"Exactly how old are you?" Brick asked.

"Eighteen."

I whistled. I knew I was older than her, but I hadn't realized by how much. My dick didn't seem to care about her age. I'd been hard as fuck since she'd walked in. Although, if she was friends with Lilian, that meant she might very well be friends with the Devil's Fury. I wasn't about to cause trouble with the other club by sticking my cock where I shouldn't.

I heard the pipes on several bikes pull up outside. When Saint, Zipper, and Grimm came inside, I knew I'd have to put the angel on hold. I'd sit down and hear what she had to say, figure out how best to help her, but right now I had Dixie Reapers to deal with. Whatever they wanted, I hoped it didn't take long.

"Are you shitting me?" Saint asked, his gaze narrowed on the woman who'd moved up beside me. "Lyssa, what the fuck are you doing here?"

"Visiting?" She moved a little closer to me, pressing her arm against mine.

Saint's gaze moved from her to me. I didn't like the look one bit, and I was about to tear into him. Then his next words froze me in place.

"Torch know you're fucking his daughter?" Saint asked.

Holy. Fucking. Shit.

Lyssa crossed her arms. "I'm not a kid, Saint. I can be with whoever I want. I don't need my daddy's permission. Or did all of you miss that memo when I packed my shit and left?"

"You were supposed to be in college," he said.

"Torch know she's here?" Zipper asked.

"He doesn't," Lyssa said. "And you aren't going to tell him. Because if you do, I'm going to tell Delphine about the chocolate lava cake you ate without sharing any with her last week."

Zipper opened and shut his mouth.

Grimm cocked his head to the side. "And how would you know about that since you've been gone for months?"

"I hired assassins when I was a kid. You really think hacking into the clubhouse feed is all that difficult?" she asked.

Wait. She'd what? I didn't dare take my eyes off the three Dixie Reapers, but I definitely wanted to know about the assassins. Why had she hired them? And how?

"No more time with Wire and Lavender. They've ruined you," Saint said.

"You're not my daddy, or my old man. You don't get a say," she said.

"Thank fuck," Saint muttered.

"As entertaining as all this is, I don't think you asked for my help because Lyssa is here. So why don't you get a drink, take a seat, and as soon as I have her settled, I'll hear what you have to say." I placed my hand at the small of her back. I had no clue what was going on, but I'd find out before the day was over.

I urged her to the front door, keeping my hand against her. My steps didn't even falter when Zipper decided to throw in a parting shot.

"Torch finds out you're fucking his little girl, you better make sure you have a ring on her finger. And for fuck's sake, don't knock her up!"

I kept going and when we stepped outside, I looked down at her. "We're going to have a little chat as soon as I hear what Saint, Zipper, and Grimm have to say. Until then, I want you to stay at my place. Don't even think of fucking leaving. I'll make sure the Prospects know you aren't to leave the compound."

"I've spent my whole life doing the exact opposite of what bossy men told me to do. Always hated having someone dictate what I could and couldn't do." She leaned closer. "But I kind of like it when you do it. Are you bossy in other situations too?"

"You're like a little powder keg, aren't you?"

She shrugged a shoulder. "I just know what I want and don't see the point in denying it. Besides, I need your help. I wasn't lying about that part. The fact my dad's club showed wasn't in my plans, but I can work around it."

I pointed to my house. It was hard to miss. After Charlotte had left, I'd decided to move out of the home we'd shared. She may not have been in my bed, but I still couldn't live there after she'd moved away. I'd seen her in every room and thought of what might have been. So I'd built a new home. The huge stone monstrosity sat back from the bend in the road. "Door's unlocked. Make yourself at home. I'll be there as soon as I'm done with business."

She flashed me a smile before going up on her tiptoes and pressing her lips to mine again. "Yes, sir."

I curled my fingers into my palms so I wouldn't be tempted to swat her on the ass. I liked her sass, and how bold she was. A little too much. I hoped I hadn't bitten off more than I could chew, but only time would tell.

She climbed into a black Cadillac Escalade, gave me a little salute, then backed out and headed for my house. I didn't see Torch buying a car like that for her, so I was more than a little curious where she'd gotten it. After I made sure she was doing exactly as I'd said, I turned and went back inside, wondering for a moment if I should have warned her about Bandit and Pirate.

"Thought Venom was coming," I said as I joined the men at a table.

"He is. He should be here any minute. Had to pull off to take a call," Zipper said.

"Then I guess we'd better wait for him." I waved a hand at some club girls waiting off to the side. "Want any entertainment?"

Saint shook his head. "I've got an old lady at home."

"Same," Zipper said.

Grimm eyed the ladies but shook his head. "Venom won't be long."

Saint ran a hand through his hair and leaned back. "I hope you know what you're doing, Beast. There are only two things in this world that will make Torch lose his shit. Anyone hurting his wife, or someone threatening his kids. Tread carefully. I have no idea what you're doing with Lyssa, but she's not like the women over there."

I saw Brick and Drifter out of the corner of my eye, both placing their hands over their weapons. I kicked my feet out in front of me and folded my arms over my abdomen as I eyed Saint. "You've got balls, I'll give you that. Walking into my house, disrespecting my woman, and giving me veiled threats? You want my help or you want a war?"

Zipper spit out his beer. "Your woman? Holy fuck."

Sunlight poured into the clubhouse as the doors opened and Venom strolled in. "Thanks for meeting with us."

I shook his hand and motioned for him to sit. "I was just getting acquainted with these three."

"Lyssa is here," Grimm said.

Venom gave a short nod. "I know. I'm glad."

He knew? I wasn't about to ask how. He'd either seen her SUV, or someone had tipped him off. Maybe the call he'd gotten on the way here? Which meant someone was most likely tracking her vehicle or phone. My money was on Wire.

"You're glad, VP?" Saint asked. "You said we needed to go get her. Did you know she would be here?"

"Yes, I'm glad, and no, I didn't know she'd come here." Venom sighed. "We've got problems. Or more accurately, Lyssa does. Some little punk has been after her, but word is he's part of the Mancini family. There's a site Wire ran across. The Mancini family is going to auction off women. Some will become wives of men with particular tastes. Others will go to brothels worldwide. Lyssa's name was recently added to the list."

"Torch received pictures of Lyssa. Some punk ass kid named Tony was trying to get in her pants, and she keeps rejecting him. Now he's out for revenge. Those pictures have been uploaded to the auction site and the description makes it clear she needs a firm hand. Bidding has already started. She's a bit old for the men wanting a wife, which means she'll likely end up in a brothel somewhere."

"Over my fucking dead body," I muttered.

Venom scratched at the beard along his jaw, his gaze intent as he watched me. Yeah, I'd said more than I should have, but one look and I already knew I'd lay down my life for that woman. I was so fucked.

"Since Lyssa is already here," Venom said, "we just need you to keep an eye on her. But if you can spare anyone, we'd appreciate some extra hands. The

Devil's Fury and Devil's Boneyard have both agreed to help us find as many of the young girls as possible, but I wouldn't be opposed to a few more men."

"Why drive all the way here? You could have just asked over the phone," I said.

"We want as many men on this as we can get. Wire and Lavender are working as fast as they can on the computer end of things, but I want as many hands available for any rescue attempts as possible." Venom folded his arms over his chest. "Look, you don't have women here other than the whores, and now Lyssa. Since she's here, I won't ask for much, but even one man could be a help. As for why I came in person, I was heading to Lyssa's next. You were on the way."

I had to wonder, if Venom had been aware Lyssa was here when he'd pulled up, that had to mean someone had been keeping tabs on her location. Why had they planned to go any farther once they got here? Or had they just known she was mobile but not her destination?

"Prospect okay?" I asked. "Our club isn't as large as yours. With Lyssa here, I don't want any patched brothers or officers leaving and putting her at risk."

"As long as it's someone you trust."

I yelled out for Iggy, one of our newer prospects. He hurried toward me and stopped by the table. "You need something, Pres?"

"These men need some help rescuing girls from the Mancini family. I want you to head out with them tomorrow and help wherever you're needed."

Iggy nodded. "I'll be ready to go whenever they are."

"Seven o'clock," Venom said. "You got a place where we can crash for the rest of today? Been riding for two days trying to gather up a few allies. I'd planned to talk to you tomorrow, after we'd had a night to rest and let Wire have a little more time to do his thing, but that call on the way here changed things. Now that I know Lyssa is handled, it's one less worry."

"If you don't mind the noise of the clubhouse, I've got a few rooms upstairs you can use," I said.

"We'll take them," Venom said.

I tapped my knuckles on the table. "All right. I'll have Brick get things set up for you. Not to be rude, but I have a woman I need to wrangle."

Venom's lips twitched. "Good luck. At least she's not as wild as my Farrah."

I stopped long enough to give instructions to Brick, then rode my bike back to my house. Although, if I'd have known about the sight that would greet me, I might have come home sooner.

Chapter Two

Lyssa

The President of the Reckless Kings was one fine man. I couldn't tell for certain how old he was, but I honestly didn't care. My dad was about thirty years older than my mom, and they adored each other. If anything, it had taught me to view people with my heart and not my eyes. Beast might be huge, and perhaps to some he seemed scary, but he'd put himself between me and Tony. He had a protective streak a mile wide, and I had a feeling he had a good heart too.

Having lived with the Dixie Reapers MC all my life, being around tough bikers wasn't anything new. I'd learned long ago most of them had a soft marshmallow center when it came to their women and kids, and by extension all other kids in the club. Well, maybe not Farrah. She'd terrorized so many people, I'd been surprised they hadn't thrown a party when she'd decided to strike out on her own. If her dad hadn't been the VP, they very well might have done just that.

After being on the run from Tony, I felt like warmed-over crap. I didn't know where Beast would want me to stay. The duffle in my hand didn't hold a lot. Just enough to get me through a few days. I dropped it on his bedroom floor and pulled out my sleep shorts and a tank. I hadn't slept in two days and knew it wouldn't be long before I crashed. Hard. At first, I hadn't wanted to come here. I'd hoped when I got on the road, I could lose the asshole. But every time I'd stopped, he'd quickly caught up to me. Finding the Reckless Kings had been a last-ditch effort.

I pulled the ends of my hair up to my nose and grimaced. I hadn't planned to wash it, but there was no way I was going to bed smelling like cigarettes. I got into the shower, marveling at the luxury of Beast's home. The shower was big enough for four or five people, with a bench seat along one of the shorter walls. It had three showerheads and a solid glass wall with a door that was so seamless it was damn near hidden. Steam billowed into the bathroom from the stall and I sighed in pleasure as the water beat down on me.

Picking up the green bar of soap, I took a quick sniff and smiled when I realized it was Irish Spring. What were the odds he'd like the same soap as me? I'd never cared for the girly shit. Simple, clean scents were my favorite. My perfume, which I seldom wore, had a warm spicy smell. If anyone gave me floral shit, or worse -- vanilla, I'd throat punch them. That crap was just nasty and gave me a damn headache.

I grabbed his two-in-one shampoo, trying not to cringe at the thought of what it would do to my hair, and washed the long tresses. Anything was better than nothing at this point. I rinsed the suds and shut off the water.

I stepped out onto the bathmat and dried off with a towel I found under the sink and pulled on my pajamas. Not a hair dryer in sight. Going to bed with wet hair was another thing I disliked, but it couldn't be helped for the moment. Yawning so wide my jaw cracked, I made my way into Beast's bedroom. I gave the covers a yank, then collapsed face first, not even bothering to pull the blankets back over me. My eyes were closed before my head hit the pillow and exhaustion weighed me down.

I heard a scratching noise and hoped like hell he didn't have rats. There were a lot of things I could handle, but rats weren't one of them. The bed covers tugged and jerked underneath my feet and I opened my eyes only to realize I was face to face with a weasel. I screamed and jerked upright, sitting on my knees as two of them jumped around me on the bed.

Not weasels. Ferrets. What the hell? Beast let these things roam free in his house?

I cautiously held out my hand for them to sniff me. I'd never seen any running free. The pet store I'd always begged Mom to take me to had them for sale, and I'd thought they were cute. After a moment, they seemed to lose interest and scampered back down, only to disappear through the bedroom door. I'd have to remember to ask him about them later. Once I knew I was alone, and my visitors weren't returning, I lay down and closed my eyes again.

A beep from the alarm system I'd spotted in the hall told me someone had opened a door. With everything going on, I should have been more concerned, but I was too tired to run anymore. I sighed and refused to budge. If someone scary came through the door, I'd find the energy to fight back. Until then, I planned to give my best impression of a corpse. Maybe they'd think I'd died and leave me alone. It worked for possums.

Footsteps came up the stairs and down the hallway. I only heard one set, so it wasn't Tony. He'd never try to come after me on his own, not inside the Reckless Kings' compound. I seriously hoped Beast had given the order to shut the gate and keep it closed. I didn't like the fact Tony had waltzed right in earlier, and same for me. There hadn't been anyone standing guard.

"Had I known I'd come home to find you in my bed, damn near naked, I'd have rushed through the meeting," Beast said.

"Tired," I mumbled.

I heard the rustle of something, a zipper, and a moment later, the mattress dipped under his weight. The hair on his legs brushed against mine and I finally managed to crack an eye open. Shirtless, he was even more beautiful, or more accurately, ruggedly handsome. For an older guy with hair going silver, he'd kept in shape. Unlike most of the guys at my dad's club, Beast didn't have a full beard. Not that I would call him clean shaven, but the whiskers along his jaw could have easily been only a day or two's growth.

His touch was gentle as he brushed my hair back from my face. "Get some sleep, beautiful. We can talk after you've rested."

He pulled the covers over both of us and tugged me into his arms. I felt oddly right, as if I'd finally found the place where I belonged. I'd never believed in fate or any of that other crap. Now I had to wonder if I'd been wrong. Were we destined to be with one person? And if that was true, had I just found my other half?

The thought was enough to make me a bit more alert. I opened both eyes and studied Beast. "Why are you here?"

"Last time I checked, this is my house and my bed."

"Okay. But why are you naked in the bed with me?" I asked.

He flexed his hips. "Not entirely naked."

I pretended I didn't notice the bulge he'd just pressed against me. Good to know the attraction I felt for him wasn't one-sided. It seemed he was every bit as interested in me.

"Thanks for playing along earlier," I said. "With Tony. I've been trying to shake him for a while, but he's like a New York cockroach and keeps coming back."

He placed his hand on my hip and tugged me closer. "What do you know about him?"

"Not much, except he gives me the creeps. He doesn't like the word 'no' and seems to think I should fall at his feet. And he's determined. You saw how he followed me here. He's been tracking my every move for weeks now. I left school because of him, and the last two days I've not slept at all for fear if I stopped to rest, he'd find me." I licked my lips. "I'm not scared of much, Beast, but Tony… there's something not right about him."

"And you came here instead of going home? Or to the Devil's Fury or Devil's Boneyard?" he asked. "Why? And don't give me that crap about Lilian."

"I was fifteen the first time I heard the story about Lilian and Dragon, and how she'd come here for help. The old ladies talk, not just amongst each other inside the club, but with the others too. One of them talked about you, how you'd helped Lilian and made sure she felt safe. I think I fell in love with the idea of you back then." I snuggled closer to him, breathing in his scent. "You were like a knight in shining armor, and while I've never been a damsel in distress, I just knew if I came here you'd help me."

"Your club is under the impression this isn't your first time here. Although, I think Venom knows otherwise. He knew you were here already, which means someone told him."

"And since someone told him, they were probably tracking me," I said. "Yeah, I'm used to it. I'm sure there's a chip somewhere on my car, in my phone. Hell, I wouldn't have put it past Dad to microchip me like a lost puppy, and if not him, then definitely my grandfather. There probably isn't much they wouldn't tag so they could find me at any given time. Shoes. Purse. Anything they could attach a tracking device to would be fair game."

He ran a hand down my back, stopping just above my ass. Was it wrong I wished he'd kept going? I pressed tighter against him, the heat of his skin seeping into my clothes. I hadn't thought I was quite as wild and crazy as my best friend, Farrah, but right now, I had to wonder -- What would Farrah do?

Climb Beast like a tree.

She'd never backed down from anything she wanted. Which explained why she was now the old lady to Demon, the Sergeant-at-Arms for the Devil's Fury MC. There probably wasn't another soul on this earth who could handle her half as well as someone like him.

"I wouldn't blame either of them for doing that. The thought of Tony, or anyone else getting their hands on you, makes me want to put my fist through something. Preferably through Tony." He kissed the top of my head. "When you walked into the clubhouse, I knew I wanted you. Even told Brick I had dibs."

I couldn't contain my snort of laughter. "You called dibs? Are you twelve?"

His hand smacked my ass and I squeaked in surprise. "Keep sassing me and see what happens."

I tipped my head to hold his gaze. "What? You going to put me in time out?"

"More like fuck you into submission."

A shiver raked me, and heat pooled in my belly. I clenched my thighs together. I hadn't ever had a man make me want him so much just with words. Hell, I'd never wanted a man ever. I'd taken my own virginity when I'd been sixteen, using a vibrator a Prospect had given me. If my dad had ever found out, he'd have booted the guy from the club, after beating his ass. Again, something Farrah had talked me into.

"With a promise like that, I may be extra bad on purpose." Like really bad, and often. I had a feeling his version of "fuck you into submission" would leave my pussy aching for days. Was it wrong I got turned-on even more just thinking about it?

Beast gave a low growl and before I knew what was happening, he had me on my back and pinned to the bed. His hips pressed to mine, and I felt the hard ridge of his cock. Holy shit! I hadn't thought he'd be small, but the length and width of his dick was a teensy bit intimidating. At least for a virgin. It seemed Beast was big everywhere. It felt like fire licked along my nerve endings and my heart slammed against my ribs. I got even wetter and felt how soaked my sleep shorts were. Could he feel it too? Did he know what he was doing to me?

"Don't tempt me, Lyssa. You have no idea how tightly I'm holding onto my control."

I took a breath to steady myself. "Then don't. Don't hold onto it. Let go, Beast."

I'd never wanted anything more. The thought of him filling me up, fucking me, made my nipples rock hard. I shifted a little, rubbing my pussy against him and couldn't hold back my moan. Jesus, the man was lethal. It should be illegal to be so damn sexy, and so… so… alpha.

"I don't do soft and gentle. Something tells me the only experience you've had is with boys. I might break you."

"You won't." I wasn't about to confess I didn't have experience with anyone. Boys, men, girls, women. None of them. Only experience I had was with my own hand and my vibrator. If Beast found out I was technically a virgin, he might very well run fast and far. I'd heard men claim it was too much responsibility being a woman's first.

His mouth slammed down on mine, his tongue thrusting between my lips. His hand gripped my wrists, keeping them over my head, and the weight of him held me in place. A raw, aching need filled me. Something I'd never felt before. I didn't just want him, I craved him. The weight of his body over mine spiked my arousal until I nearly begged him for more. I gave myself over to Beast, letting him devour me. My nipples hardened even more, and my sleep shorts got so damn soaked. I'd felt the wetness before, but it was ten times worse. I'd have to wring them out. If he could nearly make me come from a kiss, I wondered what it would be like if he took full advantage of me. And I'd willingly let him.

"Beast," I murmured.

"Eric." He kissed me again, then nipped my lip. "My name is Eric."

The significance of him sharing his legal name hit me head on. Men like him didn't hand out that information to anyone. When he'd said he called dibs, I now had to wonder if he'd meant for more than tonight. What the hell was I getting myself into?

He thrust against me and his cock rubbed against my clit. I gripped his arms, holding on tight as he did it again. Shit. I didn't care. If he wanted me tonight, tomorrow, the next week... as long as he made me feel like this, I'd stay as long as he wanted. Giving myself an orgasm with a toy was vastly different from having a flesh and blood man between my legs.

"Eric, I'm so close."

"That's it, beautiful. Come for me."

I focused on his face, holding his gaze, as he rubbed his cock against me again. The friction against my clit was almost more than I could handle, and yet I wanted to ask for more. The first time I came, crying out his name and digging my nails into his arms, it felt like I broke into a million pieces and slowly came back together again. Way better than a vibrator. It was… there were no words. I'd thought I'd come before, but compared to what Beast had just done to me? No. What I'd experienced at my own hands paled in comparison.

He worked a hand between our bodies, and I felt him shove my shorts to the side right before his fingers brushed over my pussy. He growled again, nipping the side of my neck. "All this for me?"

"Yes! You know it is."

"Shit, baby. Never had someone this wet before. I fucking love it." He released me, leaning back. "Don't move. I mean it, Lyssa."

My heart thudded against my ribs as I left my hands above my head. He reached for my tank and worked it up over my breasts, then pulled it all the way off. Beast cupped the large mounds and brushed his thumbs over my nipples. Sparks shot straight from my breasts to my clit and I wondered why it felt so much more amazing when he touched me than when I did it myself.

"Beautiful. Fucking perfection." He leaned down and nipped one breast, then the other before licking away the sting. The whiskers along his jaw scraped against my skin. I'd never understood a woman's fascination with a man who had a beard, until now, and Beast didn't even really have one. Just a few bristles from not shaving for a day or two. I wanted to beg him to rub the roughness against my nipples, but I bit my lip, holding the words back. I didn't know what I could and couldn't say. Having never been with a man, I wasn't sure if he'd be offended if I asked for something.

He managed to get my shorts off me and shoved my thighs wide, looking his fill. I felt my cheeks warm. No one had ever seen me naked before. Farrah had tried talking me into getting waxed, but I'd balked at the idea. I'd trimmed, but now I wondered if I should have listened to her.

Beast settled between my thighs, his shoulders holding my legs open. The moment his tongue touched my clit, I started coming again. I couldn't remember ever being this sensitive before. It felt like one orgasm rolled into another as he worked me with his lips and tongue.

"Please don't stop," I begged. I lost track of how many times he got me off. Each time, I thought, *Maybe just one more*. I could see how women could get addicted to having sex with men like Beast. I never wanted the pleasure to end.

He lapped at my clit before biting it gently, setting off another release. My vision blurred and I forgot to breathe. I felt the bed shift but couldn't hear anything over the buzzing in my ears. Beast settled over me again. Before I could say anything, he thrust hard and deep, filling me up.

I cried out, my body tensing at the sudden intrusion. He was far larger than any toy I'd ever used and the sheer size of him made my pussy burn as I stretched to accommodate him. He bottomed out, the head of his cock kissing my cervix. The slight spike of pain made me clench down on him. I opened my mouth, wanting to tell him it was too much, yet not wanting him to stop. The look in his eyes was intense, the muscles in his arms bulging as he held himself still.

"Should have known you'd be little everywhere," he said. "So fucking tight. You okay?"

I nodded, realizing I meant it. I only hoped he didn't comprehend exactly why I was so tight. My vibrator was more like using a pencil compared to Beast's cock. It felt huge, and so damn thick. I'd already adjusted to his size and now I wanted him to move. I'd never come so much in one day before, and never so hard. I found myself eager for more. Even though I'd heard of women having multiple orgasms, I'd never realized it was a real thing. Much less that a man would be the one to make it happen for me, instead of my trusty vibrator.

If this was what real sex was like, I was throwing the toy away. After this, I'd never be able to settle for the meager amount of pleasure I'd gotten from it. It might have seemed earth-shattering before, but only because I hadn't had anything to compare it to. Things were different now. I was different.

Awesome, Lyssa. Less than five minutes with a guy's dick inside you and you're ready to ride him from now until eternity. Or rather, let him ride me since he seemed to like being in charge. I rather liked it too.

When Beast started thrusting, I gripped the bars on the headboard. He powered into me, every stroke harder than the one before. He didn't just fuck me. He claimed me. It was like he wanted to brand himself on me. Beast rode me, taking what he wanted, and God help me but it was the sexiest thing I'd ever experienced.

"I'm coming!" I tossed my head back as the strongest orgasm I'd ever had rippled through me, leaving me breathless, blind, and deaf. Nothing existed in that moment except the pleasure zinging along my nerve endings. I felt a gush of heat between my legs as the world came back into focus and Beast stilled against me.

"Christ! Never felt anything like that before," he said, then kissed me. "I was right. You're fucking perfection."

I shifted my hips and felt something hot and wet slip from my pussy and down the crack of my ass. My breath caught as I stared up at him. He hadn't asked. Not once had he brought up protection. Oh, God! I knew he had to have been with the club sluts. What if he'd just given me something? Panic welled inside me. What if he'd gotten me pregnant?

Shit, shit, shit. Why hadn't I realized before now he hadn't used a condom? It might have been my first time, but I wasn't a complete idiot. Except maybe I was since I'd let him use me so thoroughly and had wanted to ask for more. My common sense had gone out the window the moment I'd kissed him at the clubhouse.

He kissed my jaw, my neck, then my lips as he pressed his hips tighter against me.

"Eric, we um... We didn't use anything. You know, like a condom?"

He cocked his head. "You clean?"

I slowly nodded. Hard not to be when I'd never been with anyone before. Of course, since I hadn't shared that with him, as far he knew I'd had sexual partners before him.

"So am I. Got my test results three days ago and I haven't been with anyone since I got tested. Sexy little thing like you probably hasn't lacked for male companionship, not even with your dad being who he is."

Damnit. I'd have to tell him. Right? At least, I thought I should.

I licked my lips. "Um, Eric. About that... There hasn't ever been male companionship in my life. I mean, I've never... You were my first."

His body tensed and his eyes became a darker shade of gray-blue. "What?"

"I wasn't a virgin, not in the strictest sense, but I haven't ever been with a guy before. I used a vibrator to pop my own cherry when I was sixteen."

"You telling me no other man has seen you naked? No other cock has been in this hot little pussy?" he asked. "No other guy has sucked your nipples or made you scream and beg to be fucked?"

"Right. Just you."

He lowered his weight, pressing my entire body into the mattress with his bulk until I worried he'd suffocate me. And yet, I felt a tingle I couldn't ignore. Even now my traitorous body was ready for another round. My pussy would hurt like hell after, but I didn't care. My clit throbbed and I wanted to come.

"Not smart, sweetheart."

What? What wasn't smart?

His nose trailed along my neck until he bit down my shoulder. I felt his tongue lick the same spot before he lifted off me enough to look into my eyes. "You're mine. Not for right now, but for always."

My mouth opened and shut, but I couldn't seem to form a coherent thought much less speak. His? As in... he was keeping me? I'd known there was a chance some guy in one club or another would eventually go all caveman on me and try to tell me I belonged to him and only him. It hadn't occurred to me it would be the first guy I slept with, or that he'd be the President of another club.

"Eric, I..." What could I say?

"You on birth control?"

"No," I said softly. Fine time for him to think about that. Another reason we should have used a condom.

He grunted. "Good. Makes it easier to knock you up."

Knock. Me. Up.

As in he wanted to get me pregnant on purpose? Had I fallen into an alternate reality? All I'd said was I'd never been with another man before, and now he wanted to chain me to him in any and every way possible? Sure, I'd heard the stories back home, but I hadn't realized what it would feel like to be faced with a man like Beast saying I was his and he wanted to put a baby in me.

I had to wonder if my mother had felt like this. I'd heard the story of how she and my dad got together. My grandfather had brokered her to the club President in exchange for his help. Mom had run and returned when she'd gotten a few years older. Except, she'd said the moment she saw him, she'd fallen for my dad. Was I falling for Beast? Did I want this? Want him?

"Thinking too hard," he murmured, rolling off me. He tugged me against his side, holding onto me. "Get some rest, sweetheart. You said you were tired."

Sleep. Sleep was good. Maybe when I woke up, all this would make more sense. Or maybe I'd find out I'd dreamed the entire thing. For some reason, that made me sad. I didn't like the thought of this moment with Beast not being real. I might not know if I wanted to be an old lady, especially since I was only eighteen, but I couldn't regret being with him.

I closed my eyes, breathed in his scent, and let my body relax. Worrying over the future wouldn't solve anything when I was too tired to think straight.

Besides, Venom knew I was here. If he didn't approve, he'd have come and dragged me from Beast's home himself. That had to mean something.

Chapter Three

Beast

Shit. Shit. Shit. I'd just fucked a damn virgin, and one who happened to be the princess of the Dixie Reapers MC. If her daddy didn't tear me a new asshole, the club's VP currently at my compound might do the job for him. Had Venom left her here knowing she was innocent, and counting on me to not fuck up and take her like some... well... beast?

I'd have to call Torch. It was the right thing to do, even if I did dread it. Maybe I could put it off for a bit. Jesus. All the women in the world and I had to decide I wanted to keep the daughter of another club's President. I wasn't sure how it would all play out, but I knew one thing. I wasn't giving her up. Lyssa was mine now, and they'd have to take her by force. I'd never willingly let her walk away. Not to mention she might very well be pregnant with my kid already. The thought of her swollen with my child made my cock hard again.

Even at forty-two, I could still go more than once on the nights I yanked one out, but the club whores didn't hold my interest anymore. I'd just never gotten hard thinking about knocking one of them up. Then again, Lyssa was far from being like those women. Not that there was anything wrong with them. I'd enjoyed them and had no problem with a woman embracing her sexuality. But knowing Lyssa had been innocent, that I was the only man she'd ever had between her thighs, it made me feel like King-fucking-Kong.

I eased out from under her and went to take a shower. When I'd come home, I'd had no intention of starting anything with her. I'd wanted to make sure she was all right, find out what she knew about Tony, and come up with a plan. Instead, I'd gotten balls deep inside her and decided she wasn't leaving my bed.

I heard a chatter behind me and saw my two ferrets -- Bandit and Pirate -- on their hind legs watching me. I paused to give them a scratch. My brothers gave me shit for having them as pets. I'd gone with Forge to the pet store to pick up food for the stray cats that kept wandering into the compound, only to overhear someone trying to dump their ferrets at the store, claiming they couldn't keep them anymore. I'd had them three years now, and they'd been a few years old when I'd gotten them. They wouldn't live forever, but I'd done my best to give them a good life while I had them.

"You two stay out of trouble. No snooping in her bag!"

They chattered at me again, either in agreement or the ferret version of laughter because I knew they'd damn well do as they pleased. Especially when it came to stealing shit. Anytime something went missing, I usually found it in their hoard.

I cranked the hot water until steam billowed from the glass stall and stepped under the spray. Not once in all my life had I ever lost my cool and gone bare with a woman. Until now. My high school sweetheart had ended up pregnant, but only because the condom broke. I thought about Lo and wondered what she'd think of all this. Even before she'd found out about the baby, I'd planned to hold onto her for life. I'd even worked my ass off to buy her an engagement ring right before graduation.

No one knew about her. Not here anyway. The only people who'd been part of my life back there were either dead or we'd lost track of one another. I leaned my head against the wall as the water pounded my back and thought of her sweet smile, and her gentle nature. I'd never known a woman like her and hadn't been looking for one.

I'd thought Charlotte was my second chance at happiness, but I'd been wrong. She'd wanted no part of this life, and I couldn't blame her. It had hurt like a bitch when she'd left, but I got it. She didn't feel safe, and I couldn't promise she'd never be in the line of fire again. Someone had used her to get to the club, and I knew damn well any woman one of us claimed could face the same thing in the future.

But Lyssa knew the score. She'd been raised in this life. Hell, she'd strolled into my clubhouse bold as brass and kissed me. While there had been some club whores who'd done that, they'd all been after something, like status. With Lyssa, she'd just wanted to make a point with the guy who wouldn't stop chasing her. The fact she picked me out of everyone else admittedly stroked my ego. Any of my brothers would have helped her if she'd asked.

My thoughts drifted back to Lo. My kid would be older than Lyssa by now, if he'd lived. Instead, Fate had been cruel and stolen not only my son but my wife too. And yeah, I'd married Lo first chance I'd had after graduation. The sharp pain I'd once felt when I thought of her tombstone -- Loretta Bradshaw, Wife and Mother -- had lessened over time. I'd always miss her, and some part of me would love her until I drew my last breath, but I knew she'd want me to live my life and not wallow in self-pity.

A small hand pressed against the center of my back and I glanced over my shoulder. I hadn't even heard Lyssa enter the bathroom much less the shower. I needed to get my head on straight if I was going to keep her safe. I turned and wrapped my arms around her.

"Everything all right?" she asked.

"Yeah, just taking a trip down memory lane. Not the happy kind either."

She kissed my chest, then went up on her tiptoes. I leaned down and let her kiss me. It was soft and sweet. The kind of kiss you'd expect from a woman who didn't have much experience, and for some reason, the quick brush of her lips against mine turned me on far more than getting down and dirty with any of the club whores ever had.

"I'm not taking this to the table," I said. "You're mine. End of story. Any of them has an issue with it, I'll be glad to show them the door right after I beat the hell out of them."

"So bloodthirsty." She smiled. "I think I like it."

"You're not going to try and run? Or refuse to stay with me?" I asked, thinking of Charlotte's response when I'd said I wanted to make her mine.

She tipped her head to the side and studied me. "Why would I? Am I supposed to be scared of being yours? Do you want me to fight back and say it's not what I want? I'd be lying, but..."

I didn't know what to make of her. She'd made herself at home in my bed, let me fuck her hard and without protection, and didn't balk at me laying claim to her. Yeah, she played by the same rules I did, but still... I'd expected more resistance.

"Are you lulling me into a false sense of security?" I asked.

She snorted and started laughing. "Why the hell would I do that? What's so confusing about all this? You said I was yours, I agreed, and... what? I don't get it. Should I throw a tantrum or something?"

I rubbed my hand across the whiskers on my jaw

and tried to think of the best way to put it, without pissing her off. Last thing I needed was her getting jealous when there was no reason to be. "I wanted to claim a woman a few years ago. This life wasn't right for her, and she left. Saw how Lilian ran from Dragon, and I know of others who didn't agree so easy when their man decided they were getting promoted to old lady status. You're not what I'm used to."

She'd grown still at the mention of another woman, but I didn't see any hurt in her eyes. If anything, she seemed to be attempting to puzzle things out. I could almost hear the gears whirring inside her brain as she pieced things together.

"My mom was given to my dad when she was seventeen. He didn't claim her in more than name back, then and let her go live her life with the understanding she'd return when she was eighteen. Except she didn't. She ran. When she was ready, she showed up at the clubhouse and that was it. He made her his that very night, and she's never once regretted it.

"So maybe my view of things is a little different. It never crossed my mind I'd end up with anyone other than a biker. My daddy is the President of the Dixie Reapers. My grandfather is the notorious assassin Casper VanHorne. I was born for this way of life, Eric. So if you want me to be all girly, throw a fit, and squeal about how unfair it is, you'll be waiting a long time. It's never going to happen."

Damn. She really was the perfect old lady. And I knew I was lucky to call her mine. "And the age difference? It doesn't bother you?"

"Have you ever met my parents? My dad is about thirty years older than my mom. So no, I don't have a problem with it, and neither can they unless they want to be hypocrites."

I couldn't contain my smile. "Remind me to have a front row seat if you ever decide to tell your dad he's a hypocrite. Torch isn't someone to mess with. Even if I don't personally know him all that well, most clubs within several hundred miles know of him, and not to piss the man off."

She sighed and cuddled closer. "Honestly, I'm waiting on the day he decides to step down. He's in his late sixties, and while I'd like to think he's invincible, I think he's close to wanting to retire. Or whatever the hell an MC President does when he hands the reins over to someone else. He's always muttering *I'm too old for this shit* and his bones are creaking more with each passing year. But if you tell him I said any of that, I'll kill you in your sleep."

"You think he might hand it all over to someone else?" I asked.

"I don't know. I think Mom would prefer for him to. I can tell she likes having him home. The days he doesn't do any work for the club, she smiles more. He always made time for us, but Portia, Hadrian, and Ivy are still young enough they need him more than I do. I know they'd be happy if he had less responsibility with the club."

Her dad was more than twenty years older than me, and I knew I wasn't ready to hand things over anytime soon, but would I be when I was closing in on seventy? Most likely. So why hadn't Torch done so already? Did he worry about who he'd hand the club to? Venom wasn't much younger than Torch, so even if he took the President's spot, how long would it be before he decided he'd had enough too? I'd never stuck my nose into another club's business, and I didn't want to start now, but with Lyssa being a

Reaper by blood, I felt like I needed to keep an eye on things there.

"Water's getting cold. We should wash and get out," I said. "You hungry?"

She nodded and her stomach growled. Her cheeks flushed and I couldn't help myself. I had to kiss her. She was too damn adorable. I kept it brief so I wouldn't be tempted to do far more, but I was already getting addicted to her.

As much as I wanted to wash her, and feel her soft hands on me, I knew we'd freeze in here if we played around. I washed myself while she quickly scrubbed her skin. She winced a little as she cleaned between her legs and I made a mental note to take it easy on her. Even though she said she'd taken her own innocence with a vibrator, I was betting it had been a lot smaller than me. She'd probably be sore the rest of the day and maybe tomorrow too.

I dried off and pulled on clean clothes while she did the same. I noticed there wasn't much in her bag. The Reapers had said something about her being in school. I hadn't given it a thought before now. If she wanted to continue her education, I wasn't about to tell her no, but I didn't like the idea of her being off somewhere without protection. She caught me staring and arched one eyebrow.

"Something you want to say?" she asked.

"Need to get the rest of your things," I said and motioned to her bag. "That's not enough."

"I had to drop my classes when Tony wouldn't back down and I knew I'd have to leave." She sat on the edge of the bed. "All my stuff is in a storage unit near the campus. A friend packed for me and left it all there since the university said I needed to be out by a certain day. I wasn't sticking around long enough to take care of everything when Tony was being all stalker-like. I'd thought about going home and letting my dad send someone for the stuff later, but I ended driving aimlessly in an effort to *not* need help. I ended up coming here instead."

"You could always enroll online," I said. "We may be in the middle of nowhere, but there's still Wi-Fi."

"As fancy as your clubhouse is, I wouldn't expect anything less. I'd heard this place was impressive, but I hadn't believed it until I saw it for myself. Part of me is curious how the club can afford so much, and yet I know better than to even ask about club business."

Yep. She was fucking perfect.

"It's no secret we run a few businesses nearby. Shield has a tech shop where he repairs broken computers or cleans up destruction from viruses. The club gets a cut of the profits since we helped him set it up. Forge has a metalworks place. Again, the club helped him set it up so we get a profit from it. Snake manages the pawn shop the club owns. Nitro manages the strip club, which the club owns. All legit businesses. Prospero invests a chunk of our money and always gets a good return."

"You expect me to believe everything is one hundred percent legal here?" she asked.

"Nope, but I know you won't ask what else we're into. If anyone ever wants to know where the money comes from, any of the things I just mentioned is what you can tell them." Her stomach growled again. "Time to feed you. You aren't big enough to go skipping meals. Might blow away with the next gust of wind."

She rolled her eyes and huffed. "I'm not tiny."

I patted the top of her head, which barely reached my chest. "Yeah, you are. But I think you're cute, so it's okay. I'll just call you Tinkerbell."

She patted her hips and ass. "Too much padding to be called tiny."

I grabbed her, tossed her over my shoulder, and smacked her ass. Twice. She yelped and grabbed my shirt as she squirmed. "You're not allowed to talk shit about yourself, especially when it comes to this gorgeous body. I love every curve you've got so don't even think about going on a diet or missing meals on purpose."

"I was only kidding. Sort of."

I eased her down in front of me and held her chin so she'd be forced to hold my gaze. "You had my attention the second you walked through my door. You think just anyone gets that reaction? Fuck no. I mean it, Lyssa. You're beautiful just the way you are. Stunning. Most attractive woman I've ever seen."

I realized I meant every word. No matter how much I loved Lo, even after all these years, I could admit that Lyssa was far more beautiful. Loretta had been more of a girl-next-door kind of pretty. With my little Tinkerbell, everyone took notice when she'd walked into the room. I had no doubt I'd have my hands full keeping men away for the next few decades, or however long I lived.

Her lip trembled and she hugged me tight. "That's the nicest thing anyone's ever said to me."

I made a mental note to have a chat with the Dixie Reapers. If no one had ever told her how pretty she was, or said anything else nice to her, even if her daddy was their President, I'd have to start kicking some asses. It amazed me how she'd been so tough and no-nonsense when she'd walked into the clubhouse, compared to the softer, more vulnerable woman clinging to me right now. Hard on the outside with a marshmallow center. Yep, perfect woman.

"Come on, Tink. Time to feed you. Let's see what I have in the kitchen. I have a feeling we'll need to make a grocery run, or send a Prospect out to grab some stuff. Until I know Tony isn't coming back, I'd rather you not stray too far from the compound."

"Trust me, I have no desire to see Tony again ever."

I ended up dragging some ground beef from the fridge and found noodles and a jar of sauce in the cabinet. It wasn't gourmet cooking, but it would fill her up. While I browned and seasoned the meat, I tried to think of how to best phrase my questions. I needed to know exactly how in the dark she was over Tony and why he'd been so adamant about chasing her down. Had her daddy's club told her anything at all? She didn't seem like the type to want to sit on the sidelines, blinded by anything going on around her. No, Lyssa would want to know if she was in danger. She'd want to be prepared. I might not know much about her, but it only took me a few seconds of talking to her to realize she liked being able to take care of herself, but wasn't too proud to let a man step in when she needed him.

"Why does Tony think he has a shot with you?" I asked. "It's obvious you aren't interested."

"I'm not sure. He just kind of focused on me and refuses to go away. But there's something… off. I get this feeling it's not that he wants in my pants. It's like I'm a challenge? No. Something else."

Smart girl. "A job?"

"Yeah! It's like I'm a… Oh, you've got to be kidding me." She closed her eyes and sighed. "I really am a job for him, aren't I? He's been paid to kidnap me or something."

I smirked. Definitely smart.

"Tony works for some bad people," I said. "And yes, he did target you for a reason. It's why the Dixie Reapers came here. They wanted our help. It's not just you the men are after. The fact you're here only made things easier on Venom. He said he'd been on his way to get you."

She tensed. "What's that supposed to mean?"

"Tony is part of the Mancini family. They've been gathering up girls and women to auction off. You're on the list." I shut off the burner. "Before you get some great idea to run off and try to save everyone, because that sounds like some shit you'd pull, I'll put you on lockdown if I have to. Your ass is staying right the fuck here, Tink. You hear me?"

As if in agreement, the ferrets scampered into the kitchen and shimmied up her legs to get in her lap. They stuck their little noses in her face, making Lyssa smile as she petted them. Then her nose wrinkled.

"Yeah, I know. They need another bath. Won't matter. There's a certain level of stink that just sticks to them. They're fixed, but even right after a bath they still have that eau de ferret smell."

"So why get ferrets?" she asked. "I have to admit, they scared the hell out of me when I first saw them."

I cleared my throat and looked away, not ready to admit to a level of geekiness that wasn't befitting a biker. "Kodo and Podo."

"I'm sorry, but that was supposed to make sense?"

"*The Beastmaster* was my favorite movie in the early eighties. He had two ferrets. Kodo and Podo. So when those two needed a home, I gave them one." I folded my arms. "And if you tell anyone that's why I have ferrets, I'll gag you and never let you leave the house again."

Her lips twitched and her eyes sparkled with merriment. "Are you a closet geek, Eric?"

I shrugged a shoulder and turned to finish up our food, but I heard the soft snicker behind me. If she kept that up, I might be tempted to forget she was likely sore and take her again anyway. No one got away with teasing me. Lyssa wasn't just anyone though and having her do it made me want to smile. I felt lighter than I had in a while, despite the fact trouble was on her heels. I'd keep her safe, help the Dixie Reapers any way I could to make sure those men never got their hands on her, and for once, I'd think about the future. While I usually thought ahead by a few weeks, months, or even years, it had always been about the club. For the first time in a while, I wanted to make plans with a woman.

I dished up our food and set the plates on the table, then got us each a bottle of water. After I sat down, I knew I'd need to talk to her about Lo and my son. No one here knew about them, but it wasn't right to expect her to live the rest of her life with me and keep something like that from her. It wasn't the sort of thing you just blurted out, but I wasn't sure how to ease into it. Maybe I needed to get her talking about herself first.

"You took your own virginity, so does that mean you didn't date?" I asked.

"It's hard to date when the guys are scared of your dad and grandfather. I had a Prospect who wasn't too much older than me I wouldn't have minded dating, but I knew better. My dad would have made his life hell. We hung out sometimes, but that's as far as it went. I went on some dates in college. Never saw anyone on a regular basis or had an official boyfriend if that's what you mean."

I shoved a bite of food in my mouth and wondered about the Prospect she mentioned. Did Torch know the guy was hanging out with Lyssa? That she'd wanted to date him? Probably not or he'd have been long gone.

"I mentioned a woman I'd wanted to claim. She's Brick's sister. Charlotte. You won't see her around here, so don't worry about feeling awkward or anything. And I never slept with her, just so you know. She moved to Alaska and married some nerdy wildlife guy."

"Her loss is my gain," she said.

I cleared my throat knowing this was going to be the hard part. "Before Charlotte, I hadn't been serious with anyone in a long while. When I was younger, back in high school, I had a steady girlfriend. Asked her to marry me."

Lyssa braced her arm on the table and leaned a little closer. "What happened? The two of you drift apart after school? I've heard that happens, especially if distance becomes an issue."

"No. She, um, got pregnant our senior year. We married right after high school." I set my fork down, the food feeling like lead in my belly. "She died. Her and our son. After that, I pushed people away. Didn't let a woman get close, until Charlotte. We just didn't want the same things. I think she'd have been miserable if she'd stayed. She seems happy, and that's all I want for her. Besides, if she'd stayed, you wouldn't be sitting here with me."

She slumped a little in her chair, not meeting my gaze. Had it been too much? Would she second-guess being with me now? Wouldn't matter. I wasn't letting her go, especially when there was a possibility she could be pregnant. I'd lost my shot at a family before. Lyssa was my second chance at happiness.

"Tink, it was a long time ago. Before you were even born. Hell, I wasn't even part of a club back then. It was my grief over Lo and our son that eventually led me to this way of life."

"It's a lot to take in," she said, her voice barely above a whisper.

"You wishing you'd picked another club to run to? Or maybe a different Reckless King?"

She finally looked at me. "No. I don't have any regrets, Eric. I'm sorry for all the pain you suffered, and I know Charlotte leaving had to hurt too. But I'm a selfish bitch because if your wife hadn't died, if Brick's sister hadn't left, you would have never touched me. I'd never wish for something horrible to happen to an innocent person, and yet… I'm glad you aren't married."

I reached out and took her hand. "Tink, I think you were put in my path for a reason. Just know, if I seem overly possessive or controlling, I'm not trying to dictate your every move. But I need to keep you safe, need to know you aren't in danger. I've lost too much to let anyone take you from me."

"I'm not going anywhere, Eric. You're stuck with me."

If she thought that was a threat, or supposed to make me reconsider a relationship with her, she had a lot to learn. I *wanted* to be stuck with her. Already my life seemed a little brighter. Not only would I have her in my bed every night, but we had a chance to start a family. There were a lot of rooms in this house, and I wanted to fill as many of them as we could. Since she had three siblings, I didn't think she'd mind having a big family.

And if she didn't want more than one or two kids, well... I'd just do my best to convince her we needed at least three. I'd be with her every step of the way. I didn't plan on leaving her home with the kids all the time while I escaped to the clubhouse or elsewhere. No, I wanted to experience every second of fatherhood. Even at eighteen, when I'd been scared shitless, I'd still looked forward to holding my son, watching him grow up, and teaching him stuff. I had no idea whether or not things with Lo would have lasted, but nothing would have kept me from my kid.

Maybe I needed to thank Tony. Because of his relentless pursuit of Lyssa, she'd come running to me.

Best damn day of my life.

Chapter Four

Lyssa

Beast had dropped a lot on me. I hadn't expected him to be a virgin, but knowing he'd been married, and had asked a second woman to be his had me wondering how I measured up. What had they been like? There weren't any pictures in Beast's home, not even the decorative kind. It was hard to imagine loving someone and not keeping their picture. Then again, it could be in his closet or desk. It wasn't like I was going to go snooping.

At least he'd told me about them. He'd been honest, which said a lot. If no one here knew about his wife and child, then he could have easily kept it to himself and I'd have never found out. Not unless I had a reason to go digging into his background on the computer. I tried not to do that if I didn't have to. Even if Wire and Lavender had taught me a lot, I knew I wasn't anywhere near their level.

Beast's home was incredibly clean, especially for a bachelor. I didn't have anything to do and I was quickly getting bored. He'd cleared out two drawers in the dresser for me and I had my own closet. Although, until my stuff arrived, I didn't have a lot to fill all that space. Using Beast's credit card -- at his insistence -- I'd purchased a few things online. They hadn't arrived yet, but were due sometime today. It would be nice to have a few extra outfits and another pair of shoes.

Bandit and Pirate scampered around my feet as I walked from room to room. With nothing to clean, I was quickly becoming bored. I'd left my books behind, and Beast wasn't about to let me leave the compound and go shop at the nearest bookstore. And I certainly wasn't going to ask any of the Prospects to choose something for me, especially since I liked romances. The hotter the better. Then again, the look on the guy's face would be priceless. I'd love to see one of the tough guys around here shopping in the romance section.

I bounced on my toes and twisted my upper body a few times, trying to burn off a little energy. When that didn't work, I pulled up a workout video on the living room TV and started stretching. I wasn't anywhere near as small as Beast claimed. I had curves, and those curves had a few curves of their own. It wasn't that I was out of shape. I'd exercised plenty both at home and college. I blamed my DNA. No matter what diet I tried, or workout routine, I never slimmed down all the way. My clothes made me appear slimmer, but naked? Well, you could see my soft, pudgy belly then, and the way my thighs jiggled.

At one point, my weight had bothered me. I'd let girls at school make me feel like shit all because I didn't meet their standards. My mom had figured out something was wrong and sat me down for a talk. After explaining that everyone was beautiful in their own way, no matter how big or small, it made me feel a little better about myself. Once I accepted that I was just different from the super thin girls in my class, it had become easier to be happy with who I was.

Sweat beaded on my skin as the video came to an end. My breathing was heavy, and a few drops of sweat landed on the floor at my feet, but I still felt a buzzing under my skin and a need to be on the move. I hadn't ever sat in one place for very long and being on lockdown was going to kill me. If I were at home, I'd walk the compound. Maybe watch the new Prospects exercise. They had a tendency to start stripping off clothes partway through, and every woman at the compound tried to sneak over to watch. Even the married ones like my mother.

I did a set of jumping jacks, then some lunges. The feeling in my gut wouldn't go away. It felt like if I stayed inside the house another moment, I might come apart at the seams. I was ready to scream in frustration. Beast had mentioned keeping the compound gates closed and assigning a Prospect to stand guard. Which meant it should be perfectly safe to leave the house as long as I didn't venture outside the gates.

My nose wrinkled as I caught a whiff of myself. Maybe a shower first.

I ran up the stairs and went to the master bathroom. I had to peel my clothes off since they were soaked in sweat, then tossed them into the hamper. Normally, I'd have loved a hot shower, but I left the water on cold and stepped under the spray. It cooled my heated skin and felt like heaven. I scrubbed my body, shaved, then washed and conditioned my hair. By the time I got out, I felt like a different person, although the itch to be out of the house was still there.

I pulled on a pair of my jeans and the boots Beast seemed to love, then eyed my closet. My options were slim at the moment so I pulled on my long-sleeved tee with skulls and roses down the sleeves. After I twisted my hair up into a messy knot, I put on a tinted lip balm and decided to check out the clubhouse. It had been mostly empty when I'd arrived yesterday. I didn't know if that was the norm or not. Only one way to find out, and hope Beast didn't get pissed.

I let myself out of the house and decided to walk to the clubhouse. It wasn't that far, and it was a nice day. Fresh air was always welcome, and I breathed in deep as I set off for the clubhouse. From the house, I could see a handful of bikes out front and a few cars. There was no way in hell those cars belonged to any of the Reckless Kings, or the Prospects, which meant there were probably club whores inside. Lovely.

It wasn't that I had a problem with those women. They served a purpose, and I didn't begrudge them a little fun. But I'd also heard about the ones who didn't care if a brother was taken and tried to dig her claws in just the same. Anyone who so much as looked at Beast in a way I didn't like, I'd be happy to show her the error of her ways. And if Beast had a problem with it, I'd see how he liked having blue balls. I'd never disrespect him in front of his club, but at home? That was another matter. When it was just us, I'd have no problem telling him exactly what I thought.

I pushed my way inside, my eyes adjusting to the dim interior. Despite the sun shining outside, very little light seemed to pour through the windows. I scanned the room and didn't notice Beast. A few brothers were scattered around the room, more than one with a naked woman on his lap. I ignored them and went up to the bar. The Prospect eyed me before leaning closer.

"You're not the sort we usually see in here," he said.

No shit. "I'll take a bourbon."

"You got some ID? Because the Pres would have my balls if I served a minor alcohol."

A minor? Seriously? "First, I'm a legal adult. Second, I didn't ask you to think. Give me the damn drink."

"You're in for a rude awakening, doll. Women don't give orders around here. You either turn around and leave, or I'd suggest you take a look around and get with the program. The only place you have here is on your knees."

I felt a spark light up inside me and I used the

stool for leverage as I went halfway over the bar, grabbed the asshole by his cut, and dragged him closer. My nose was nearly touching his and I hoped he could see the fury in my eyes.

"I'm not a fucking whore, and I damn sure won't take any shit from you. You're a motherfucking Prospect. Don't act like you're someone because around here, you're no one. There are two options. You pour my fucking drink, or... I embarrass you in front of all the men you want to impress."

I released him and leaned back.

"That was a stupid move," he said, sneering at me. Before I had time to react, he'd leapt the bar and grabbed my arm. "The only value you have are your tits and your pussy. If you aren't offering up a nice view at the very least, you need to leave."

"Get. Your. Hands. Off. Me." I held back a growl as I narrowed my eyes at him. He shook me like I was a damn rag doll, then started hauling me to the back hall. It hit me that he was probably trying to take me to a room. His? Oh fuck no. "You were warned."

I twisted in his grasp and punched him in the throat before kneeing him in the balls. He dropped to the ground, gasping for air, one hand on his throat and the other between his legs. I heard the scrape of chairs and heavy footsteps. Looking up from the shithead on the floor, I saw three Reckless Kings heading my way.

"Before any of you lay a hand on me, you might want to check in with your Pres," I said. "He won't be happy if you hurt me."

"Fucking whore," the Prospect said, still gasping at my feet.

I drew back my foot and kicked him in the ribs, giving him another reason to bitch and moan. One of the patched members folded his arms over his chest. I eyed his cut and saw the *Sergeant-at-Arms* patch just under his name. *Forge*. If anything, he seemed slightly amused I'd gotten the drop on the man at my feet.

"You need better Prospects," I said. "This one is weak."

"And what would you know about it?" one of the others asked. I eyed his cut too. *Snake*.

"I know my daddy would have hauled his ass out of here and beat the shit out of him for treating me the way he did," I said, nudging the downed Prospect with the toe of my boot. "Assuming he let him live, he'd have been banned from the club."

"Who's your dad?" Forge asked.

"Torch." I braced my feet shoulder-width apart and crossed my arms. "I'm a Dixie Reaper by blood, but your Pres has decided to make me part of the Reckless Kings."

Snake's jaw slackened. "Holy shit. You're Beast's Tinkerbell?"

I sighed. "I don't know why he insists on calling me that, but yes. I belong to Beast."

Forge snorted and kicked the Prospect on the floor. "You done fucked up, boy. Manhandling the Pres's woman? You'll be lucky if you're breathing by the end of the night."

"I didn't know."

I eyed him. "You were trying to take me down the back hall. To where? A room?"

He paled and didn't answer, which told me enough.

"That's what I thought. And if I'd said no? If I'd fought and told you to let me go?" I asked. If anything, he looked like he might throw up or pass out at any moment. "Forge, tell me right now if your club permits rapists. Because if you do, I don't give a shit what Beast thinks, my ass will be out of here so fucking fast his head will spin."

"We don't," Forge said, a coldness seeping into his gaze. "Beast is in his office. Down the hall, last door on the left. I'll take out the trash while you find your man."

I gave him a little salute and hustled down the hallway. My first official day with the club and things were already going to shit. I wasn't sure if I should mention the incident to Beast, or let Forge tell him. For one, I didn't know what he'd think about me putting his Prospect on the floor. On the other hand, they now knew they had a rapist in their midst. If the Reckless Kings were anything like my dad's club, I had a feeling that guy wouldn't be seen ever again.

Outside Beast's office, I heard the murmur of his voice. I didn't know if he was on the phone or had someone in there. I lifted my hand to knock, but before my knuckles met the wood, I froze.

"I don't know what to do with her. It's not like I can just toss her out," Beast said to whomever he was speaking to. Who was he going to throw out? Was he sorry he'd said he wanted me to stay? "Look, it's not that simple. I'll piss off a lot of people if I tell her to leave."

Right. Like my dad and grandfather? I took a breath and pushed open his door. Beast glowered a moment, until he got a good look at me. He flashed me a smile and waved me in. I took the seat across from his desk and decided he must have been talking about someone else.

"Just come get her," Beast said. "I don't give a shit if she's a pain in your ass. She's too much fucking trouble and I have enough on my plate. She's your fucking cousin, not mine."

He hung up the call and motioned for me to come around the desk. I stood and walked to him, letting out a gasp of surprise when he tugged my arm. I lost my balance and fell on him. Beast grunted and I jabbed my elbow into his stomach.

"Be nice. It's your fault I fell."

He kissed my neck. "You can fall on me anytime, Tink. What brings you to the clubhouse?"

"Got restless. I thought I'd get a drink, but Forge told me where your office was so I came to see you." I paused. "I'd thought at first you were talking about me when you said to come get *her*."

He kissed my cheek, then my lips. "No, Tink. Not you. One of the club whores is related to someone I know. She's always causing problems, so I need her gone. Guess I need to formally introduce you to everyone. Except the club girls. You have any problems when you came in?" he asked.

I debated telling him, but decided I needed to be honest with him. "The Prospect behind the bar gave me some trouble, but Forge is handling it."

"What kind of trouble?"

"He didn't want to serve me a drink, then said the only place a woman had in the clubhouse was on her knees. When I refused and basically told him to fuck off, he tried to drag me down the hall."

Beast tensed and the look in his eyes would have scared most people. Not me because I'd seen that same look in my dad's eyes plenty of times. I also knew it didn't bode well for the Prospect if Beast got his hands on him.

"Forge said your club doesn't tolerate rapists." I cuddled closer to Beast, hoping it would keep him from jumping out of the chair and charging after the guy. "I have a feeling the Prospect will be buried in a shallow grave somewhere before nightfall."

"Fucking hell," Beast muttered. "Bad enough I need to protect you from that rat Tony, but now I can't even trust my own men? Glad I found out about that kid before he patched in, but it makes me wonder if there are others we need to cull."

He pulled out his phone and I peered down at it, since he wasn't hiding the screen from me. *Get rid of the Prospect. Permanently.*

Now I knew for sure the guy wasn't going to be breathing much longer. If he went around raping women, I honestly couldn't say I was broken up about him dying. Might make me cynical, but I knew there were some men who were just born wrong. Those were the ones my dad's club had taken out at every opportunity.

"I don't envy you. I know running the Dixie Reapers hasn't always been easy for my dad. Seems like it would be a giant headache, and that's without having traitors or assholes you have to deal with."

Beast squeezed me. "I'll get it handled, Tink. There's always someone new wanting a shot at a patch. I'll make this a safe place for you, but for now… exactly what sort of drink did you order?"

"Bourbon."

He smacked my thigh, making me yelp. "No alcohol, Tink. What if I knocked you up yesterday? And if I didn't, well… I plan on practicing as often as necessary until I get it right. How many kids do you want? Three? Five? Enough for a baseball team?"

I couldn't hold back my laughter. "A baseball team? Seriously? Do you want an old lady or a broodmare?"

"Just don't want anything between us. I liked taking you bare. Whenever you decide you don't want more kids, I'll go get fixed. Until then, I'm going to fill as many rooms in the house as you'll permit. But just so you know, I'm hoping you want at least three kids."

Kids. I'd known the man for a day, and he was already talking about getting me pregnant. I smiled, and knew I'd found the one man I was supposed to be with. While I'd never doubted I'd end up with a biker, it hadn't occurred to me I'd nab myself a President. Still, there was no point letting him know I wanted a houseful of kids. Not yet. I'd make him squirm and work for it a bit. I'd tell him… eventually. Like maybe after the third baby was born. I'd always wanted a big family, so four or even five kids wouldn't be so bad.

"Guess we better practice a lot, then, in case you didn't get me pregnant yesterday. How much more work do you need to do here?" I asked.

"None. For today, anyway. I had to sign off on some papers, make sure everyone would get paid this week, and deal with a club whore who isn't really a club whore. She's the cousin to someone in another club, and trouble with a capital T. I'm ready for her to go before she causes another blowup."

"Blowup?" I asked.

"She decided to play two brothers off each other. Shit apparently went sideways last night, but it's sorted for the time being. Until she does it again. I'm hoping she's gone long before that can happen." He kissed me, his lips lingering a moment. "Come on, Tink. Let's head home. If you're restless, it means I need to wear you out."

I squirmed on his lap, knowing exactly what he meant, and I was more than ready.

Chapter Five

Beast

I locked Pirate and Bandit in their room. Lyssa thought it was cruel, but I'd ferret-proofed one of the bedrooms. They had a cage they could go into whenever they wanted, a litter pan, and a shit ton of toys and tunnels. What they didn't have were cords to chew, or open outlets. I'd made it as secure as I could so they would have a space to roam free without getting hurt, although I had a tendency to give them free run of the house. Or I had when it was just me.

By the time I walked into my bedroom, Lyssa had already stripped out of her clothes and lounged on the bed. Fuck but she looked sexy! I loved everything about her. Not just her soft skin and curves for days, but her sharp wit, her sarcastic tongue, and the way she didn't hesitate to stand up for herself. My woman was the entire package, and I was one lucky bastard.

"Someone seems eager," I said as I toed off my boots and shrugged out of my cut. "Did you miss me? Or just my cock?"

A smile slowly spread across her lips. "Well, I missed you, but I definitely missed your cock too."

"Hmm. Does that mean you're going to show me how much?"

She tipped her head to the side and I could tell she wasn't entirely sure what I meant. Knowing she'd been an innocent just made my blood heat more. I'd get to show her things, explore sex toys with her, and find all the ways to make her scream my name. Maybe she'd even be open to checking out the special room I had downstairs. I couldn't fucking wait!

"What was it that dipshit at the clubhouse said? Women belong where?" I asked. Christ, she might very well hand me my balls for saying that to her. Or it could turn her on. I was hoping for the latter.

"On our knees."

I pointed to the floor at my feet once I finished stripping. Pre-cum leaked from my cock I was so fucking turned-on at the mere thought of her obeying my every command, giving herself over to me, and letting me corrupt her. "Right here, Tink. Drop and show me how much you love my cock."

Her eyebrows rose. "You want me to do what?"

I waited until she'd gotten off the bed and sank to her knees in front of me. Prettiest damn picture ever. I reached out and gripped a fistful of her hair and tipped her head back. Holding my cock with my other hand, I used the pre-cum on the head to paint her lips. She licked it off, her eyes darkening with need.

"Open up, baby."

Her lips parted and I slowly worked my cock into her mouth. Knowing this was her first time, that she'd never tasted another man, had my dick hard as steel. Her tongue flicked back and forth as I sank deeper, and I couldn't hold back a groan. How the hell had she known to do that? It made my balls draw up and I found myself widening my stance to give her more access. Fuck but she felt amazing. Her hands lifted and gripped my thighs. I tightened my hold on her hair, angling her head a little more so I could slide in deeper.

"Put your hand on my balls, Tink," I said, my voice sounding harsh even to my own ears. I felt her small fingers close around me, her touch light. "Now gently roll them in your hand."

She made soft little sounds that sent vibrations down my shaft.

"Fuck, yes! Just like that, sweetheart. You're

doing so damn good. Gonna give you more."

I flexed my hips, going deeper until I felt the head of my cock at the back of her throat. She gagged a little and I pulled back only to thrust in again. The next time she gagged, I held still, my dick twitching as her throat convulsed around me.

"Jesus! Yes, baby. Gag on it. Feels fucking amazing."

I pulled out almost all the way, giving her a second to suck in a breath, before I thrust back in. She had drool leaking from the corner of her mouth, and my dick was so sloppy wet. Even if she didn't have a clue what she was doing, it was the best fucking blowjob I'd ever had. I felt my balls draw up and I knew I'd be coming before I was ready. I planned to be balls-deep inside her when I came, and I didn't mean in her mouth.

"We are definitely doing this again," I said.

She smiled around my cock, her gaze lifting to mine. It wasn't like I'd never had my dick sucked. The club whores had more experience than my little Tink, and they'd served a purpose, but it had never felt like this before. Maybe the difference was being with someone I actually wanted to keep. The others had been a convenience and nothing more. Except my wife, but that was so long ago there were times I struggled to remember what she looked like.

"Come on, Tink." I tugged her off my cock. "I don't want to come in that pretty mouth. Not this time. But one day, baby. One day, you're going to suck me off and I'm going to make you swallow it all."

I helped her to her feet and kissed the hell out of her before bending her over the side of the bed. I pressed my chest to her back and placed my lips by her ear. I gave it a nip as I rubbed my cock against her ass.

If she'd had a virgin pussy, that meant her ass hadn't had a cock in it either. Had she put her toy back here? I couldn't wait to play around and eventually fuck her tight little ass.

"Eric, I need you."

"I'm all yours, Tink." I bit her shoulder and licked the red spot I'd left behind. "One of these days, I'm tying you to the bed. I'll fuck every hole you have, make you scream until you're hoarse, and still you'll want more."

Goose bumps erupted over her skin and I chuckled, knowing my words had turned her on. I worked my hand between our bodies and squeezed her ass. She pushed back against me and wiggled her hips. If she kept that up, I'd think she wanted me to fuck her somewhere other than her warm, wet pussy. Then again, she wasn't exactly predictable. For all I knew, she wanted me to take her ass every bit as much as I wanted to. If she hadn't told me she'd never been with a man before, I'd have never known it.

"Eric, please."

"Please what?" I asked.

"I need you inside me."

I rubbed the lips of her pussy. "Here?"

She made a keening sound as I thrust a finger inside her. I worked it in and out, feeling the tight clasp of her pussy. My dick jerked and I pulled my finger free before slipping between her ass cheeks. "Or here?"

"Eric!" Using the slickness from her pussy, I worked the tip of my finger into her ass. Jesus! Yeah, I'd be taking her here soon enough. She struggled under me, but she wasn't trying to get away. No, my fierce little woman was silently asking for more, lifting her ass and wiggling against me.

"I was going to wait, give you more time, but I

think you're ready now. Get in the center of the bed and put your hands by the headboard."

I backed away and went to the closet. I had some restraints I'd wanted to use for a long time, but I never had the opportunity. They were still brand-new and sitting in a box on my top shelf. I took down the cardboard and opened the flaps, withdrawing the fur-lined leather cuffs. I only took out one pair for now. Eventually, I'd use the others to shackle her ankles and hold her legs apart. More precum seeped from the head of my cock just thinking about it.

I approached the bed and ran the handcuffs through the spindles before fastening one around each wrist. I buckled them tight enough she couldn't break free, but made sure they wouldn't hurt her. Gathering her hair in my hand, I pulled it to the side and kissed her neck. I slid my hand down her side, my fingers digging into her hip as I lifted her ass in the air.

"Stay exactly like this, Tink."

I drew back and put my hands on the inside of her thighs and spread her wider. Her pussy was soaked, the pink lips glistening. I toyed with her clit until she trembled and whimpered with need. Just in case we needed it, I grabbed the lube out of the bedside table and set it on the bed. I ran my hand over her ass and gave it a light swat. The way she gasped and arched her back told me enough. With a grin, I smacked her harder, leaving her skin a rosy pink.

"Yes! Eric, don't stop. Please don't stop."

I lined my cock up and thrust hard and deep, making her yelp. I brought my hand down on her ass cheeks, alternating between the two. *Smack. Smack. Smack.*

She screamed and thrashed as I slammed into her. Sweat slicked our skin. My hand tightened on her hip as I rode her, wanting the moment to last forever. She gripped me tighter as she came, chanting my name as the heat of her release nearly sent me over the edge. I smacked her ass again.

Fuck. As responsive as she was, I knew I'd eventually show her my playroom. It might be too much for her, or it might intrigue her enough to try it at least once. The thought of her tied up down there, and all the things I could do to her would fuel my fantasies until the time was right. For now, I'd fuck her as often as she'd let me. I might be an asshole sometimes, but I'd never take a woman who wasn't willing. I liked them begging and pleading for more.

"Come for me again, Tink. Get me nice and wet, then I'll give you what you really want." I grabbed the lube and popped the top before letting some drip between her cheeks. I worked it into her until I could thrust my finger in and out without resistance. If she'd played back here before, she wasn't saying. The way she lifted her ass told me plenty. Whether this was her first time or not, she was enjoying it. It wasn't long before she squeezed my dick again, coming even harder than before. The gush of her release slicked my cock and trickled down her thighs.

Pulling free of her pussy, I spread her ass cheeks and placed the head of my cock against her rosette. Pushing slowly, I breached the tight ring of muscle. My body tensed as I fought for control. She squeaked at the intrusion and stiffened a moment. I didn't want to hurt her. It wasn't like I was a small man. Even if she'd used her toy back here before, I doubted it was as big as me. If it had been, she wouldn't have been so fucking tight.

I slid my hand around her belly and down between her legs, brushing my fingers over her clit. I stroked her until she pressed back against me, taking more of my dick. When I knew she was ready for more, I sank into her deeper, not stopping until she'd taken all of me. My eyes damn near crossed at how tight she was. Never felt anything like it. If she enjoyed this as much as I did, I'd definitely be fucking her ass again. Multiple times.

"That's it, Tink. Fucking beautiful. I love seeing your ass stretched tight around my cock." I ran a hand down her spine while my fingers still worked her clit. The hard little bud was swollen and slippery. I rubbed it in small circles, pressing a little harder every fourth stroke before lightening my touch again. "You okay?"

She nodded. "Keep going."

"You sure? If it's too soon..." *Jesus fuck please don't let her tell me to stop!* I would, but I would fucking hate it. As it was, it took everything I had to hold back and not slam into her ass over and over. I wanted to pin her down, use my body to press her into the mattress, and fuck her like the beast I'd been named for. When it came to sex, sometimes I was more animal than man, or so I'd been told.

"No! Please, Eric. I want this."

I braced a hand by her head, leaning over her back. I pinched and rubbed her clit as I fucked her, riding her tight ass, my hips slapping against her with every thrust. "Fuck!"

She squirmed under me and I wished I had more hands. I wanted to play with her nipples, work her pussy, and be able to hold myself up while I fucked her. Mostly, I wanted her screaming in pleasure.

"Come for me, Lyssa. Need you to come."

"Eric, I... I need..."

"What do you need? Tell me." I'd give her anything she wanted as long as she came for me again.

"More. I need more."

I groaned. Christ. More of my cock? More fucking? "More what, Tink?"

"Harder." I heard her audibly swallow. "Fuck me harder. Use me. I… I liked feeling your weight over me, holding me down. I want to feel you come inside me."

Her words lit a fire inside me and I knew there would be no holding back. I wrapped my arm around her waist and took what I wanted. I drove into her with hard, deep strokes until I came, filling her ass with my cum. My cock twitched and I wished I could stay buried in her a while longer, but I worried I'd hurt her. She hadn't uttered a word of complaint. Had seemed to enjoy herself. Still, it wasn't like she'd ever done this before, and I'd already thoroughly used her pussy. She'd be hurting more than likely.

I eased out of her and unfastened the cuffs before lifting her into my arms. I carried her into the bathroom and started the shower. Before she could get in, I stopped her, pressing my hand to her back so she'd bend over.

"Spread your ass cheeks, Tink. Let me see."

She did as I commanded and the sight of my cum leaking out of her was enough to make me hard again. With her, it was like I was a decade younger and ready to go all the damn time. Couldn't remember the last time I'd gone more than once in a night, except with my hand, or even wanted to. The club whores were good for a quick release, but it wasn't like I wanted to linger with any of them. Most times, I gave them a wide berth. The novelty had worn off long ago.

"Fucking beautiful," I said.

She stood and looked at me over her shoulder. "What is it with men getting off on seeing their cum on a woman? I'd always thought that was just a thing in books."

"Exactly what books have you been reading?"

She grinned at me. "The naughty kind."

"I think I need to read these books. Maybe there's stuff in there we can try."

She waggled her eyebrows at me. "Oh, yeah. Lots of stuff. But I don't think you'll want to try the ones that require more than one guy. Unless you like sharing?"

I growled at her, narrowing my eyes.

"Right," she said. "No sharing. So much for having lots of hands on me and more than one cock in me at the same time."

I tossed her over my shoulder, smacking her ass several times before I stepped into the shower with her. I set her on her feet with a glare.

"Don't even joke about another man's cock being anywhere near you much less inside you. I will fucking end anyone who dares touch you."

She trailed her fingers down my chest, giving me an innocent smile. "Guess you better make sure I don't have a reason to ever need more."

"Careful, Tink. You're treading a very fine line. If your ass is sore right now, it's nothing compared to how it will feel if you piss me off and even so much as eye another man like he's your favorite dessert."

I saw the curiosity in her eyes and knew she might very well push me just to see what I'd do. And I'd show her. It would be a lesson she'd never forget. The thought of punishing her made me hard as granite. Corrupting my innocent little Tink was going to be fun as hell.

I pointed to the bench along the wall. "Go. Sit. And don't move until I tell you to."

She looked like she might argue, but she did as I

said. I quickly soaped my cock, not want to chance giving her an infection by fucking her again without cleaning up first. When I'd finished, I knelt at her feet, spreading her legs. The lips of her pussy parted, her clit still hard and protruding. Leaning down, I lapped at the little bud before biting it gently.

Her thighs squeezed my head. "So good, Eric."

I didn't stop until she'd come twice, then I flipped her over, bending her over the bench, and drove into her wet pussy. My body pressed against hers as I thrust into her. I couldn't draw this one out, making it last as long as I had before. My need for her was still sharp. And the thought of her even thinking of another man's dick made me want to claim her all over again, cover her in my cum.

I powered into her, holding her down. She'd wanted to be used so I told myself I was only giving her what she'd wanted. I'd always needed to be in charge in the bedroom. With her, it was a little different. Oh, I still wanted to be in charge, but there was something more. A need to possess her, to own every part of her, and make her want it just as much. It wasn't just my dick I wanted her to beg for. No, I wanted her to crave submission, as long as it was only to me, and only during sex. The rest of the time, I liked her fire.

The tile was hell on my knees, but I didn't care right then. I made her come again before I filled her with my cum.

"Christ, Tink. I'm too fucking old for this." I groaned as I slipped free of her body and staggered to my feet. She giggled as she stood, then turned to kiss me.

"Not old. I think you're just right," she said, twining her arms around my neck. "Seasoned to perfection. My sexy, almost-silver fox. Even now, as sore as my pussy is, I still wouldn't tell you no if you bent me over again."

Seasoned to perfection? I nearly snorted. She made me sound like a damn steak. Then again, I could easily make a snack of her, so maybe she felt the same about me. She hadn't exactly disliked having my cock in her mouth, or anywhere else.

"Come on, beautiful. Let's get cleaned up. We can make a bunch of finger foods, grab some drinks, and watch TV for a while."

"Sounds like the perfect way to spend a day."

I took my time washing her, loving the soft feel of her skin against my hands. She'd only been part of my life for one fucking night, and already I knew it would feel like someone had ripped my chest open if she were to leave. The moment she'd walked into the clubhouse, my life had changed. I'd known then I wanted her. I just hadn't realized I'd be keeping her. I still had to order her a property cut, and I needed to call Church to make an official announcement. I wasn't asking their permission, but I needed it on the record that Tink was mine.

"My beautiful Tink." I kissed her softly. "Thank you."

"For what?" she asked.

"For coming here. You changed my life with that kiss. Now you're mine, and I'm never letting you go. I think I lost Lo, and Charlotte left, because I was supposed to wait for you. It was fate you walked in yesterday. I only hope you don't come to regret being here."

She cupped my cheek. "Never. I will never regret it. I'm right where I'm supposed to be."

I kissed her again, then shut off the water.

Whatever it took, I'd make her happy, give her a life she loved. She was used to being part of a club, but she'd been their princess before. Now she was my queen.

Chapter Six

Lyssa -- One Week Later

Beast had sent a Prospect to gather my things from storage, which meant I also had my laptop and e-reader. I'd looked into online classes like he'd suggested, but there was plenty of time to make a decision. It wasn't like I could jump in the middle of the semester. I'd have to wait until the next term.

I pressed a hand to my stomach. What if I was pregnant? He'd been doing his best to knock me up. I'd wanted to take classes to help with the club, in any capacity my dad would allow, so I'd taken finance and tax courses. Boring as hell, but honestly, there wasn't anything I wanted to do with my life. I didn't have a career in mind, something that made me excited to get up in the morning.

Except for what I was doing now. Being Beast's woman, and possibly a mom, filled me with joy. I'd talked to my mother and assured her I was fine. I'd left out the part where I wasn't coming home. She hadn't mentioned anything about me moving, which made me wonder if Dad knew and just hadn't told her. If Beast hadn't talked to my dad yet, I wasn't going to be the one to drop that bomb on my family. I had a feeling my dad would have plenty to say on the matter.

My phone rang and I saw the display. *Portia*. Yeah, my parents had given my twelve-year-old sister her own phone. She only had family and the club programmed into it, so she couldn't get into much trouble. It didn't even have access to apps or anything. With danger lurking around the corner, it was probably a good idea to give her a way to reach out if something happened.

"What's up, squirt?" I asked when I answered.

"When are you coming home? You are still coming back, right?"

"Um. Why? Is something wrong?"

"Hwan said he heard his parents talking and his dad said you were going to live with the Reckless Kings now. It's not true is it? Did you really move? Are they far away? If you don't live here anymore, when will I see you?"

My heart melted a little. "You'll still see me, Portia. I love you, all of you. You're my baby sister and no matter whether I live at home or elsewhere, I'll always be here for you."

"Love you too, Lyssa. I miss you."

"Miss you too." My throat tightened with unshed tears. It had been one thing to be away at college, but it hadn't hit me until just now. This was my home now, and we weren't exactly around the corner from my family. I wouldn't be able to pop over anytime I wanted.

Wait. If Zipper was talking about me living here… That meant my dad and my mom knew. Why hadn't they said anything? Were they waiting on me to bring it up?

"Can I come stay there sometime?" Portia asked.

"I'd love that, but not right now. You do what Dad says and you stay inside the compound fence. You hear me?"

She was quiet a moment. "Bad men are out there?"

"Yeah, squirt. Bad men are outside the gates. You stay home and stay safe." I didn't know for sure if Tony would go after my sisters, but I wasn't willing to risk it. He'd followed me to the Reckless Kings, and I didn't exactly advertise I was related to the Dixie Reapers. Still, I didn't want to take any chances. What if he knew more than I realized?

"Okay, Lyssa. I gotta go. Mom is calling."

The line went dead, and I gripped my phone tight. I hadn't realized how much I'd miss her, Hadrian, and Ivy. Being away at school was different. I'd known I was going home for holidays and I'd only be gone four years. This wasn't the same, not even a little.

The front door chimed, and I rushed to see if Beast was home. I skidded to a stop when I saw Ranger. I hadn't had a chance to get to know the Reckless Kings all that well, but Beast had introduced me to a few. Beast wouldn't send someone here unless trouble was coming. Had Tony come back again? We hadn't heard from him since that first day. I'd thought it odd he'd been so relentless, then ran with his tail tucked the first time he saw Beast. Especially since I knew now why he'd wanted me.

"What's wrong?" I asked.

"Beast asked me to keep an eye on you," Ranger said.

Keep an eye on me? I'd been home alone several times since I came here. Why was he suddenly worried about me being by myself? Had trouble come knocking and he was concerned I'd get hurt?

"Should we arm ourselves or something? Did Tony breach the compound?"

He shifted on his feet. "Um, no. We don't need weapons."

My eyes narrowed. "We don't need weapons, and I'm not in danger. But you have to keep an eye on me?"

I wasn't sure I liked where this was going. The only reason Beast would ask him to watch me, without danger being present, would be to keep me on lockdown in the house. Or report my every move when I walked out the door. "So then I'm free to leave and go for a walk?"

He shook his head and pressed his lips together. It seemed he wasn't going to tell me exactly why I had to stay home. I didn't mind following orders, but I didn't want to do it blindly either. I knew Beast wanted to keep me safe, but if I wasn't in danger, what was the point in making me stay home? Unless there was something he didn't want me to see.

My hands fisted at my sides as I imagined him with some other woman. "Just know that I'm real sorry about this."

Ranger's eyes went wide when I launched myself at him. My knee hit his groin as I gripped the pressure point at his shoulder near his neck, making him drop to the floor. I stood and stepped over his body. My property cut hung on a hook by the door and I grabbed it, slipping it on, before I went outside. I hadn't thought to grab my keys, but it wasn't a far walk to the clubhouse, as long as no one tried to stall me.

I started walking and realized there were too many bikes out front. Quite a few I hadn't seen since coming here. And... I faltered a moment. That car. I knew the shiny silver Tesla. I'd recognize it anywhere. I broke out in a run, heading straight for the clubhouse. As soon as I burst through the doors, I realized why Beast had wanted me to stay home.

My dad and my grandfather were both landing blow after blow. Beast had a bloody lip and nose and seemed to be favoring his right side. What the hell was going on? My dad cracked a fist against Beast's jaw, making my man's head whip to the side. Before he could recover, my grandfather landed a blow to his ribs.

"Have you lost your minds?" I asked, raising my voice to be heard. Beast glanced my way, giving my dad another opening. I winced when he slammed his fist into Beast's cheek. "Daddy! Stop it!"

My dad and grandfather turned to face me. At least my grandfather had the sense to look embarrassed. My dad not so much. He glowered at me and stalked over, not stopping until we were toe to toe. I tipped my head back to look up at him.

"Why the hell didn't you tell me?" he asked. "Or did you know I wouldn't approve?"

"Why don't you?" I asked. "He's a President like you. You've said before the Reckless Kings were allies. So why don't you want me to be with him?"

"He's too broken! Everyone knows he wanted Charlotte, and she left. You shouldn't be anyone's second choice," he said.

"Third," I murmured, thinking of Beast's wife. My dad's face flushed a deep purple and he turned, but I reached out to grab his arm. "Daddy, stop. Please. Does Mom know you're here? Did she approve of you riding all this way to beat on Beast? Don't you have better things to do?"

He drew himself up to his full height and the look he gave me would have scared a lesser person. Yeah, I'd called him out in front of the Reckless Kings, my grandfather, and it looked like at least one visiting club, which explained the extra bikes. I'd probably pay for it later, but I needed him to stop pounding on my old man. Beast was too honorable to fight back. Neither my dad nor grandfather had a mark on them.

I eyed my grandfather. "Your wife know where you are?"

He shrugged a shoulder. "Not so much."

"Is this the lesson you want Hadrian to learn?" I

asked my dad. "That it's okay to pound on someone who isn't even going to defend themselves? I know he didn't hit back. Not only are you both still standing, but there isn't a bruise anywhere on you. Does that make you proud?"

My dad tensed and my grandfather walked over to me, pulling me against his chest. He gave me a tight hug. "You're my first grandchild, Lyssa. I'm allowed to protect you."

"Fine. Except I don't need protecting from Beast. Instead, I need you to keep me safe from a lunatic who's set his sights on me."

Beast came over, moving a little slower than usual, to stand beside me. I pried myself out of my grandfather's arms and reached up to touch Beast's face. He winced and I had a feeling he'd have a black eye later. I looked around and spotted a Prospect near the bar. He gave me a chin lift and I saw he had something in his hand. He tossed it over and I caught it. An ice pack! I smiled my thanks and pressed it against Beast's battered face.

"I'm sorry the men in my family are still kids," I said. "I'm pretty sure Hadrian is more mature."

My dad grumbled. "Not too big for me to make you find a switch."

My grandfather snorted. "Since when have you ever used a switch on any of your kids? Not even when this one sent killers after my wife. Why start now?"

My cheeks grew warm. I hadn't exactly known what I was doing at the time. Farrah and I had gotten into my dad's computer and sent men after the woman my grandfather had married. I just hadn't realized at the time they were going to kill her, or try to. Thankfully, she had my grandfather there to keep her safe.

"One day you're going to tell me about that," Beast said.

"She only got into trouble when Farrah was around. Well, most of the time," my dad said. "I raised a good girl. A sweet daughter who thinks of others. Which is why I'm surprised she didn't think I needed to know she'd been seeing someone."

I didn't like the fact I'd hurt him. It hadn't been intentional. On the one hand, I didn't want to admit I hadn't really been seeing Beast and he'd claimed me the first time I walked through his door. On the other, I didn't want him to think I'd kept something important from him. Either way, I'd let Beast claim me and I hadn't said a word to my parents.

"Daddy, I'm old enough to have a life of my own now. I love you, and the rest of the family, but I can't live with you forever. I'd thought you understood that when I left for college." I curled my fingers against my palms so I wouldn't reach for him. "I never meant to hurt you by not telling you what was happening in my life."

"It's not that you're starting your life he objects to," my grandfather said. "It's the man you picked."

I let Beast hold his own ice pack so I could focus on my dad and grandfather. They objected to Beast in particular? I didn't understand why. He'd been amazing, if a bit overbearing, but I'd known to expect that. I'd grown up surrounded by men just like him.

"There isn't a single thing wrong with me picking Beast. He's helped whenever other clubs have asked. Even though he doesn't have anywhere near the manpower you do, he's sent help whenever it's been needed, including when you've requested assistance before. Maybe I wasn't his first choice, but I wasn't alive when he fell in love the first time. I can't hold that against him, Daddy. And I didn't know him when he was chasing after Charlotte."

"But that doesn't…"

I lifted a hand to stop my dad. "What about Mom?"

His brow furrowed. "What the hell does your mother have to do with any of this?"

"How many women were you with before her? Does that make her any less in your eyes? Is she somehow not as good as the others?" I asked. My grandfather's eyebrows rose as he stared at my dad, obviously eager to hear his answer. When my dad didn't say anything, I knew I had him. "You adore Mom. And everyone knows it. If she could reform you, why can't I be enough for Beast? Besides, do you honestly think I'd stand by and do nothing if he slept around behind my back?"

My grandfather coughed to cover a laugh. Which reminded me…

"I told Ranger I was sorry, by the way," I said, glancing up at Beast.

"What did you do to Ranger?" he asked.

"Um. Well… he won't be too interested in the club whores for a bit, and I left him napping by the front door."

My dad burst out laughing until he had to double over and brace his hands on his knees. So glad I could amuse him. Even Beast's lips twitched as if he fought back a smile. My grandfather patted me on the head, but the twinkle in his eyes told me he was proud.

"You dropped Ranger?" Hawk asked, joining the conversation.

I hadn't had much of a chance to interact with the VP of the Reckless Kings. He didn't look impressed by what I'd done. If anything, he looked pissed.

"If Ranger was laid low by my little Tink, then he deserved what he got." Beast tugged me against his side. "I kind of like knowing she can take care of herself. If anyone slips past us, she won't be entirely defenseless."

"My girl knows how to take a man down with her bare hands, and she can shoot as well, if not better, than any man in your club and mine," my dad said. "And thanks to Wire and Lavender, she can wreak havoc with a computer. Maybe not on par with them or your Shield, but she knows enough to get revenge."

My nose wrinkled. "Do we have to bring that up?"

Damn. They were going to spill all my secrets. I hadn't been an angel, despite what my dad seemed to think. The thing was I knew he didn't consider what I'd done bad. To him, it was great I could handle myself and had some skills. It wasn't Farrah who had led me astray. I'd always wanted to be a rebel, but I'd known my dad would do far worse than lock me up and throw away the key.

"Bring what up?" Beast asked.

"In high school, some girl slipped a laxative in Lyssa's food at lunch. My girl had Wire and Lavender help her hack into the school security system. They saw who did it and let her get even in her own way. Let's just say the girl hadn't been keeping her legs closed and some of the encounters had been recorded. Lyssa made sure the girl's boyfriend got a copy of each video that had occurred after she'd started dating the guy." My dad winked at me. "My girl doesn't need a knight in shining armor. She can slay her own dragons."

I leaned against Beast. "Sometimes it's nice to not have to, though. If Beast wants to rescue me, I'm okay with it."

My grandfather made a fake gagging noise, but I saw the wink he gave me. Even if he wasn't happy about the fact I was growing up, I think he actually liked knowing Beast would be taking care of me. He and my dad had both made sure I could handle any problems that came up, but deep down, they both believed it was a man's job to take care of his woman, and his family. It made them cavemen, but I loved them.

"So why are you here?" I asked them.

"I was visiting when your dad found out about you and Beast," my grandfather said. "Thought I'd tag along and see how he handled the situation. I might have gotten carried away, but the thought of Beast defiling my precious granddaughter made me take a few swings."

I rolled my eyes. "Defile? Really? When were you born again?"

He eyed my dad. "You're right. We should send her out for a switch."

"No one is spanking Tink except me," Beast said, making my grandfather gag again.

One thing was for certain. There would never be a dull moment when my family was around. I hoped Beast realized exactly what he'd signed up for by claiming me. It wasn't just me he'd taken on, but my entire family.

Chapter Seven

Beast

My club knew why I hadn't fought back when Torch and Casper attacked. I'd understood their need to take a pound of flesh. I hoped I'd have a daughter someday, and if she got claimed by a biker, I'd be sure to pound his ass into the ground as a reminder if he fucked up I'd be there to make sure he learned a valuable lesson. Although, having the infamous Torch and Casper VanHorne come at me at the same time had been something to see.

Neither man was as young as they'd once been, and thankfully they didn't hit as hard as they would have a decade or more ago. I'd never say as much to their faces. I admired both of them, especially for coming here to put me in my place when it came to Lyssa. If anything ever happened to me, I knew they'd be there for her. Hell, my club would be too. Despite Hawk's grumbling over her dropping Ranger, I knew he'd make sure Lyssa was taken care of if I ever didn't make it back home.

Lyssa winced when she put the ice against my jaw. It didn't hurt. Well, not much. From the quick peek I'd had when we first got home, I had to admit it looked far worse. The skin had already started to bruise, and my split lip kept bleeding. Maybe I should have at least blocked better, but I hadn't wanted to embarrass them by not letting them get any hits in.

"Why did you let them do this to you?" she asked.

I placed my hand over hers, where she held the ice pack to my face. "How do you think they would have reacted if I'd kicked their asses? Not to mention, they're both older than me, made a name for themselves long before I got into this way of life. They deserve my respect, Lyssa, and they only wanted to show they'd protect you from any threats, even if it meant they had to come after me."

"I still think it's absurd they came all the way here just to throw a punch at you." She kissed my brow. "But thank you for not hurting them. I know you could have."

I wrapped an arm around her waist and tugged her closer. "They're your family, Tink, and you're mine. That means by default, those two are my family now too. They'll get used to it. Eventually."

"Was it wise to leave them in the clubhouse? Neither one is likely to party with your brothers, and the noise..." She nibbled her lower lip. "Should we have let them stay here?"

I snorted and swatted her ass. "Hell, no. Last thing I want is those two down the hall when I'm making you scream my name."

"Is sex all you think about?" she asked, giving me a mock glare. I could see the humor in her eyes and knew she wasn't really upset about it.

"No. Not always. I also think about you being pregnant with my kid. I wasn't joking about filling this house with kids, Tink."

She sighed and shook her head. "I want kids too, Eric, but that's still thinking about sex considering how babies are made."

I grinned at her. "So it is. Does that mean you want to head to the bedroom and practice? Might have to try lots of times before I knock you up."

She backed up and dropped the ice pack on the table. Folding her arms, she stared at me, looking too damn adorable for words. Whatever she was about to say, I probably wasn't going to like nearly as much as stripping her naked. Still, as long as whatever she wanted wasn't dangerous, I knew I'd be agreeing to it. There wasn't much I wanted more right now than to see her smile, to make her happy. Except keeping her safe. That would always be my priority.

"What do you want, Tink?"

"I want to make lunch and invite my dad and grandfather over. I don't like the thought of them being at the clubhouse all day. I doubt the rooms are very big. Besides, I don't know when I'll see them again. Especially my grandfather."

"Instead of cooking, want me to get something delivered? Chinese? Pizza? Or I could place an order somewhere and have a Prospect pick it up. Any restaurant in town."

Her stance softened and she came closer again, sitting on my lap. "Really?"

"Tink, I told you. They're my family now too. I have no problem with you spending time with them. I just don't want them sleeping down the hall."

"Eventually they'll need a place to stay when they visit," she said. "I don't want to be separated from my family, Eric. It didn't hit me until I spoke to Portia. I'll hardly ever see them, especially if I don't have room for them to come stay with us. Portia already asked if she could come visit."

"All right, Tink. There's something I haven't shown you. It's not perfect right now, but we can make it work." I tapped her thigh. "Let me up."

She stood and I took her hand, leading her through the laundry room and out the door on the back wall. She'd probably assumed it went into the backyard, and it sort of did. There was a large room built onto the back of the house. I hadn't filled it yet, not having any idea what to do with it. At first, I'd thought to make it a weight room, but now I had a better idea. We stepped out onto the back patio and I opened the door to the extra space.

I ushered Lyssa inside and eyed the space. It had ceramic tile flooring and plain white walls at the moment, with two windows that looked out over the backyard. It wouldn't be hard to add a small bathroom and a kitchenette. I told her as much.

"We could put a queen bed in here and a sleeper sofa. A small dresser would give them a place to put their things and we could set a TV on top. No reason I can't set up a guest account for the streaming services so they could watch whatever they wanted. Maybe a small table with four chairs? And a bookshelf with a variety of paperbacks for adults, kids, and teens." I wrapped my arm around her shoulders. "Think it will work?"

"It's perfect, Eric. It keeps them close, without putting them in the clubhouse, but also gives them a space to feel like they have their own little studio apartment. I don't think I'd want Portia out here alone, though, if she came to visit without my parents." She leaned against me. "Maybe we could set up a guest room downstairs too? You have more rooms than we could ever need."

"You're right. There's one I've been using for storage, but there's no reason I can't clear it out and put bedroom furniture in there." I kissed her temple. "Now, what do you want to order for lunch? I'll call it in, ask Kye to pick it up, and I'll get your family to come over and hang out with us for the rest of the day. I think I need a chance to get to know them better and assure them you'll be safe with me."

"Catch Tony and you'll convince them," she said. She shrugged a shoulder. "Actions speak louder with them. Don't tell them you'll protect me, Eric. Show them."

It wasn't that I had forgotten about the little shit who'd chased Lyssa into my arms. The fucker had gone underground and dropped off the radar. Shield hadn't been able to catch him on any surveillance or traffic cameras around town, which made me think he'd split for the time being. I had no doubt he'd return for Lyssa, but at the moment something seemed more important to him. But what?

"Tony isn't just after you, Tink. He has other women and girls he's auctioning off. We'd assumed he needed you before he made his next move. Maybe we were wrong. What if the auction is already happening?"

"Those poor women." She looked up at me. "Eric, we have to do something."

"Your father's club was working on it, with several others. If they haven't found them yet, I'm not sure we'll be able to do much better. They have Wire and Lavender. While Shield is great, he's not on par with them, and he'd be the first to admit it."

"So they're just lost?" she asked. "We give up and don't even try?"

I leaned down to kiss her, trying not to groan at the ache in my ribs. "Tink, I'll make sure every club hacker I know or have even just heard of is working on it. We might not rescue them today, but eventually we'll get them out of that hell. It will take time, if they've already been sold, but it's not necessarily impossible."

"I guess that's an issue for another day," she said. "For now, food. I know Mom watches what my dad eats, when he's home. And I'm sure Carmella watches my grandfather like a hawk. So no pizza, and probably no Chinese."

I ran my hand over my jaw, my fingers rasping against the whiskers coming in. No junk food, which meant no fast food either. Italian with the heavy sauces most likely was out too. It didn't leave many options. Then again, I could order salads and soup with a pasta order.

"I'll put a call in to the little Italian place and ask Kye to pick it up. Anything they can't eat for medical reasons?" I asked, knowing some people had food allergies.

"No. They'll eat anything. Probably shouldn't, but they will," she said.

"All right. Make sure we have enough beer in the fridge, and anything else they like, and I'll place the order."

She went up on her tiptoes and pressed her lips to mine, flashing me a smile before she walked off. At least she was easy to please. I called in the order, then let Kye know he needed to make a run. I looked around the empty room again, getting an idea of what I'd need. One of the Prospects had worked construction and had some carpentry skills. I'd get him to start framing out the bathroom and adding the kitchenette. It wouldn't get finished overnight, but it wouldn't take too long. The last thing I wanted was to keep Lyssa from her family. I could tell they were close, and I wanted her to be happy. If she couldn't visit with them at least a few times a year, I had a feeling she'd be miserable and maybe even come to resent being here someday.

Before I went to find my woman, I sent off a text to Shield.

Look into the auctions for the women and girls. Think it's going down now.

It only took him a moment to respond. *On it.*

Since Torch would be visiting with his daughter, I didn't want to bring up the issue of Tony. Not with him. Not right now. Instead, I pulled up Venom's number in my phone and hit the call button before I changed my mind. He answered almost immediately.

"Who the fuck is this?" he asked.

"Don't you check your caller ID, old man? It's Beast."

Venom snorted. "Torch didn't kill you?"

"No. He tried, but Lyssa stepped in. Which is part of why I'm calling. I don't want to take away from the time they have until Torch returns home. But Tony has been too fucking quiet after the scene he made when Lyssa showed up that first day. Something's wrong. There's no fucking way he just forgot about her, so what's he doing? Or worse, planning?" I asked.

"I've been wondering about that. Wire detected some movement on that auction site for the women and girls, but then everything went dark, like they'd taken it down."

"Which means they probably know someone is on to them, even if they don't know who," I said.

"That's what I'm thinking. We've got nothing to go on right now, but if Tony hasn't made his presence known there he could be anywhere, or just lying in wait. He may be lurking in the shadows hoping you drop your guard. With Lyssa, it's not just business but personal. She turned him down, repeatedly, which dented his fragile ego."

"That's because he's a punk-ass little boy who doesn't know the first thing about being a man."

"So true, brother," Venom said. "Look, with Lyssa being your old lady, far as I'm concerned that makes you and your club family. Same for the Devil's

Fury since Demon decided to take on my daughter, poor bastard. That girl is more than just a handful. Be thankful you got Torch's daughter. She's at least somewhat reasonable. Takes after her Momma."

"I don't know. She was bold as brass the day she came here. Walked right up to me and kissed the hell out of me." I smiled. "But she had my attention before that."

"Don't mention that to Torch if you like keeping your teeth," Venom said.

"Last thing I want is to build tension between us. It's why we're having him and Casper over for lunch. I figure Lyssa needs some time with them, and maybe they just need a chance to see I'm not going to hurt her. But I wanted to handle the Tony situation first, or at least make sure someone was working on it. I have Shield digging around a bit."

"I'll get Wire to call him. I know he's been in touch with all the hackers he knows, both club affiliated and not. It's not just our two clubs working on this. Devil's Boneyard, Hades Abyss, Devil's Fury, and even the Savage Raptors and Broken Bastards are doing what they can." Venom sighed. "I hate this shit. People never learn. The world just gets darker and uglier every fucking day."

"That's the damn truth. Let me know if you hear anything on Tony?"

"You got it and give Lyssa a hug from us. She's missed around here. It was different when she was at college because all the kids knew she'd be back. Now everyone knows she's staying with you, and I think her younger siblings aren't taking it too well. Heard Portia already called and asked when she could come visit."

"I'm working on getting some things situated at the house. In the next few months, I should have a small studio off the back patio for when the adults come to visit and a bedroom downstairs for when the kids come to stay for a bit. Lyssa really wants Portia to come stay with us."

"Listen, you want to win over Torch, just show him how much his daughter means to you. All he wants is for her to be happy and safe. You prove you can do both those things, and you'll have his blessing," Venom said.

"Working on it. Thanks, Venom. Not just for help with Tony, but for the advice."

Venom chuckled. "I have a feeling you'll need all the help you can get."

The call disconnected and I gave Kye a quick call, wanting to touch base to check on the food and make sure my new in-laws would be coming over. Although, since I wasn't married to Lyssa, they weren't technically in-laws in the strictest sense. Shit. Did she want to get married? Was that part of why Torch seemed so pissed? I'd heard he'd married his old lady. Maybe he expected me to do the same.

I followed the sound of her cursing and smiled when I saw her pawing through the fridge. "Keep shaking that ass and I'll cancel lunch with your family."

She gasped and whirled to face me. "Don't sneak up on me!"

"I don't know. If I get to see a view like that, I may have to do it more often. And convince you to run around the house naked." I waggled my eyebrows at her, making her crack a smile and eventually laugh. Good. She seemed far too tense, and I knew I didn't have time to give her an orgasm to loosen her up before her family got here. Hell, as rough as I felt, I wasn't sure I was even up to the task right now.

"Stop being bad and help me! I can't fit the beer in the fridge, but there's nothing I can take out that we don't need."

I shook my head before going to her. I shifted her out of the way and looked into the fridge. Since she'd moved in, I'd gone from cold leftovers, beer, and occasionally sweet tea, to finding fruit, juice, milk, and a host of other healthy things in there. I wasn't sure if they were just her preference, or if she was trying to make me live longer. Either way, it had reduced the space for beer by quite a bit.

"Looks like I need to buy another fridge just for alcohol," I said.

"And put it where?"

"Well, with that pretty SUV you have, I'd imagine I'll need a rather large garage now. It would be nice to have one for the bike anyway. Might need a second vehicle too, once we start having kids. No reason I can't go ahead and plan for enough room to add an extra fridge and maybe one of those big chest freezers out there."

She leaned against me, wrapping her arms around my waist. "Only been here a week and look at you... already getting domesticated."

I swatted her ass. "Watch it or I'll show you just how *un*domesticated I am."

"Promises, promises." She giggled and pulled away when the doorbell chimed. "Looks like you'll have to hold that thought for later. Much later. Once my dad and grandfather step inside this house, they won't leave until it's time to go to bed. And despite their age, neither one heads to bed at nine o'clock."

"And just how do you know how late your dad stays up? Watching and waiting for a chance to sneak out?" I asked.

Her cheeks turned bright red. "No. More like the entire house and neighbors can hear him and my mom going at it. Definitely no issues with their sex life, and they're noisy as hell. All. Damn. Night."

I couldn't contain my laughter, and I still hadn't gotten control of myself by the time she let her family into the house. I wiped the tears from my eyes and went to greet them. One look at my face and Casper seemed highly amused.

"And what has you laughing like a hyena?" he asked.

"Trust me. You don't want to know." I shook my head. "Seriously. Leave this one alone."

"Now you have to tell us," Torch said.

"All right." I glanced at Tink, who was frantically motioning for me to shut up. "Lyssa here was just telling me that she knows her dad stays up late because she, and apparently all the houses nearby, can hear him and her mom going at it all night long. It was the look on her face when she said it that made me laugh."

Torch ran a hand down his face, but not before I saw the smirk. "Well, it's not like she thinks the stork dropped her off."

"You know, just because I'm old enough to know about sex and babies, it doesn't mean I want to *hear* my parents down the hall every night," Lyssa said. "It's traumatizing."

Torch winked at her. "Just remember that when you start having kids. Better only plan on having one and then abstaining the rest of your life. Can't have you traumatizing my grandkids."

I narrowed my eyes at him, knowing he'd mentioned one grandkid, then no sex ever again on purpose. If he thought I was keeping my hands off Lyssa, he was going to be sorely disappointed. "We already decided we're filling the house with kids. I'll hire a therapist for them."

Lyssa groaned and buried her face in her hands. "Why did I think it was a good idea to have them over? Now the three of you are going to team up on me."

Casper patted her shoulder. "Better have girls or you'll always be outnumbered."

I smiled, thinking of a girl who looked just like her mother. Yeah, I definitely wanted that. Until it was time for her to date. Then I'd make sure I was armed to the teeth and whatever punk took her out knew the consequences of hurting her. I wasn't about to let some unworthy motherfucker hurt my baby.

Shit.

I glanced at Torch, suddenly understanding how he felt.

Looked like I had a long road to travel, but one day, he'd realize his daughter meant the world to me and I'd do anything for her. Even die to protect her.

Chapter Eight

Lyssa

I eyed the items I'd pulled from the hobby store sacks and wondered what I'd gotten myself into. *Note to self: Never complain I'm bored.*

I picked up a small mallet, which was far heavier than I'd anticipated. I assumed it went with the large metal block and other items I'd found in that particular sack. Looked like I'd be Googling how to use it. It wasn't that the idea of crafting something didn't intrigue me. I'd just never tried it before.

Whoever had shopped for the items had also picked up kits for making soap, candles, jewelry, and even all the basics I'd need for painting canvas. Not that I had any artistic talent. I had no idea how to even start using any of the stuff, but I had to admit, Beast had ensured I'd have something to do. He'd even had Forge drop off a box of books, a combination of romance and mystery.

"Now I just need someone to talk to other than myself," I said, looking around the empty house. My dad and grandfather had left three days ago. Ever since, Beast had holed up at the clubhouse trying to do his part to track down Tony and find the women who'd been auctioned. Which left me completely alone.

I turned on the radio so the house wouldn't be so quiet, then I decided to read the soap and candle instructions. If nothing else, I could make some for gifts for my family and set them aside for birthdays or Christmas. Unless I was terrible at crafting. I knew how to defend myself, with my body or weapons. And thanks to Wire and Lavender, I knew my way around a computer. Math had always come easy to me, but things like this? Being creative? I was stepping outside my comfort zone.

It looked like they'd bought everything I'd need for making glycerin soap bars. I melted the cubes, then played around with colors, adding decorative pieces to the insides, and tried out every mold they'd bought me. Hours had passed before I realized the sun had set and I hadn't eaten since breakfast.

I heard the front door slam and a heavy tread coming my way.

"Tink?" Beast called out.

"In the kitchen."

He came through the doorway and halted, staring at the mess I'd made. "I see you found a use for some of the stuff I had Iggy drop by the house. We won't need soap for a while."

I shrugged a shoulder. "I got carried away trying it all out. I think I'll get some sort of paper to wrap them in? Or maybe small boxes."

He pressed a kiss to the top of my head. "Did you have fun?"

"Yeah, surprisingly I did. I've never really done this sort of thing, but once I started I didn't want to stop. Maybe I can find a place to store stuff as I make it? I thought I might put a bunch of soap and candles aside for presents over the upcoming year."

"Or sell them at the local craft fair," he said, picking up one of the first sets I'd made with an indigo color. "Charlotte liked that sort of thing. She couldn't make any of it herself, but she'd run off to every fair that came to town. I think there's quite a few over the year."

"That could be fun," I said, thinking it over. I'd never been to anything like that before. Then again, until today, I hadn't known I was capable of making something like soap.

"Since your stuff has exploded all over the kitchen counters and table, I guess this means we're ordering dinner out."

"Or…" I leaned my hip against the counter. "Your clubhouse has a kitchen and I know you have burgers and stuff. Why don't we go over there and eat tonight? It will almost be like going out to a restaurant. If it was a place with naked women and sex."

He pinched the bridge of his nose. "I know you grew up around a club, but Tink, I'm not sure I want to take you to the clubhouse when my brothers are partying with the club whores."

"I'll wear my property cut," I said.

"And if one of the girls decides to put her hands on me?" he asked.

"Then the bitch better be ready for a lesson in manners. I don't share. For that matter, just so we're perfectly clear, my dad has been faithful to my mom all these years and I expect the same from you. The moment your dick accidently slips into someone else, you'd better learn to sleep with one eye open because I'll be biding my time for revenge."

He growled soft and low. "Fuck but you're sexy when you get all bloodthirsty. Like a damn Valkyrie."

I shoved his chest to get him to back up a bit. "You're not right in the head."

He grinned. "Yeah, but you like me just the way I am. If I were all normal and shit, you'd be out of here so fast my head would spin."

He wasn't wrong. Normal was highly overrated, whatever the hell "normal" actually was. Having been raised by the President of the Dixie Reapers MC, what I wanted in a man was slightly different from the girls I'd met in high school and college. I'd never understood women who swooned over a man in a suit. Give me a guy in a leather cut, grease-stained ripped jeans, and a tight T-shirt and I was in heaven. Granted, my grandfather had worn suits for the longest time and still tended to dress more business casual than anything else. As much as I loved my grandfather, I was definitely a daddy's girl.

"So can we? Go eat at the clubhouse?" I asked.

"Sure, Tink. Put up what you can of this mess, then get ready. I think it's going to rain so we'll drive over in your Cadillac. Don't want you getting soaked on the bike, even if it is a short trip."

"The big, bad Pres is going to show up at the clubhouse in an Escalade? You sure you can handle the fallout?"

He swatted my ass. "Yep. Be ready in an hour. I need to check on Pirate and Bandit."

Now why the hell hadn't I thought to let them out of their room? It wasn't like they could talk back, but at least I wouldn't have looked like an idiot talking to myself today. Of course, I'd have to make sure they couldn't reach any of the soap stuff. I wouldn't want them to get sick if they tried to eat or drink it.

I cleaned up what I could without having a place to pack it all away, then ran upstairs to shower and change. It was cold outside so I dried my hair before pulling it back in a ponytail. I left a few wisps of hair around my face. Even though I wasn't big on makeup, I did take the time to at least enhance my eyes and use a lip stain in a deep raspberry. If I was going in there on Beast's arm, as his old lady, I wanted to make sure I wouldn't embarrass him. Well, not with the way I looked at any rate. I couldn't make any promises when it came to my behavior or my mouth.

The long-sleeved black shirt I'd chosen had

cutouts down the arms with little silver buttons holding the pieces together. It fit snug across my breasts and nipped in at the waist. I'd always felt chunky in it, but Beast was slowly showing me I was sexy just the way I was. He loved my curves, and I was starting to like them more too.

My skinny jeans clung to me like a second skin, and I'd tucked them into the boots I'd been wearing the first day I'd met Beast, since he seemed to like them so much. Or rather, he'd said something along the lines of every time he saw me in these boots he wanted to fuck me. I wasn't sure it was the boots to be honest. He seemed to be set to "want to fuck" default whenever we were in the same room. I couldn't complain. The man had given me so many orgasms there were nights I thought I might die from pleasure.

I hurried downstairs and nearly tripped over my feet when I saw him standing by the front door. He'd apparently changed clothes while I was in the shower. The jeans he'd put on hugged his thighs in a way that made me tingle. His shirt was tight across his chest and biceps. But the leather cuff on his wrist nearly made me melt into a puddle at his feet. Well, that and his scent. I didn't know what cologne he'd put on, but it made me want to rip my clothes off and beg him to take me right here. Holy. Shit.

"You all right, Tink?" he asked, a smirk gracing his lips.

"Y-Yeah. Just need my property cut."

He took it off the hook by the door and helped me into it. His fingers brushed the bare skin peeking through the cutouts on my shirtsleeves and a shiver raked my spine. It was going to be a long damn night. Maybe we could eat fast and come back home. Did he have any idea the impact he had on me? The way just looking at him made my knees weak? That his scent made my panties damp and my nipples hard?

The heat in his eyes suggested he knew damn well what he was doing to me and was loving every second of it. Fucker.

I handed him the keys to my Escalade, then pulled open the door. He slammed his hand against the wood, making it shut as he gripped my hip with his other hand. He leaned in, the heat of him pressing against me, his lips by my ear.

"You're mine, Tink. Mine to touch. To kiss. To fuck. Anyone touches you tonight, and I'll remove their hands."

I glanced at him over my shoulder. "You really think your club would do that?"

"Not mine, but we have some visitors. I haven't dealt with them much in the past so I can't say for sure they'll behave."

"Do I have permission to teach them a lesson if they get out of hand?" I asked. It was second nature to protect myself, but for Beast, I'd hold back if I needed to. Back home, my dad wouldn't have had an issue with me putting a man on his ass. But this wasn't the Dixie Reapers, and I was still feeling my way when it came to the Reckless Kings. As the only old lady, there wasn't much for me to go on.

"You won't have to, Tink. I protect what's mine, and, baby, my name is written all over you."

I snorted because I knew he meant that literally since "Property of Beast" was in huge letters across my back. He opened the door and ushered me outside. Since I could see the clubhouse from our driveway, it was a quick trip and soon enough I was getting out and heading up the steps. My heart slammed against my ribs and my palms felt a little damp. I rubbed them on my jeans and hoped I didn't do anything to embarrass Beast. It was one thing knowing his club was inside, but guests too? It wasn't like I didn't know how to act. Sort of. My dad gave me a lot of freedom when it came to my interaction with other clubs. As long as I didn't do anything like flirt with them, or act like a hussy -- his words -- then he hadn't minded me putting a few bikers in their place. As the daughter of the President, they'd expected a certain amount of feistiness and confidence.

I felt the heat of Beast against my back as I stepped through the door. Music blared from the speakers in the corners of the room and smoke hung heavy in the air. My eyes burned and I fought not to cough as I made my way up to the bar. Beast put a hand on either side of me, leaning into my space.

"We aren't staying long. Give Logan your order. I'm going to secure a table in the corner."

"What about you?" I asked. "Shouldn't you order some food too?"

"Just tell him I want my usual. And, Tink, I will hurt a motherfucker if they put their hands on you."

I eyed the club whores mingling with the crowd. "Same goes. Any of those bitches touch you and it won't be pretty."

He pressed a kiss to the side of my neck before backing off. Damn the man! He left me all tingly and aching. Why had I wanted to leave the house? I suddenly couldn't remember and wanted nothing more than to be back home, preferably in bed. Naked. Then my stomach rumbled and reminded me why that hadn't been the best idea, unless I wanted to cook, which would have meant spending an hour cleaning up the mess I'd made of the kitchen.

Damnit.

Beast walked off, leaving me at the bar alone. The Prospect made his way over to me, his gaze scanning the crowd. I figured he wondered why Beast had left me alone. As the first and only old lady for the Reckless Kings, I was having to learn how these men thought and worked, and what they expected of me. So far, I still felt like I was floundering.

"Beast wants his usual order, and I'll take a bacon cheeseburger, pink in the center, with a side of fries," I said.

"Drink?" he asked.

"Beast didn't say what he wanted, but I'll take whatever soda you have available."

His lips tipped up a little on one corner and he nodded. "Coming right up. Better get over to your man before someone decides he's fair game. I'm hoping I can make it through the night without cleaning up any broken furniture or blood. Something tells me you won't just sit idly by when someone puts their hands on Beast."

"You would be right. I already warned him too, so he won't be surprised if I have to beat one of these whores."

He winked and went to get my drink, handing off a sealed can before making his way to the kitchen, hopefully to place our order. I couldn't see over all the men in the room, but Beast had mentioned a table in the corner. That narrowed it down to four locations. I worked my way along the bar but I didn't see him so I quickly turned to head for the next wall. Someone stepped into my path, making me eye-level with a patch that read *Savage Knights MC*. I noticed he went by Seeker. I lifted my gaze and raised my eyebrows as I stared him down.

"You going to move or are your feet stuck to the

floor?" I asked.

"You must be Beast's old lady," he said.

"Last time I checked."

He crowded in closer, nearly pressing up against me. I clutched the soda to my stomach wondering if I was about to have to put him on the floor. I really didn't want to do anything that might mess up whatever Beast had going with this guy's club, but I also wouldn't be intimidated.

"Brought your old man a present. You keep clear until they're done."

They? I leaned to the side and peered around him, finally spotting Beast at a table. A blonde was pawing at him, her tits out and in his face. To his credit, he seemed to be doing his best to ignore her without knocking her to the floor. But if she'd been a gift, he wouldn't want to be rough with her and offend his guests. I looked up at Seeker.

"Yeah, sorry. Not happening."

He folded his arms. "Really? What's a tiny little thing like you going to do about it? Be a good girl, and just wait. You obviously need a lesson in how things work in a club."

"Wow. Just... wow. You don't do your homework at all, do you?" Brick came to stand next to me and I handed him my soda. He took it, his brows lowering as he eyed the can, then me. Before he could ask why I'd handed the beverage to him, I decided to teach Seeker a lesson.

I brought my knee up like I was going to nail him in the balls, and predictably, he shifted to cover his dick. I took the opportunity to nail him in his temple with my fist. He staggered but didn't go down. He let out an enraged roar and swung at me, but I ducked and gave his balls a nice uppercut. The big man fell to the ground, cupping his bruised testicles. I took my can back from Brick and used Seeker as a stepping stone, putting my foot on his stomach as I walked over him.

"FYI, I'm not just Beast's old lady. I'm also Torch's daughter. You think the President of the Dixie Reapers didn't teach his kids how to protect themselves? Fucking idiot." I stalked off, making my way to Beast. He'd stood at some point, his gaze shooting from me to Seeker, then back again. I grabbed the blonde by her hair and yanked her away from my man. "Run along. Your services aren't needed."

She huffed, but took one look at the cut over my shoulders and turned to leave. At least the woman they'd brought was smart. Wasn't sure I could say the same for the Savage Knights themselves. Then again, it wasn't fair to judge them all based on the actions of one. I noticed a man sitting to Beast's right, wearing the same cut as Seeker. *Claus* was stitched on his cut and I almost snickered. The man really did look like Santa. Well, if Santa were sexy.

"Looks like Seeker said the wrong thing," Claus said. "It's impressive you took him down."

"What can I say? I'm my daddy's girl, and my grandfather helped train me too." I held out my hand to him. "Lyssa."

I heard a groan behind me as Claus wrapped his fingers around mine in a brief shake. There was no doubt in my mind Seeker had either come to bitch, or maybe get revenge. I fought not to tense as I waited to see what he'd do.

"No one said a fucking thing about her being a damn princess," Seeker said. "Shit, woman. Next time lead with the fact you're Torch's kid."

"Better yet," Beast said. "Make sure they know you're Casper VanHorne's granddaughter. Nothing against your dad, but your grandfather scares more men."

Claus whistled and Seeker collapsed into the chair beside me, a wince on his face. I wasn't sure if it was from physical pain, or the knowledge I could have my grandfather wipe out him and his entire club with one phone call. I'd never used my connections to get anywhere, or fight my battles. Until now. I didn't like the way it felt. But at barely over five feet, I knew I didn't look very intimidating. And the names Torch and Casper carried a lot of weight.

"If you'd like to still be able to produce children, you might want to *not* offer up naked women to a man who has an old lady. Not everyone is willing to fuck around with just any woman. Beast said I'm his, and that makes him mine. If that whore had even tried to get her hands on his dick, she'd be filling a shallow grave out back. And I know I'm not the only woman who feels that way. Any of the Dixie Reaper ladies would cut a bitch for daring to touch her man."

"She's hot as fuck, right?" Beast asked, a smile spreading across his lips. "I'm so fucking lucky. My little kitten has claws and knows how to use them. Sexiest thing ever."

He wrapped his arm around my waist, then sat, tugging me down onto his lap. I opened my soda and took a swallow. Claus seemed amused by the situation, and Seeker looked embarrassed as hell, which hadn't been my intention.

"I'm sorry I dropped you," I said.

He shook his head, a slight smile flickering for a moment. "Guess I deserved it. And you're right, I should have done more research on who you were before I brought a whore to offer your old man."

"Any more women like you?" Claus asked.

"Single ones who might like to make a home in Vegas?"

"Not that I know of. Farrah was the closest, but she's already with Demon at the Devil's Fury. Her sister, Mariah, is the next closest to my age. Actually, we're only a few months apart. After that, the next oldest isn't even sixteen yet." I tilted my head a moment, thinking. "Of course, there's Janessa. She's Tex's daughter from a different woman. She's older than me, but very much taken by Irish over at Devil's Boneyard."

"Just how many girls do the Reapers have over there?" Seeker asked, looking slightly ill. "Damn. Remind me not to reproduce if we're only going to have daughters. I don't think I could handle it."

"Why?" I asked. "Worried they won't be able to protect themselves?"

"If they're like you, I won't worry so much," he said. "But yeah... a girl would be like waving a red flag in front of a bull. Our enemies would jump at their chance to get their hands on one of our daughters. If we had any."

"We probably do," Claus said. "We just don't know it. Condoms aren't foolproof, and neither is pulling out. So unless you're going to abstain, you run the risk of knocking someone up."

"Shit," Seeker muttered. "Talk about a boner killer."

I wanted to laugh at the forlorn expression on his face, but I knew it wouldn't be long before he was balls-deep inside a woman again. It was just the way men like him operated. Except maybe for one biker. No one knew for sure if Grizzly, the ex-President for Devil's Fury, took any women to his bed or not. There'd been speculation, but from what I'd gathered, after his wife had passed from cancer, he'd decided to focus on raising his kids. I didn't think for a second if I were to die that Beast would never touch another woman. It was sweet what Grizzly was doing, and maybe a little sad too. What would it be like to lose the love of your life?

Talk turned to other things and our food arrived. I noticed Beast seemed to be inhaling his burger, and I ate as quickly as I could. I had no idea why the Savage Knights were here, and I wasn't stupid enough to ask. If Beast wanted me to know, he'd tell me. For now, I had other things on my mind… like how fast we could get undressed when we got home.

As much as I wanted to worry about Tony popping up or the women he wanted to sell, I knew it was out of my hands. I refused to live every day of my life in fear because of what could happen. I'd enjoy my time with Beast and trust him and the other clubs to do their jobs. This wasn't my first rodeo. I'd seen what could happen to women in this world, and I also knew that no matter how vigilant you were, it would only take one second of being distracted for something to go horribly wrong. All I could do was be prepared to fight if the need arose. But secretly, I hoped Beast and the others handled it without me having to lift a finger. After all, it's what they did best.

Chapter Nine

Beast

I'd forgotten about asking the Savage Knights to come. Having Lyssa fall into my lap, and the trouble she'd brought with her, had shifted my priorities a bit. With Tony in the wind, there wasn't much I could do right now, and I didn't want the club to miss out on deals I'd already put into motion. We weren't hurting for money, but I wasn't about to sit on my ass and not proactively bring more funds in either.

Thankfully, Seeker hadn't been pissed about Lyssa dropping him on his ass. I could have reprimanded her in front of everyone, made a big show of how sorry I was my woman was out of control, but it would have been a lie. I liked the fact she could handle herself. As my old lady, I needed her to be strong and resourceful, and Lyssa was both.

I knew she was curious why they were here. Since it wasn't related to her issue, I wasn't saying shit about it. The Savage Knights owned a few strip clubs in Nevada and were looking to expand. Except theirs were a little different from the one we ran here. I wasn't sure if Lyssa would approve. They offered certain services to special clients. All completely consensual. The girls would never be forced to do anything they didn't want to do, but those who wanted extra cash would have the opportunity, which also meant more money going to the club's pocket since both clubs would take a percentage.

I'd offered to purchase a place nearby for a split of the profits. We were going in fifty-fifty on Cherry Pie, which was set to open within the next month. I'd put an offer in on the building a month before Lyssa had strolled through my door, and I'd signed the papers shortly thereafter.

Seeker would be hanging around for a little while to help get the strip club off the ground and bring in some talent. The "gift" he'd given me had been one of their girls from back home, looking for a change of scenery. I knew Brick had two others lined up from around here, but we needed more than three dancers. It was an issue for another day, or better yet, one someone else could handle. It wasn't like I needed to micromanage my brothers. Once I gave them a task, they knew what the fuck to do and left me in peace unless I had to sign off on something.

Which meant I should have the rest of the night alone with Lyssa.

We'd barely cleared the door before she'd started removing her shoes and clothes. I followed the trail up the stairs to our bedroom except she wasn't in the bed like I'd expected. I heard the shower going and removed my clothes before heading that way. I opened the shower door and stepped inside as she tipped her head back and rinsed the shampoo from her long tresses.

"Didn't you shower before we left?" I asked. "Not that I don't enjoy seeing you all naked and wet."

"I smelled like smoke. I can't stand cigarettes. They smell horrible, and if I die from secondhand smoke one day, I'll come back to haunt every bastard responsible."

Right. I'd found out the hard way she didn't like cigarettes and I'd made sure I didn't smoke around her. Granted, I hadn't realized exactly how much she hated the smell until just now. I'd thought it was more of an irritation to her eyes since I'd seen her blink rapidly whenever someone was smoking near her. It just gave me a good reason to quit. I'd tried before, and succeeded for several months, until I'd caved and lit one up.

I reached for her soap and decided to wash her myself. Any excuse to get my hands on her curves. She felt like silk as I glided my hands down her ribs, up her back, and down over her shoulders. Cupping her breasts, I felt her nipples harden against my palms. She was the perfect fucking woman for a randy asshole like me. All I had to do was touch her, whisper dirty things in her ear, or press my cock against her and she was ready to go. I hadn't lied when I'd told the Savage Knights that I was fucking lucky to call Lyssa mine. She was every biker's wet dream, and the perfect old lady. Even though she'd put Seeker on his ass, I knew if I'd told her to behave and come to me with any issues, she'd have backed down. She might have hated it, and given me an earful later, but she'd have done it.

"You're gorgeous," I said, pinching her nipples before trailing my hands down her belly. I dipped one between her legs while I held her hip with the other. She moaned and spread her thighs a little more. We'd have to fuck in front of a mirror… soon. I wanted to see my hands on her tits, see her pussy spread wide around my cock, and watch her face as I took her from behind. It made me even hotter to think of her watching all the things I would do to her.

"If we keep fucking like rabbits, we'll be setting up a nursery really soon," she murmured.

"You like fucking me," I pointed out, and I seriously had no issue with having kids with her. In fact, I wanted it. Badly.

"Yeah." She smiled. "I really do."

I kissed her, slipping my tongue between her lips. She opened to me, giving in, bending to my will. I dominated her mouth while I worked her clit, feeling the little bud harden. It wouldn't take much to get her off. It never did.

"Come for me, beautiful." I nipped her lip. "Right the fuck now, Tink."

She gave a little cry, and I felt her tremble. Her hips jerked against my hand and I plunged two fingers inside her. Her pussy gripped me tight, as she rode out her orgasm. When the last of her tremors had subsided, I spun her to face the wall and pressed against her back, urging her to bend over. She gripped the bench and spread her thighs.

I tugged on my cock, smearing the pre-cum over the head before I held onto her waist with one hand and guided my dick into her wet heat with the other. Even if I lived to be one hundred, I'd never grow tired of the way she felt. So tight. Hot. Fucking perfect. And the way she looked? Her pussy was fucking beautiful taking me deep. I didn't stop until she'd taken every inch. My muscles strained as I held back. I wanted to take her hard and fast, pounding her sweet pussy until I filled her up with my cum.

"Tink, I think you must have a magic pussy."

She snorted, then giggled, glancing at me over her shoulder. "And why is that?"

"Because once I'm inside you I never want to come back out. At the same time, I want to fuck you so hard it would border on painful. For you." Need flared inside me at the thought of holding her down and taking her hard. Only if it was what she wanted too. I liked getting a little rough sometimes, but I'd never cross the line. If she wasn't into it, then it wasn't any fun for me.

"I can take it, Eric. Show me what you've got."

I tightened my hold on her. "Tink, you have no idea what you're asking for."

"I'll never know at this rate. I won't break, Eric. If it's too much, I promise I'll say something. Do I need a safe word? Is that the sort of pain you mean?"

I smacked her hip. "What the fuck do you know about safe words?"

"I read. I'm not stupid."

I drew back my hips and slammed back in. "Didn't say you were."

She wanted to see what I was like when I let go? Then maybe I'd give her a taste. She'd experienced a small measure of it in the bedroom before, when I'd tied her to the headboard. Still, what I wanted to do to her went far beyond that. I'd always held myself back, even with the club whores, afraid it would freak them out.

I gripped her hair and pulled her head back until she looked me in the eye. "You want this? Want all of me? Every dark, twisted part?"

She nodded eagerly.

"Want to know why they call me Beast? Be sure, Tink."

"I'm sure."

I pulled free of her body and smacked her ass. "Then let's dry off and go downstairs."

Her brow furrowed. "Downstairs?"

"Ever notice the locked door?"

She nodded. "I figured it was an office or something."

More along the lines of the *or something*. She'd find out soon enough. I shut off the water and briskly dried the both of us. Opening the closet, I yanked out a duffle bag I'd been prepping the last week, on the off chance my old lady ever got adventurous enough to try a few things. I carried it downstairs and led her to the locked room. It wasn't an ordinary knob and latch.

It required a code to gain access.

"They call me Beast because the women have always said I'm a beast in bed. I've always been a little rough when it comes to sex." Her eyes narrowed. "You wanted to know, Tink. I want honesty between us, remember? What I'm about to show you is a side of me I don't share with anyone else, or haven't in a really long time."

I punched in the numbers and pushed the door open, then flicked on the lights.

I heard her sharp inhalation as she stepped over the threshold, her eyes wide as she took everything in. I'd discovered what a few women had called my darker side at a rather young age, shortly after my wife had passed. At the time, I'd had a much older woman who showed me the ropes, no pun intended. Since then, I hadn't trusted anyone enough to share this part of my life with them. I'd known Charlotte would never be able to handle it, assuming she'd ever accepted anything more than friendship from me, so I'd kept the few pieces I'd had made under lock and key in a storage room. Then I'd built this house and set up this room in the hopes I'd get to use it someday.

I'd come in here a few times, made sure the place stayed clean and ready on the off chance I ever found someone to share it with. Now my old lady was eyeing the space while she chewed on her lower lip. I reached out and tugged it from between her teeth, worried she'd make herself bleed.

"Still up for it, Tink?" I asked.

"Yeah, I think I am, just… go slow. I've read about some of this stuff, but I never thought I'd actually try it. I trust you, Eric. I'd never let anyone else bring me to a place like this. Just keep that in mind."

I nodded and motioned to a small bench. "Why

don't we start there?"

It was my favorite piece. One I'd designed myself and paid a fuck ton to have made to my specifications. I honestly didn't need anything else in this room as long as I had this one piece of furniture. Although, I was eager to try out everything in here, as long as Lyssa was willing.

She walked over and I shut the door, making sure it locked again in case anyone stopped by the house uninvited. I set the bag down and unzipped it. The rasp was loud in the otherwise quiet room. Deciding I needed to change the atmosphere a bit, I lit a row of candles on a cabinet across the room, and another set on the opposite side of the room before I shut off the light. The flames flickered and cast a soft glow on the space. Lyssa visibly relaxed, and I knew I'd done the right thing.

"Tink, I'm going to give you a choice starting out. You want to be tied down, or free to move?"

"Um. Maybe free to move? Wait." She looked around, probably trying to figure out what I was about to do to her. "Tie me down."

"I won't be using ropes. To be completely transparent, no one has used anything in this room. It's all brand new, and I've never trusted anyone enough to bring them in here. Same for the stuff in the bag. The few things I've opened I've only used on you."

She took a deep breath and let it out slowly. I positioned her body the way I wanted her, with her tits hanging over the padded top, the leather supporting her stomach. I used the wide leather cuffs to anchor her wrists in front of her. Even if she tried to rise up, she wouldn't be able to. Next I used the leather straps and buckles to spread her legs and locked down each thigh, making sure they weren't so tight they'd hurt, but good enough she wouldn't be able to budge.

The padded bench where she kneeled was just high enough that her ass stuck up in the air, her pussy lips parted. One of these days, I'd video a session with her in this room so I could play it back later. If she ever cut me off, I'd have the perfect material for yanking one out.

I pulled the duffle closer to her and took out the items I wanted. I curved my back over hers, letting her feel my hard cock between her legs as I tweaked her nipples. Lyssa made the sweetest sounds as I tugged and twisted the hard tips. I grabbed the vibrating nipple clamps and adjusted the screws on each before attaching them. She made a squeak as I tightened them a little more and turned them on.

"Oh, shit! Eric! I… I…"

"Don't you even think of coming yet, Tink, or I'll punish you. Now, about that safe word. What's it going to be?"

"Bunny."

My lips quirked in amusement, but I said the word back to her, making sure we were on the same page. Normally, I'd have blindfolded my partner. Since this was her first time, I was going to go a little light on her. I wanted to use every single thing I owned, drag this out for hours if not days, but for now, I'd settle for making her scream and beg for more. I needed her to want to come back here. Often.

"Ar-are you like a Dom or something?" she asked.

"I don't put a label on it, Tink. It's not like I go hang out at BDSM clubs or anything. This is just a part of who I am, and I'd hoped to one day find the right woman to share it with. If I'm lucky, that's you. And if you hate all this, then I'll lock the room up and we won't use it ever again."

I ran my hand down her spine and spread her ass cheeks. Her tight hole clenched, and I knew I'd be playing there soon enough. She'd liked it when I'd spanked her before. It was time to see whether she only liked my hand, or if she liked her ass burning and bright red no matter what I used.

I selected a leather paddle and lightly swatted her ass twice, watching for her reaction. The next swing was a little harder and I noticed her pussy got wetter. Good to know. With a smile, I smacked her ass again. "Count it out, Tink. Think we'll start with ten and see how juicy this pussy gets."

Smack. "One."

Smack. Smack. "Two. Three."

By the seventh spanking, I was making sure each was harder than the one before. Her ass was cherry red, and I could feel the heat coming off it. She was so fucking soaked her thighs were slick. She begged me to let her come, pleaded for release.

"You want a good, hard fucking, Tink?" I asked.

She nodded so hard I worried she'd hurt herself. "Yes! Yes, Eric. Please."

I grabbed the lube and let it dip between her cheeks before I started working it in, stretching her a little. "You're about to come so fucking hard, Tink."

I went through the duffle bag until I found what I wanted, pulling out the double vibrator. One cock was a little longer and thicker than the other, but they'd both stretch her pretty good. I couldn't wait to fucking see her taking both dicks at once, hear her screams as she came.

I lubed both shafts, then placed them against both holes. She sucked in a breath and her body tensed. I ran my hand down her spine, soothing her.

After she'd relaxed again, I eased the toy inside her, giving her time to adjust. I waited until she'd taken all the toy before I switched on the vibrations. Maybe I should have started them out low, but fuck that. I turned it all the way up and started thrusting it in and out. Long, deep strokes. I'd give anything to be able to fuck her mouth at the same time, but the last thing I wanted was for her to bite down if she came as hard as I thought she might.

"Want to film you like this, Tink. Get a video of you taking two cocks. Fuck, baby. I'm so damn hard right now."

I plunged the toy into her harder and faster, fucking her with driving strokes that had her crying, whimpering, and begging. I'd been right. She was made for this. Made for me.

"That's it, Tink. Let me hear it all."

"Oh, God. Eric, I can't... I can't... So close. I need to come."

I reached over to tug on the nipple clamps, one, then the other. It was just what she needed, and she screamed as she came so hard she squirted around the vibrator, soaking my hand. I didn't stop, didn't slow. I kept a steady pace, wringing out every bit of pleasure I could. When she sobbed and begged me to stop, claimed she couldn't take any more, I proved her wrong and made her come again.

I pulled the toy free and set it aside, only to pick up a thicker vibrating butt plug. I slipped it inside her before kneeling on the bench behind her. Holding her cheeks open so I could see the toy, I lined my cock up with her pussy and thrust into her.

Lyssa made nonsensical noises as I fucked her, making sure every stroke pressed against the toy in her ass. She came so many times she soaked the both of us and the bench, and I fucking loved every second of it. I came inside her, but my dick was still more than ready to keep going. Pulling the toy from her ass, I placed the head of my cock at her entrance and pushed inside.

"Eric! Fuck, yes! Don't stop. Please don't stop."

I took her ass, growling as I slammed into her over and over. It didn't take long before I was coming again. I pinched her clit, making her cry out again as her ass clenched down on me.

"Fucking perfect," I muttered, leaning down to kiss her shoulder, her neck, then gave her a little nip.

"Can I get up now?" she mumbled. "I think you broke me."

"Oh, Tink. We're just getting started. Give me a little bit and I'll be ready to go again."

"Again?" Her voice went up an octave with her question.

"Yeah, again. In the meantime, I think I'll see how many times you can come in one night. I have lots of toys to try, Tink, and I plan to use them all." I heard a mumbled *oh fuck* and grinned. "All night long, baby. If you're not knocked up by tomorrow, then I guess we'll just have to come down here again. And again. We'll get it right eventually."

She gave a half-hearted laugh. "Eric, I've heard people joke about death by sex, but if we do this every night you may very well kill me with pleasure."

"Is that a no?" I asked.

"No. Damn you. I loved all this and I'm definitely ready for more. Do your worst. But if you keep making me come, I'm going to expect no less than ten orgasms a day after this."

I swatted her ass making her yelp. "Challenge accepted, Tink." She had no idea what she'd just done. But she would soon enough.

Chapter Ten

Lyssa

I stared at my phone thinking I'd misheard. "Excuse me but what did you say?"

I knew I shouldn't have answered when I didn't recognize the number. That's what I got for getting complacent. Then again, Beast had fucked me damn near into a coma the last three nights, taking me to his playroom each time. I must have lost some brain cells along the way. Was that a thing? Being fucked stupid? I loved that room as much as he did. Or rather, I liked coming so many times I lost my voice every night. He'd accepted my challenge of ten orgasms a day and then proved he could do so much more. My pussy hurt, but I wasn't about to complain about it.

"You heard me, stupid bitch. If you don't come out here to me right the fuck now, I'm going to snatch that pretty little sister of yours to take your place."

I opened and shut my mouth twice before responding. He had to mean Portia, right? Or did he not know I had two sisters? Ivy was only six. Maybe he hadn't wanted someone that young? I knew there were perverted men out there, but... "Um, Tony, you do realize if you so much as touch my sister that they'll never find your body, right?"

"Don't threaten me, you little whore. I'd planned to auction off a virgin. Instead, I get someone who can't keep their legs closed. Letting him fuck you outside was really stupid, Lyssa. One of my men got it all on video. It's amazing what technology can do these days. He didn't even have to be close to the house. The only upside is that I have a buyer who's more than eager to have a woman like you under him. Well, under him and all his men."

My stomach soured and bile rose in my throat. He'd had someone watch me? And they'd not only taken a video, but apparently it had been shared too. What the fuck? When Beast found out, he'd blow a gasket. I remembered that day. I'd gone outside with Beast to tell him my ideas for the yard when the weather warmed. One thing had led to another and... Well, I hadn't had a chance to tell him my plans. He'd sidetracked me.

"I'm not coming out there, Tony."

"All right. Then I guess I'll just have someone snatch your little sister on her way home from school. Should be easy enough, and I have plenty of men who like pretty young girls."

"You're a sick, twisted bastard! Leave Portia alone."

"Then come outside the gates, Lyssa. I won't ask again. You have five minutes, then the deal is off."

Five minutes? That might be enough time to get a message to Beast. Even still, the second I approached the gates, whoever was standing guard wouldn't let me through. Unless I knocked him out like I had with Ranger. I really didn't want to. It wasn't like Tony was giving me much of a choice. It was either go to him, or risk Portia being grabbed.

"Lyssa, the clock is ticking, and don't even think of warning anyone. I'll find out, and then you *and* your sister will pay the price."

I looked around, realizing the only window in the kitchen faced the back property. There was no way anyone was watching from there. I grabbed the pad from the kitchen drawer and a pen, quickly scribbled a note to Beast, then walked out of the house to face my fate. Taking a deep breath, I approached the gate on foot. The Prospect standing guard was Logan, and I knew damn well he'd never let me leave without permission from his Pres. Damnit.

"I don't have time to explain, but I need you to open the gate," I said.

"Beast know you're leaving?"

"Logan, I really don't want to hurt you, but I need to leave right now. Like, right this very second. Please. Open the gate."

He stood a little straighter, his lips firming into a tight line. "That sick fuck contacted you, didn't he? Is that it? He demanded you leave and go to him?"

"Logan, please," I said softly. "He'll hurt my little sister."

He leaned down, dropping his voice to a soft whisper. "You have ten seconds, then I'm alerting Beast, Hawk, and Forge."

He stepped back and opened the gate, watching me as I walked through. The second I'd cleared the entry, Logan shut the gate and stepped into the little guard booth. I didn't dare look at him again, but I hoped he was staying true to his word and alerting the club officers. It was stupid to come out here, to hand myself over to Tony, even if he did claim to have a way to grab Portia. Regardless, I wasn't about to put my little sister at risk.

"I'm here," I yelled out. "Come get me, you sorry rat bastard."

"Not until you come closer," someone yelled back. It sounded like Tony, but I couldn't be sure. I walked a little farther down the driveway, scanning the area around me.

Tony stepped out of the wooded area, two men flanking him. I recognized them as the ones who'd come with him before, when he'd chased me to the Reckless Kings. I tipped my chin up and stared down my nose at them. They might have coaxed me out here, even if I knew it was a dumb move, but it didn't mean I would go down without a fight.

Tony tossed a pair of handcuffs at my feet. "Put them on."

"You want me to handcuff myself? I'm not that bendy. One wrist sure. Both? Not happening. Sorry. You'll have to get closer." I smirked, trying to appear far braver than I felt. I'd come here for a reason. I'd been worried Tony was trouble and hoped Beast would protect me. Even I didn't think I could go up against three guys and come out unscathed. "Or are you scared?"

I heard the click of a gun cocking and eyed the one who'd drawn his weapon. Tony sauntered over. Any plan I'd had to drop him went out the window the second a 9mm had been aimed at my head. I stood meekly as he fastened the cuffs around my wrists, then he gripped my upper arm tight and hauled me down the long driveway. The brisk pace had me tripping over my feet and nearly falling twice. A blacked-out SUV idled on the side of the street and Tony shoved me inside.

The driver didn't even acknowledge my presence. Tony got in next to me, with one of his goons squishing me on the other side. The last guy climbed into the passenger seat up front. I squirmed in my seat. The sound of pipes had me perking up a little. It meant Logan had kept his word and notified Beast and the others. A rescue was already on the way.

"Fucking bikers!" Tony slammed his fist against the window. "Go! Get us the hell out of here before they show up."

The tires spun, spitting gravel as the SUV rocketed forward. It ate up the miles as the driver put as much distance between us and the Reckless Kings as possible, except I knew Beast wouldn't give up. I could still hear the bikes in the distance and hoped like hell they were closing in. Had they even noticed which way we went? Or had the SUV been out of sight before they'd reached the road? If it weren't for all the damn trees, Logan would have been able to see us all the way to the vehicle.

My stomach knotted again, and I fought not to throw up. Tony put his hand on my thigh, giving it a squeeze before sliding it up. His fingers brushed my pussy. Revulsion rolled through me. I'd have moved away, but there was nowhere to go. With Tony pressed against one side of me and his man on the other, I was well and truly stuck. He stroked me through the material of my jeans.

"Since you're no longer an innocent, there's no reason we can't have some fun before I hand you over to your new owner." He leaned in closer. "You'd like that, wouldn't you? I saw the things you let him do to you. Such a wild one!"

"Get your hands off me before I puke all over you," I warned.

"Now, now. Is that any way to speak to the man who holds your fate in his hands? If you're extra good, maybe I'll keep you instead. What's it to be, Lyssa? Only one cock filling you up day after day, or do you want to go to your new owner and be shared amongst the men who work for him?" Tony leered. "Maybe you like playing the part of a whore. Is that it? You need multiple men to keep you satisfied?"

I spat in his face. "You're not a man. Real men don't act the way you do. You disgust me, Tony. I bet you have to pay the women you fuck. Do they charge you extra for having such a small dick?"

His hand clenched tighter on me and I knew it would leave bruises. "If it's so small, you won't mind where I put it."

"You even think of raping me and you won't have to worry about what Beast will do to you. My dad and grandfather will get to you first." I caught the gaze of the driver in the rearview mirror. "You sure you want to throw your lot in with this guy? Because Casper VanHorne doesn't play around, not when it comes to his family. My grandfather is going to fuck all of you up."

The vehicle swerved and then came to a stop on the side of the road. The man turned in his seat, glaring at Tony. "What the fuck? You didn't say shit about her being related to Casper VanHorne. I don't care how old that fucker is, he's still deadly."

"I don't pay you to think." Tony snarled at him. "Get this car back on the road."

"I'm not dying because you have a hard-on for this woman," he said, then opened the door and got out. "You want the car to move? You drive it!"

The door slammed and the man walked off. He didn't make it very far before the guy in the passenger seat leaned out the window and fired off two shots. The guy staggered and dropped to his knees. Another pop from the gun and he fell face-first onto the road. My heart raced and I knew I couldn't hold back the puke any longer. I threw up all over Tony's pants and shoes.

"Bitch!" He backhanded me, which only caused me to spew again. He got out of the car and removed his shoes, then his pants, tossing the garment down on the gravel shoulder and kicking them away. The man who'd shot the other one dragged the body off into the bushes, then got into the SUV on the driver side. Once

Tony was back in the car, this time up front, the SUV was once again in motion.

The worst part was that I didn't hear the bikes anymore. Had they gone the wrong way? If they didn't find me, would I really end up being sold to someone? Turned into their whore? I scooted away from the man to my left and hugged the door. I didn't care if I sat in my own puke or not. I didn't want any of them touching me.

"How can you do this?" I asked to no one in particular. "Do none of you have a soul? What happened to you that it made you think something like this was okay?"

"If you don't shut up, I'll let Leo find a way to occupy your mouth," Tony said.

The guy sitting next to me snickered, then blew me a kiss.

I'd joked more than once that my family must have me microchipped like a pet, but right now I really hoped that it was true. I didn't have my phone or car with me. Was there another way they could trace me? I really, really hoped so. If not, then leaving the compound to meet Tony had been even dumber than I'd thought. What if I never saw my family again? What about Beast? Would he keep searching for me, or would he give up and move on?

I pressed a hand to my stomach, hoping there wasn't a baby in there. It would only give them another way to control me, and I'd never want to raise a child in that environment. As much as I wanted a baby with Beast, I couldn't handle the thought of any of these men, or ones like them, getting their hands on someone so innocent.

At some point, I fell asleep, my head resting against the window. The door opened and I nearly fell out, landing right in a man's arms. His cologne teased my nose as he helped me stand. The fact he wore a suit didn't exactly ease my nerves. I knew plenty of men who dressed nice but hid a black heart under their clothing. When I looked into his eyes, I knew he'd either never had a soul, or it had burned out long ago. There was nothing there except darkness and pain.

"Lyssa, meet your new owner. I'd advise you be nicer to him than you were to me," Tony said, giving me a smirk before he walked off. I stared a moment, trying to process the fact he was wandering around without pants and didn't seem the least bit concerned. Then again, maybe he hadn't brought a change of clothes with him.

The man who'd bought me smoothed my hair from my face, then gripped my chin, turning my face one way, then the other. "Let's get you upstairs and get a better look at you, pet."

I closed my eyes and took a breath before he led me into the biggest house I'd ever seen. With every step I took, I prayed. *Please find me. Someone save me, before it's too late.*

If ever there was a time for God to answer my prayers, this would be it. I only hoped he didn't leave me here with these monsters. I'd rather die than be with anyone other than Beast. And with men like these, death was a real possibility.

Chapter Eleven

Beast

"Explain to me again why I had to fall back?" I asked as I glared at Casper, Torch, and Venom.

The fuckers had shown up about the same time I'd been notified Lyssa was gone. They had yet to tell me why they were here. Honestly, I didn't give a shit, as long as they helped me get my woman back. If I had to guess, I'd say Wire had notified them of Tony's location, or had spotted him heading our way. I just didn't know why they wouldn't have called to let me know. Maybe I could have stopped Lyssa from going out to meet him.

"Because I have men who owe me favors. They're going to extract Lyssa," Casper said. "It's better this way. You won't be tied to any of the dead bodies left behind, and neither will I or the Dixie Reapers."

Torch cracked his neck. "As if that's ever bothered any of us before."

Casper glowered. "Maybe not, but we're not exactly getting any younger. You want to leave a mess behind when you kick the bucket?"

"Really? Now you have me dying any day?" Torch shot back. "Fucker."

The two of them bickered like an old married couple. While it would normally be entertaining, right now I needed them to focus.

"You think I give a shit about that? I want Lyssa back, and I want those fuckers to bleed. They threatened her little sister or she'd have never gone to them willingly."

Torch stood silently, but I noticed the tension in his jaw. He wasn't too happy about this either. For whatever reason, he was letting Casper take the lead on this. I fucking hated it. She was my old lady, my everything. I hadn't had a chance to tell her what she meant to me. It ate at me. She'd been gone too fucking long. They'd had her for hours, and from what we'd heard, she'd reached the home of her new owner.

I snarled just thinking about someone putting their hands on her.

"Every second she's with them gives them another opportunity to hurt her. They could be doing anything right now. What if your men are too late?" I demanded. "What's wrong with using the guys who gave you the intel on this place? Aren't they still here?"

"Jesus," Torch muttered. "Would the two of you shut the fuck up? Do you have any idea how hard it is to stand here while my baby is in that house with all those soulless bastards? Hearing the two of you snipe at each other isn't helping anything. All you're going to do is make me have a fucking stroke."

"If you don't want to stand on the sidelines, why are you?" I asked.

"Fuck this shit. I'm not." He pulled his gun and marched through the wooded lot toward the house. Casper had sent scouts and we already knew the location of all the guards, assuming they hadn't had a recent rotation.

I followed Torch, my own weapon in my hand and a knife strapped to my thigh. He'd already taken out the guard at the back door by the time I caught up to him. I heard Casper behind me, muttering about fools not listening, and I went back to ignoring him. How could he leave his granddaughter in this place? It seemed cold even for him, and I'd heard some horror stories over the years.

Torch shot at anyone who moved, the silencer on

his gun keeping this relatively quiet, while I rushed up the stairs to the second floor. I didn't know for certain if Lyssa was up here, but my gut said she was. I went door to door, taking care of anyone who wasn't my woman, leaving them bleeding out on the floor. All the fuckers needed to die.

I knocked down the last door on the hall, and what I saw made my blood boil and rage filled me. A man had pinned Lyssa to the bed and had been in the process of ripping her clothes off her. With a snarl, I launched myself into the room and went after him. Sorry son of a bitch didn't even have a weapon on him. Shooting him would be easier, but I needed him to suffer.

I yanked the knife from the sheath on my thigh and slashed at him. I drew blood across his abdomen and his bicep.

"Well, if it isn't my whore's first love." He smiled. "You should sit back and enjoy the show. I'm about to show this bitch how a real man fucks."

I glanced at Lyssa and noticed she was entirely too still and hadn't said a damn word yet. Her eyes were glassy and unfocused. "What the hell did you do to her?"

"Gave her a little something to make her more docile. Once I've been inside her, she won't be as inclined to fight me. I always break them the first time, make sure they understand there's no escape."

"Oh, she has an escape. Me."

"You?" He threw back his head and laughed. "Boy, I'm older than you and I haven't stayed alive this long by being stupid. You think I'm scared of some low-life biker?"

"I beg to differ. If you were smart, you'd have never bought my woman. You signed your death warrant the second you touched her."

I went after him again, not holding back. I watched his blood flow, sent him to his knees. The moment he realized I was going to kill him, I saw a flash in his eyes. Anger. No, more like fury. He was more than just pissed. He'd thought himself invincible, which made me wonder why. He'd been unarmed and hadn't fought back very hard.

"Why did you think you'd win?" I asked. I was missing something.

"There are thirty men in this house, all armed. The fact you slipped past them is admirable, but you can't kill them all."

"And why do you think I'm here alone?"

The man waved his hand, blood dripping from his fingertips. "Your men are no match for mine."

My men were... I laughed. I couldn't help myself. "Exactly who do you think you've bought?"

"A biker's whore," he said. "I saw the way you've trained her. I was impressed, and more than willing to pay top dollar for such a treasure."

I gripped my knife tighter. "A whore. Right. You really are a dumb shit, aren't you? Lyssa isn't a Goddamn whore. She's my old lady, and the daughter of Torch, President of the Dixie Reapers. If that isn't enough to make you realize the error of your ways, you should know she's also the granddaughter of --"

"Me," Casper said, stepping into the room. "I'd say it's nice to see you again, but I'd be lying."

My shoulders stiffened. "You know him?"

Casper gave a regal nod. "Dealt with him a time or two. Slimy fucker who doesn't like to play by the rules. Right now, he's waiting for help to arrive. Sorry, Carlos. No one is coming because they're all too busy bleeding all over your floors."

"She's your family?" Carlos asked, tipping his head in Lyssa's direction. "Well, that will make her submission even sweeter."

"Are you really so arrogant you think you can walk away from this?" I asked. "Or are you just stupid?"

"I'm going with stupid," Casper said. "Only an ignorant motherfucker would go after Lyssa. First, it was clear she'd been claimed by you, the President of Reckless Kings MC. Did they think you'd just let them take her without repercussion? And anyone who did even a little digging would find her connection to Torch and me."

I eyed my woman, worried that she still hadn't moved or registered the fact I was in the room with her. While Casper toyed with Carlos, I crept closer to the bed. She lay so still, if her chest hadn't been rising and falling, I'd have thought he'd killed her.

"Tink, you with me?" I asked, running my fingers through her hair.

I glanced at Casper when I heard a fist hitting flesh, but it seemed he was just taking his time with Carlos. I wasn't worried. The top-rated assassin in the world could surely handle a two-bit human trafficker. I lifted Lyssa into my arms and walked out of the room. As much as I wanted to end Carlos myself, the woman in my arms was far more important. I met Torch on the stairs, and he made me stop so he could check on his daughter, running his hands over her arms and checking her eyes.

"Drugged," I said. "I need to get her the fuck out of here."

"I'm going to give Casper a hand. If you trust me to have your bike returned to your compound, pick any vehicle outside and use it to get our girl home."

"I can give them a ride." The guy shoved his hands into his pockets. No cut. Not wearing a suit. And he wasn't dressed in head to toe black like the men Casper had called in. So who the fuck was this guy?

Torch ran a hand down his face. "Fuck my life."

"You know him?" I asked.

"Yeah. Punk-ass keeps sniffing around Venom's daughter. I trust him to get the two of you home safely. If nothing else, he'll want a way to earn points with my VP."

"Fine. Get us the fuck out of here." I followed him out to the driveway and climbed into the backseat of one of the SUVs.

"My name's Tyson," the guy said. "I'll have you home as quick as I can."

"Don't need any cops pulling us over," I warned.

He snorted and flashed a badge at me. "No worries. I've got it covered."

What. The. Fuck. Casper and Torch had let a cop come along for this trip? And the guy wanted to date Venom's daughter? What was it Charlotte had always said? Not my circus, not my monkeys. I shook my head and turned my attention to Lyssa.

"Beast?" she asked, slurring my name like she'd drank half the clubhouse's stash of liquor.

"Yeah, Tink. I've got you." I held her a little closer. "Anyone hurt you?"

"Tony touched me," she said.

My teeth ground together. "Where?"

She tried to grab my hand but fumbled it a few times before she dropped it between her legs. My gaze clashed with hers. Was she saying what I thought she was? Had he…

"Tink, I need you to tell me. What exactly did he

do?"

"Touched me there." She turned her face into me so her words were muffled. "Sorry. So stupid."

"No, baby. You're not stupid. You were protecting your family." I kissed her forehead. "Need to tell you something. I'm so fucking proud of you. Not only for staying alive, but for thinking of others. You're my fierce Tinkerbell, and I love you."

She turned her head to look up at me. "You love me?"

"Yeah. I do."

She reached up, her fingers brushing my jaw. "Love you too."

"We'll get through this, Tink. Your dad and grandfather are cleaning things up, making sure there's no one left alive who could come after you. You're safe. I'm only sorry I didn't get to you sooner."

She fingered her shirt, poking at the slices from where Carlos had tried to cut her clothes from her. "What happened?"

She was starting to sound more like herself and I hoped it meant the drugs were wearing off. I took her hand in mind, closing my fingers over hers. "Don't worry about it, baby. I got there before he did anything else. We'll burn these clothes. Hell, I'll buy an entire new wardrobe if you want."

We rode the rest of the way in silence, with her snuggled against me. It gave me time to think of all the ways I'd fucked up. Logan had let her walk out, and I'd understood why, but it also showed me I needed to up our security measures. I needed a way to make sure men like Tony couldn't get anywhere near the gates. Lyssa might be the only old lady at the compound, but I knew there would be more in the upcoming years. And children. There was no fucking way I was going to bring a child into this dark world without a better way to protect them.

I shot off a few texts to the other officers in my club, hoping they'd read them when they had a chance and come up with some ideas. We had a lot of planning to do between now and when my first kid was born. With the way Lyssa and I had been going at it, I would honestly be surprised if she wasn't pregnant already. She hadn't had a period since she'd been with me, but maybe it was just too soon. I knew she hadn't asked for a pregnancy test yet.

The SUV pulled up to the gate and I leaned forward to shout out to Logan through the window. He let us through, and I directed Tyson to my house. I got out with Lyssa in my arms and went inside, going straight to our bathroom.

"We'll get you cleaned up, Tink."

"Can we use the tub?" she asked. "I need you to hold me, Eric. I know it sounds whiny and needy, but... I was so damn worried I'd never see you again."

"I'll fill the tub." I kissed her cheek, then her lips. Just a soft brush of my mouth against hers. When I released her, I leaned over to put the stopper in the tub and turned on the water, making sure it wasn't too hot. I carefully removed her clothes, worried if I moved too fast or got too rough she might fall apart. They'd been torn, and it looked like she'd gotten sick on herself. My gut clenched at all she'd suffered in the short time those bastards had her in their grasp. Once I had her undressed, I stripped.

I lifted her into my arms again and sat in the tub, holding her in my lap. She clung to me, not acting at all like the badass I'd known her to be so far. It worried me. Had Carlos been right? Had he broken her? He'd mentioned fucking her first, and he hadn't gotten that far yet, but had the entire ordeal just been too much for her to handle?

I shut off the water and waited for her to relax at least a little. As much as I wanted to run my hands over her, I didn't want to risk scaring her more. My strong, beautiful woman had been through hell. I'd give her whatever she needed, even if it was space. Eventually, she sagged against me, all the tension drained from her body.

I washed her, using slow gentle strokes to clean every inch of her. When my fingers brushed her pussy, she shook and I realized she was crying, her nails biting into me. I wrapped my arms around her and murmured words of comfort to her.

"You're safe, Tink. They're gone, and none of them will hurt you again."

"Make me forget, Eric. Please. I need to forget what their hands felt like."

Their? So Tony hadn't been the only one to touch her. I wished I could bring them all back from the dead just to kill them all over again. If I hadn't seen Tony's bloody corpse on my way out of that damn house, I'd have personally sent him to hell. Looked like Torch or Casper had beat me to it. They'd taken her confidence. I was just glad they hadn't done more damage. If any of them had raped her before I got there, I wasn't sure she'd have recovered. Hell, I wouldn't have either. It would have eaten at me until I finally lost my mind.

It made me realize the missing women, those auctioned off, had families who probably felt the same way. I didn't know how long it would take to find them, but I'd lend whatever support I could to the clubs trying to reunite them with their families.

"Come on, baby. Let's dry off and go lie down. I don't know about you, but I think I want a nice, quiet day in bed. Just the two of us snuggled under the covers."

"You won't leave?" she asked.

"No, Tink. I'm not going anywhere."

I dried us off, then took her to bed. With my arms wrapped around her, she managed to fall asleep. I didn't know what I'd need to do for her to feel safe here again. Whatever it took, I'd make sure the shadows left her eyes. I wanted my Tink whole again. It might take time, but I'd make sure she healed. She was my woman, my love, and I'd do anything for her.

Epilogue

Lyssa -- Six months later

I ran my hand over the small bump under my shirt. A daughter. I smiled when I recalled Beast's reaction. He'd gone from amazed to terrified in the blink of an eye. If I'd thought he'd strengthened the compound in the weeks after he'd rescued me, it was nothing compared to what he'd done since finding out the gender of our baby. The fence line was slowly being replaced with a large stone wall. He'd had spikes mounted across the top of it as well as motion-activated cameras. To some, it might feel more like a prison, but I knew he'd done it to keep us safe.

My mother stood beside me, her arms folded as she watched our family. My siblings ran across the grass while my dad and Beast headed for us. Mom pursed her lips, and I had a feeling she was about to give my dad hell.

"Why haven't you put up a wall like this one? All the trouble we've had over the years and we still have chain-link fencing."

My dad snorted. "Because we have more land than the Reckless Kings. Do you have any idea what it would cost to put up a wall like this?"

My mother sniffled and pouted. More than once I'd seen her cry on demand, and her eyes welled with tears now. "Our family isn't worth the cost of a sturdy wall? Do we mean so little to you?"

"Oh hell." My dad stalked closer and yanked my mom into his arms. "You don't play fair, woman. You know damn well I love you and our kids. If you want a big-ass fucking wall like this one, I'll figure it out."

I rolled my lips in and pressed down so I wouldn't smile or laugh. Mom winked at me over my dad's shoulder and I rushed over to Beast before I couldn't stay composed. He opened his arms and I cuddled close.

"She do that often?" he asked, his voice low enough my dad wouldn't hear.

"Yep. And he falls for it every single time. It's a thing of beauty to watch."

He smacked my ass. "Don't go getting any ideas."

I looked up at him. "But I don't need to trick you into doing what I want. All I ever do is ask and you give me anything and everything I could ever want or need."

His lips grazed mine, then he kissed me fully. "Because I love you and I want you to be happy. Should we show them what else we've been building?"

I nodded. Instead of making an in-law suite out of the empty room out back, Beast had decided to put up a set of guest cottages. Even though I was the only one with family who would come visit, sooner or later we'd have more families here. If the women who fell for the other Reckless Kings had big families like mine, they'd need a place with plenty of room when their family stopped by. The first cottage was complete and the second was already underway.

"If you two are finished, we have something to show you," Beast said, raising his voice to be heard over my brother and sisters.

We walked a little farther down the road past our house. Beast stopped in front of the completed cottage and handed my dad a key.

"What's this for?" my dad asked.

"The cottage is yours to use while you're here. I'll need the key back when you leave. It's the first of three guest homes we're putting in. Lyssa wanted to make sure you had plenty of space when you came to visit, and I think she's hoping some of my brothers will settle down. She wants more women around, which could mean more families visiting." Beast placed his hand over my baby bump. "Besides, you'll want to come back when little Madison is born, won't you?"

My mother was already nodding. "Of course we will! I can't wait to hold my first granddaughter."

Torch looked heavenward and sighed before coming to shake Beast's hand. "Looks like I can't get rid of you now. You not only knocked up my daughter, but you've made my wife happy. Welcome to the family, Beast."

Portia shyly approached, the look she gave Beast was full of adoration. "Does that mean you're my big brother now?"

He released me to kneel down to her level. "Absolutely, Sprite. I hope you come to visit us often. Your sister has been fixing up one of the rooms at our house just for you. Maybe after the baby is here, and we've adjusted to being parents, you can come stay for a week or two. Would you like that?"

Portia nodded eagerly.

"Can I go play with the ferrets some more?" she asked.

"Sure you can," Beast said.

"I'm heading back to the house," I said, feeling an ache start in my lower back. I'd found that standing or walking for long periods of time didn't agree with me during my pregnancy. If I'd known all those months ago, when I'd left with Tony, that I'd been carrying Beast's baby, I might have rethought my strategy. Thankfully, the drugs I'd been given hadn't hurt our child, and my old man had come for me before anything worse happened.

I still had the occasional nightmare from that day, but Beast was always there to chase the shadows away. I loved him more and more each day. When I'd come here that first day, I'd only hoped for some help getting Tony to leave me alone. Yeah, I'd fallen in love with the idea of him when I'd first heard about his part in saving Lilian. It had been about the same as falling for a movie or book character. Meeting him in person had changed things. I never thought I'd find my soulmate. There wasn't any other way to think of Beast. He completed me, as sappy as that sounded.

He looped my arm through his and led me home, my family following with excited chatter from Portia and Hadrian. Little Ivy was quiet. I figured she wasn't sure what to make of Beast and the other Reckless Kings just yet. Eventually, she'd come to trust them and realize they were family.

"Thank you," I murmured.

"For making sure you don't trip over your own feet?" he asked.

"No. For loving me. The day you made me yours was the happiest I'd ever been, until we found out about Madison." I rubbed my belly again. "You've made me so happy. I can never tell you enough times how much you mean to me. You're my entire world, Eric."

He glowered and I smiled up at him, knowing he didn't like me calling him by his given name when others were around. Although, I knew Wire and Lavender could find out anything they wanted when it came to Beast or anyone else. Still, it was a sign of respect to use his road name, and I usually did. This time was a little different.

"I know. You've earned the name Beast, and I'll use it when necessary, but right now I'm telling Eric how much I adore him. The man who sleeps beside me at night, dries my tears, gives me more pleasure than I can stand sometimes, and for some reason loves me just as I am."

He drew me to a stop and pulled me into his arms. "Love you too, Tink. More than all the stars in the sky. You and Madison have given me something I never thought I'd have again. Family. You're the greatest gift I could have ever received, and I will cherish the two of you until I draw my last breath."

"Such a sweet talker." I smiled and then pushed up on my toes to kiss him. I heard Hadrian make a gagging noise, which just egged Beast on. He growled and deepened the kiss, making a big production of it. Until my dad started gagging alongside Hadrian. "Seriously? Mom, can't you make them behave?"

She gave a bark of laughter. "Yeah, right. About as much as you can make your man do as he's told. Give it up, daughter. They're wild and untamed, and you know damn well that's exactly how you like Beast. You wouldn't change him for anything, just as I would never try to change your father. We love them, rough edges and all."

"Damn straight," my dad said, smacking my mom's ass.

"Now you're going to make *me* gag, except there's a good chance breakfast will come up when I do."

"Stork didn't drop you off, Lyssa," my dad said.

"No shit," I muttered, thinking of all the nights I'd had to listen to him make my mother scream his name. There were some things it was just better for children to remain ignorant about. The fact your mother screamed out "Oh God" as your dad made their headboard slam into the wall repeatedly was definitely on that list.

Beast leaned down and whispered rather loudly. "One day that will be us. Just think of all the fun we can have terrorizing our kids with talk about sex."

"You're terrible."

"Maybe." He winked at me. "But admit it sounds fun. And sixty years from now, our daughter can do the same to her kids."

"Sixty years?" I asked.

He nodded. "Yep because she's not dating until she's forty. Then I'm going to demand a long engagement."

I nudged his shoulder. "Careful there, old man. In sixty years, you'd be over one hundred. Might want to rethink your timeline."

"Watch it, Tink. You might be pregnant, but that doesn't mean I can't spank you."

My cheeks warmed, as did other parts of me. We hadn't been able to use the playroom much the last month, mostly because he worried he'd hurt me while I was pregnant, but Beast still enjoyed using his hands to make my ass burn. I liked it too. A lot.

I leaned in closer. "How long before we can tell them to go back to the cottage for the rest of the day?"

"If you're offering up sex, then... in about two seconds."

"We aren't having sex right now."

"Don't challenge me, Tink. You'll lose."

I knew he was right, all too well. Every challenge I issued, he met head-on. Of course, I liked the ones where I demanded lots of orgasms. My pussy ached for a good day or two afterward, but it was so worth it. I sighed and leaned against him. "Fine. But I still say we wait until after dinner."

"Whatever my woman wants, she'll have," he

murmured. "Even if it means I get blue balls."

I buried my face against his arm and laughed. My dad had always kept things interesting, but I could tell Beast would too. And the two of them together? Never a dull moment for sure. If our daughter took after him, she'd be hell to deal with later. I looked forward to watching the mighty Beast fall with the crook of her tiny finger. And heaven help whatever boys decided to look her way.

Life was never perfect. It was messy, often painful, and full of mistakes. But it was in all the imperfectness that you could find true joy, and that's exactly what I had with Beast. Our lives were just starting, and I had no doubt it would be a bumpy, winding road. As long as I had him by my side, I'd face everything head-on. With him, I was invincible, but only because that was how he saw me.

My dad and mom chased after my siblings in the front yard, making my heart feel full. I remembered the days when I'd been one of the kids being chased. Now that I was all grown up, I'd be the one doing the chasing. When my pregnant belly wasn't slowing me down.

I pressed my hand to my baby bump again. "I can't wait to meet you, Madison. There's so much to show you, tell you, and teach you. But mostly, I can't wait to build a life with you and your daddy, filled with tons of memories."

Beast stopped and dropped to his knees, kissing my belly. I ran my fingers through his hair as he talked to our daughter. He always whispered his conversations with her, so it remained between them. I found it endearing, and it made my big, fierce biker all that more special to me. Beast was a force to be reckoned with, but with me -- and now with our daughter -- he was a gentle giant.

I'd found myself a biker with a heart of gold and a soft mushy center. It didn't get more perfect than that.

Hawk (Reckless Kings MC 2)
Harley Wylde

Hayley -- Having both a father and brother who are in law enforcement, and overprotective, doesn't make it easy to date. Which is why I was still a virgin at eighteen and had never had a serious boyfriend. If I'd realized chasing Cuddles through the biker compound would result in the hottest night of my life, I might have fixed my hair and dressed a little better. Not that Hawk seemed to mind. He made my knees weak and blew my mind. I just didn't realize the night would end with a free gift with purchase -- one that's an eighteen-year-long commitment.

Hawk -- Never thought I'd make it to the age of forty without ever finding someone special. But I did. Then I met Hayley. She's the last woman I should fall for, but I can't seem to help myself. Too bad I figured it out after she disappeared. If I'd known our one night had repercussions, I'd have tried harder to find her. Finding out I have a daughter is the best and scariest thing, but it means I get what I want most. A family.

Prologue

Hayley

There were some things you just didn't tell your family, at least when your dad was the chief of police and your brother was also a cop. It would have been smart to clue them in, except I didn't want them to cage me. I'd be under house arrest until the problem had been resolved. So far, the person hadn't exactly been threatening. Just creepy. I'd seen enough movies to know how fast it could all change, and as stupid as I felt for keeping it to myself, I just couldn't tell my family. I'd tried twice before, and the words died on my tongue.

I eyed the pink rose under my windshield wiper, knowing it was from my secret admirer. At least, that's the term I used when I didn't want to freak the hell out over the fact I'd apparently picked up a stalker. Other than cryptic notes and flowers, he hadn't really done much of anything. At least, I assumed it was a guy, but could be a girl.

I yanked the flower from under the wiper and glanced around. Would the person hang around to make sure I received their gift? I scanned the area and didn't see anyone noticeably watching me. Didn't mean anything. They could be inside a shop or restaurant, or hiding out of my line of sight. I twirled the flower between my fingers before opening the driver's side door and setting the rose on my seat. I locked up the car and went about my business, hoping nothing else would be left for me while I was gone.

I heard the buzz of whispering busybodies and glanced around again. Across the street, Delilah and her man, Titan, were walking past. I hadn't heard they would be visiting, but I didn't exactly keep in touch.

Delilah had been a few years ahead of me in school, so we hadn't been friends. More acquaintances. This was a small town, so everyone knew everybody else. When she'd hooked up with a biker in another state, the rumor mill had started to churn full speed ahead. I had to admit she seemed happy.

I shoved my hands into my pockets and trudged down the sidewalk toward the Farmer's Market. Cuddles needed more fruit, and I'd promised my mom I'd grab some fresh veggies for her while I was out. The hair on my nape stood up, and it felt like someone was following me. I wouldn't turn around. If I really was being followed, I didn't want them to know I was aware of their presence.

I entered the open market and grabbed a small handcart. I added some apples and oranges for Cuddles before perusing the peppers, carrots, and celery for my mother. When I'd gathered everything I needed and had paid for it all, I carried the bags to my car. I could hear footsteps behind me, and I twitched with the urge to run, but it was a busy day and tons of people were out shopping. It was probably my overactive imagination.

Except I remembered the rose on my car, and all the other gifts I'd been left over the past month. I picked up the pace and put the sacks on my back seat. I tried to nonchalantly look around as I got into the car, and my heart stalled in my chest. The shadow of a man was hidden in a nearby alley, and he seemed to be looking my way. Not moving. Just watching. Goose bumps raced along my arms and my hands shook as I got into the car and turned over the engine. I locked the doors and pulled away.

My heart hammered against my ribs, and my palms grew slick with sweat. I needed to tell someone.

But if my dad or brother got involved, I'd end up with an escort all the time, if I were permitted to go anywhere at all. And since Cuddles had a tendency to run into the Dixie Reapers' compound, the one place my dad forbade me from ever going, I didn't exactly need someone reporting back to him that I frequented the place every week. Granted, I only chased after my pet, but my dad wouldn't see the difference.

If he thought Cuddles was putting me in danger, he'd make me get rid of him. I couldn't do it! I'd raised Cuddles since he was a baby, and I refused to give him up. He'd bonded to me and was my best friend. No, I'd have to figure out the stalker thing on my own. Until then, I'd be extra vigilant.

But maybe just in case anything went wrong, I should tell *someone* what was happening. I didn't have any friends I'd consider close, or a bestie. So I did the only thing I could think of. I dialed the only person near my age I talked to somewhat frequently, and only because Cuddles kept running off. He loved going to the Dixie Reapers' compound, even though I didn't know why. I called Mariah and hoped she could keep a secret, at least for a little while. If she told her dad, he'd tell mine, and then I'd be screwed.

"Hayley?" she asked when she picked up.

Yeah, I knew it wasn't common for me to call. Her surprise wasn't unexpected.

"Yeah, it's me. I, um... I need to tell someone something, and I don't want my family to know yet. Can you keep it a secret?" I asked.

"What kind of secret? Because if you need to bury a body, I'm not helping. Although, a few of the guys around here might just for the hell of it."

I tried not to think about why they'd do something like that for fun. The bikers were a different breed to be sure.

"I have an admirer who's... creepy?"

"Are you asking me or telling me?" she asked.

"Telling. I keep finding gifts on my car, on the front porch, and in various places. And today it felt like someone was watching me."

Mariah sucked in a breath. "Hayley, you need to tell your dad if you have a stalker. This is some serious shit! Do you know just how badly this could end?"

"Yeah, I do. Which is why I needed someone to know, but he hasn't done anything scary, or to try and hurt me. I'm not ready to tell anyone yet."

"I don't want to be in the middle of this. Your dad already doesn't exactly like my family, and now you want me to keep a secret from him?" she asked.

"I didn't have anyone else to call," I admitted softly. "I don't... I don't have friends in town. No one wants to hang out with the daughter of the chief of police. But if I'm wrong and this blows up in my face, I need someone to know what's going on. If I go missing..."

"Jesus, Hayley," she muttered. "Fine. I've got your back, but don't let this keep going indefinitely. If it escalates, or you start to feel threatened, tell someone! Even if you come talk to my dad."

"Thanks, Mariah."

I disconnected the call as I pulled up to my parents' house. I still lived at home, even though I had a small studio type apartment in the basement. I had a huge closet, small bedroom, living area, and tiny bathroom. There was even a kitchenette with a counter, sink, mini fridge, and microwave. It was the closest my dad had let me get to being independent. Why was it my brother could chase after bad guys, but I had to live with my family? Because I had girl parts? Total bullshit.

I carried the bags into the house and set the veggies on the counter in the main kitchen where Mom would find them. Then I carried my fruit downstairs for Cuddles. He raced over to greet me as I entered the apartment and I bent to scratch behind his ears.

"I missed you too!"

He chittered at me and scurried over to his bowl, waiting. I smiled, thinking I at least had one friend, even if he did have fur.

One day I'd have more… As soon as I found a way to break free of my overprotective father.

Chapter One

Hawk

I leaned against the back of the Dixie Reapers' clubhouse, enjoying a cigarette and a little alone time. We'd been here two days with Beast and his woman. I understood the reason behind the trip to Alabama, but I was ready to get back home. Nothing against the Reapers, but the men with old ladies only wanted to do family-oriented shit and the single ones were all about the free pussy in the clubhouse. I'd have preferred the middle of the road. Or maybe I was getting old. The women in the clubhouse only wanted to sink their teeth into someone in hopes of getting claimed.

Nothing against the club whores, but they didn't have a snowball's chance in hell of getting claimed by me. I wanted a woman who looked like an angel on the outside, but clawed my back and screamed my name in the bedroom. Someone respectable to the outside world who only showed that devilish side in private. I was starting to think she was a damn unicorn and I'd never find her.

I inhaled another lungful of nicotine before letting it out. Beast had mostly given up smoking since he'd found out Lyssa was pregnant. Before that, he'd have been out here with me. I had no problem with his priorities changing, as long as he focused on the club when we needed him. But I sometimes felt like I'd lost my brother. He wasn't down to party like he'd been before, even though he'd slowed down a bit even before Lyssa showed up.

I heard something rustling through the grass and a muttered "I'm going to kill you when I find you." Definitely a woman's voice. Since I doubted it was a club whore, it had to be one of the old ladies or some other family member of the Dixie Reapers. Which meant I needed to give her a wide berth.

A fat raccoon went waddling by me wearing a harness and dragging a leash. I stared at it, wondering if I'd had more to drink than I thought or if I'd gone crazy. Who the fuck leashed a raccoon?

A moment later a goddess stepped into the moonlight. Cut-off shorts clung to her like a second skin, and the tank she had on left little to the imagination. Her long, blonde hair fell in curls nearly to her waist.

"I swear to God, Cuddles, I'm going to turn you into a fur muff when I catch you."

I nearly choked as I tried to hold back a laugh. *Cuddles?* She might be beautiful, but she was damn sure peculiar if she'd made a pet of that raccoon and named it something so ridiculous. Oddly, I found her intriguing, even if she was crazy as a bedbug.

I watched her stomp past me, mesmerized by the sway of her ass. The shorts barely covered her ass cheeks, and fuck if I wasn't jealous of them for getting to cup the tempting globes. I reached down to adjust myself, my cock getting uncomfortably hard.

"Cuddles? Cuddles! Goddamnit! We're not supposed to be in here to begin with. Are you trying to get me killed?" She huffed and stamped her foot.

"Need some help, beautiful?" I asked, pushing away from the wall and stepping out of the shadows.

She whirled to face me, hand at her throat, and her blue eyes wide. "Who are you?"

"Name's Hawk. My club is here visiting the Dixie Reapers. I think the question is who are you?"

She folded her arms, like she was trying to hold herself together. Her lips pressed together, and she glanced away. It was clear she didn't want to give me her name, which made me want to know even more.

"Guess I should go get Tank," I said. "I'm sure he can spare a few men to help you find your pet."

She jolted. "No! Wait, I... I'm not supposed to be inside the gates, but Cuddles took off and I needed to find him."

Now we were getting somewhere.

"I'll help you find Cuddles, on one condition."

"What's that?" she asked.

"Your name, for one."

She licked her lips and shifted on her feet. "Hayley. Hayley Daniels."

"That wasn't so painful, was it? All right, Hayley. My second condition is that you spend some time with me while my club is here."

She jolted and took a step back. "I can't! I... you don't understand."

I moved closer until I could reach out and wrap a lock of her honey-colored hair around my fingers. "Can't? Or won't?"

"My family tolerates the Dixie Reapers, but my dad and brother will go through the roof if they find out I'm hanging around bikers. You said you're only here visiting. Why bother spending time with me?"

"Because I find you fascinating."

"When you say spend time... what exactly do you mean? Because if it's sex, I don't do one-night stands."

"I don't take what isn't offered, beautiful. Just want to get to know you. Not asking for anything more."

"All right. I need to catch Cuddles before he gets into trouble."

I took her hand and led her farther into the darkness. I couldn't believe I was going to spend the night chasing after a fucking raccoon. We finally found the beast, tail up in a trash can. It might have been funny, if Preacher didn't have a gun trained on it.

"No!" Hayley screamed and took off.

Preacher swung his gun toward her before seeing me and lowering the weapon. "Christ, Hawk. All those women at the clubhouse and you had to go and find the most innocent girl in town? What the hell are you doing inside the compound, Hayley? Your dad and brother know you're here?"

"Not exactly," she said, reaching into the trash and pulling out her pet. She gripped the leash when she set Cuddles on the ground. The raccoon reached up and wrapped its front paws around her leg, brushing his head against her. "Cuddles ran off. He came in here and I had to catch him."

Preacher ran a hand over his head. "Who the fuck is on the damn gate tonight?"

She danced from foot to foot again. "Spencer."

Preacher rolled his eyes. "Of-fucking-course. Naturally he let you waltz right in without telling anyone."

I glanced from Preacher to Hayley and back again. "What the fuck does that mean?"

"It means Spencer would do anything for Hayley. They were best friends until he started to prospect for us. Her brother had a shit fit and read Spencer the riot act, forbidding him to go anywhere near Hayley."

"Your brother sounds like an asshole," I said.

Hayley snickered. "You're not wrong. He has a god complex."

"Take Cuddles and get the fuck out of here, Hayley. We don't need your dad and brother putting us under a microscope. We may be more legit these days, but old habits die hard."

She gave a jerky nod, picked up her pet, and walked off. I watched her a moment before deciding to follow. I tried to tell myself we'd made a deal and she needed to uphold her end. I had to wonder if it was more. I hadn't liked the idea of her and some punk ass wannabe being close. No, if she was going to have a biker between her thighs, it would be me.

I was starting to understand how Beast had fallen so hard and fast for his woman. Seeing Hayley tramp through the compound, chasing a raccoon of all things, something inside me had twisted into a pretzel. I didn't like the feeling in my gut, or the way my heart beat a little faster in her presence.

"Exactly how old are you?" I asked. "Don't know too many grown women who let their families rule their lives."

"I'm eighteen," she said, looking at me over her shoulder. "And my dad and brother don't exactly ask permission. They just step in and take over."

I reached out and tugged on her beltloops, spinning her until she crashed against me, the raccoon smashed between us. "Don't go."

"You heard Preacher. I need to leave before I cause trouble." The raccoon squirmed between us, but she scratched his ears and he settled.

"And I think you need to stay." Before I could talk myself out of it, I lowered my head and claimed her lips. She tasted so fucking sweet! She whimpered and dropped her pet, the raccoon chittering his displeasure. Her arms went up around my neck. Her nipples pebbled and I felt the hard points brush against me. I slid my hand down her back to cup her ass, giving it a squeeze. Gripping her thigh, I brought it over my hip and ground my hard cock against her.

"Yes! Yes, please." She pressed closer. "Hawk, I need... need..."

"You need to come, beautiful?"

She nodded.

I laid her down in the grass, knowing she deserved better, and definitely more private, but we were both burning so hot. It was risky being this close to the road, but I counted on the family men being home and the others partying at the clubhouse. I unfastened her shorts and worked them over her hips before I cupped her pussy. Her panties were damp, and I couldn't wait to feel her on my fingers. I yanked the silky material down, exposing her. She shivered and clung to me as I rubbed her slit.

"So wet, beautiful." I leaned down to kiss her again, while using my thumb to circle her clit. I teased her opening with my finger before sliding it in. Jesus! I'd never felt a woman so tight before, so fucking perfect. I worked her pussy while I devoured her lips. She cried out, her body bowing as I felt the gush of her release.

I shoved her tank over her breasts, growling when I saw she didn't wear a bra. I took one of the hard tips into my mouth and gave it a long, hard suck. She squirmed under me, silently begging for more. A buzzing filled my head as I made her come again and before I realized what I was doing, I'd unfastened my pants and had my cock sliding along the wet lips of her pussy.

"Hayley. My beautiful Hayley," I murmured. I notched my cock at her entrance and pushed inside, moving slow, and taking my time to savor how fucking incredible she felt. She tensed and whimpered, her nails biting into me. "What's wrong, angel?"

"Don't stop," she said.

I thrust deep and hard, silencing her cry with my lips. I took her like some savage beast, driving my cock into her. I'd never wanted anyone as much as I craved her in this moment. I came, grunting with my release. It wasn't until the haze in my brain cleared that I realized I'd fucked up. Shit.

"Dammit!" I pulled out and looked down at our mingled release sliding out of her and noticed the tinge of pink on my dick in the moonlight. "What the fuck? Were you... Shit. Hayley, was this your first time?"

My gaze found hers and I saw the fear in her eyes. It nearly gutted me. Preacher had called her innocent, but I hadn't realized exactly what he'd meant. What the hell had she been thinking, letting me fuck her in the damn grass where anyone could walk past? If she'd said something, I'd have stopped, or at least waited until there was a bed available.

"I'm sorry," she said, scrambling to tug down her shirt and yank up her panties. I reached to grip her hands and keep her still.

"Hayley. Angel, there's nothing for you to apologize for. I'm the one who took you like some possessed demon. I didn't even ask, just took what I wanted. Fuck!" I sat up, raking my hair back. My chest heaved as I realized exactly what I'd done. "I didn't give you a chance to say anything."

"Wait, do you think you... raped me?" Her jaw dropped and sat on her knees next to me, no longer caring about her state of undress. "Hawk, look at me."

I turned to face her. "What, Hayley?"

"I wanted this, wanted *you*. I should have told you I was a virgin, and I'm sorry I didn't, but don't think for one second you did anything wrong."

"You deserved better. I didn't even use a fucking condom!" I growled at myself, at my stupidity. "I'm clean. Got tested not too long ago. Are you... I mean..."

Her cheeks flushed and she looked away. "We should be fine."

I gripped her chin and turned her to face me again before kissing her once more. "You gave me a gift, Hayley. One I'll cherish for the rest of my life."

She leaned into me a moment, taking a deep breath before pressing her lips to mine. "I should find Cuddles and get home before I'm missed. He's wandered off again, and there's no telling where he went. Thank you, Hawk. You aren't the only one who will always remember tonight."

I watched her stand and finish righting her clothes. With one last smile in my direction, she went off to find her pet again. I zipped up my pants and lay back in the grass, looking up at the moon. I was forty fucking years old and just took the virginity of an eighteen-year-old. I should feel dirty, wrong, like a bastard who'd crossed a line. Instead, it just felt oddly right.

I smiled and wondered if I'd get a chance to see her again before we headed home. I had a feeling I'd never meet another woman like Hayley. Sweethearts like her didn't come along all that often. Not in my world.

* * *

Hayley

What had I done? At the time, it had seemed like the perfect opportunity. A hot guy had taken my virginity, and the sex had been incredible. So why did I feel like I needed to keep it a secret? I was a grown woman and could make my own decisions. Maybe it was the fact I knew my dad would completely lose it.

Not only because his precious daughter wasn't a virgin anymore, but the guy I'd picked was definitely not on my dad's approved boyfriend list.

Then again, I didn't think anyone was on the list. He didn't want me dating cops because he worried they were trying to gain favor with him, or he claimed they'd cheat on me. Anyone else around town wasn't good enough. He had a laundry list of offenses for every guy I'd ever mentioned. They drove too fast, drank too much, got caught with marijuana, ran a stop sign. The list was never-ending.

So letting my dad find out I'd slept with a biker? Not a good idea. I slipped through the back door and down to my apartment with Cuddles in my arms. Once I'd set him free, I ran my hands up and down my arms. Shower. I should shower, right? Did I smell like Hawk? Would my dad take one look at me and know what I'd been doing?

I pulled out my favorite set of pajamas and rushed into the bathroom, cranking the hot water in the small shower stall. Steam billowed out as I stripped off my clothes. I soaked myself under the spray and shampooed my hair. The suds swirled down the drain, along with no little amount of dirt. I worked the conditioner through the long mess and scrubbed my body while it set. Wincing as my fingers brushed over my nipples, I realized Hawk had lavished a little too much attention on them. They were redder than usual and a bit sore.

I slid my soapy hand between my legs and hissed as the soap stung my skin. I felt like I'd been rubbed raw, even though it had been amazing at the time. Now the adrenaline had worn off, I could feel the burn from taking his large cock. Too bad I didn't have a tub down here. A soak would have been much better.

After I rinsed my hair and body, I got out and dried off.

I pulled on my pajamas and padded into the living room. Cuddles chittered at me from his bowl and I detoured to the kitchenette. Pulling his fruit from the fridge, I sliced a few pieces of apple and placed them in his dish, then refreshed his water bowl. He washed his snack before eating it. I smiled and ran my fingers over his head.

"Love you, Cuddles. You're the only man I need in my life, right?"

He crunched another bite of apple, ignoring me. I shook my head and sat on the couch. I could either find a movie, or read a book. I eyed the romance sitting on the cushion next to me. Somehow, reading about another woman's adventure after just having one of my own, didn't seem all that thrilling. I picked up the remote and flipped through Netflix until I found something to watch.

Cuddles finished his snack, washed his paws, and came to curl up in my lap. I ran my fingers through his fur as the comedy played on the TV. A thud overhead made me look up at the ceiling. When it repeated, then took up a rhythm, my cheeks burned and I turned up the sound on the TV. Since my brother didn't live at home anymore, I now knew it was my parents, and there were some things I really didn't need to hear.

The noises got louder, and I groaned, shutting my eyes and wishing I could turn off my ears. I looked up at the ceiling again, narrowing my eyes.

"Seriously? You're going to scar for me life," I bellowed.

I heard my dad's laughter, but did the headboard stop slamming into the wall? Nope. Fuck my life. I really needed a job so I could move out. An actual job, not just the odd jobs I did here and there to pay for gas and Cuddles' food. I was old enough to stand on my own two feet, but my dad was doing his best to keep me home. I knew he thought of me as his baby girl. He said it often enough. I'd hoped when I graduated high school, he'd realize I wasn't a kid anymore. I was beginning to think he'd consider me a child even when I was forty.

The headboard stopped slamming into the wall and a few minutes later I heard the water start running upstairs. My face felt like it was on fire. For a man who wanted his daughter to be a virgin forever, my dad was never shy about how much he couldn't keep his hands off my mom. It was kind of sweet. As long as you weren't their kid.

I heard my dad jogging down the stairs and knew he'd be making an appearance at any moment. He burst through my door, without knocking as usual, and didn't seem the least bit remorseful for giving me a good reason to need therapy.

"Hi, Dad."

He leaned against the doorframe, arms folded over his chest. "Did you think you and your brother were dropped on the doorstep by a stork?"

I scrunched my nose. "Ew. And no, but you can't tell me you're seriously trying to have more kids at this stage of your lives."

"Hey, your mom is every bit as sexy as she was the day I first noticed her. I'm sorry if we grossed you out, but there's nothing wrong with showing your mom how much I still love her."

"Right. Maybe we could schedule it? So I'll know when not to be home?"

Dad rolled his eyes. "Really, Hayley?"

I shrugged. It wasn't like I didn't realize they still had sex, and I had no problem with it. I just didn't want to have to *hear* them going at it. Some things should remain a mystery.

"Did you have a good night?" my dad asked. "I noticed you went out earlier."

"I took a walk with Cuddles. It's not good for him to be cooped up in here all the time. He'll get fat if he doesn't get some exercise."

My dad eyed the raccoon in my lap.

"All right. Fat-ter," I conceded.

My dad looked at the floor and heaved a sigh. He rubbed a hand over his head before holding my gaze. "Look, Hayley. I know you're at an age where you want to date and find someone special. If you want to see someone, I'm okay with that. I just would prefer you let me check the guy out first. You're going to get your heart broken and there's nothing I can do to stop it from happening, but I'd like to at least make sure you'll be physically safe."

Aww. That was actually kind of sweet. And it was the first time my dad had said he'd let me date without making a huge deal out of it. I figured my mom must have had a talk with him. He was quite a bit older than she was and watched over me like a pit bull. I knew he meant well. Sometimes I felt a little suffocated.

"I appreciate that, Dad. I know you want to protect me. I understand. But I won't learn anything if I don't ever get a chance to make mistakes."

He came into the room and leaned down to kiss my forehead. "I know, Hayley. Your mom reminds me of that all the time, but you're my little girl and I'm not ready to let go. One day you'll get married, have a family of your own, and won't have time for your old dad. I'll just be left to molder in the corner."

I snorted. "Dad, you still have women check you out everywhere we go. Have you not noticed the death grip Mom has on your arm when we go out as a family? She's trying to stake her claim."

"She already did, long ago. Haven't wanted to look at another woman since, and I never will."

And that's what I wanted. A love like my parents had.

It didn't mean I wouldn't like to date. Going out meant I'd have the opportunity to find my Mr. Perfect. My mom had once told me she believed everyone had a soul mate. She'd found hers in my dad. Since neither my brother nor I had ever had a serious relationship, I had to wonder if she wasn't completely wrong. Maybe some people had a soul mate, but it didn't mean everyone did. What if that sort of thing was rare? A once in a lifetime love that not everyone discovered before they died?

My dad hugged me, then went back upstairs. I snuggled with Cuddles and blindly watched the TV. I couldn't have told you what was playing. In my mind, I relived my moments with Hawk. He'd made me laugh, and I'd felt special even if just for a little while. The way he'd seemed freaked over the lack of protection told me plenty. I wasn't his forever, and I hadn't expected to be. I'd known I was just a good time for tonight. If he'd thought we might have a chance at something more, I didn't think he'd have been quite so worried. Besides, I'd stopped believing in fairy tales a while ago.

No, the guy clearly didn't want to make babies with me, which meant he didn't want me around long-term. He'd mentioned being in town a bit longer, and while I was tempted to drop by and see him once more, I figured it was better if I didn't. I had enough going on in my life to not get my heart broken by a biker who was only in town for a short while.

Like my stalker.

As much as I didn't want to admit someone was following me, I couldn't pretty it up. What if things escalated? I didn't want to freak out my family, but I wondered if maybe it was time to come clean. I set Cuddles aside and gathered the notes I'd found on my car and at home. Carrying them upstairs, I hesitated on the top landing, trying to gather my courage.

"Need something?" my dad asked, making me jump.

I peered through the darkness and saw him sitting at the kitchen table. "Since when do you hide in the dark?"

He slid something across the table. I inched closer, trying to figure out what it was. When I saw the note, the blood in my veins went ice cold.

I saw what you did. Whore.

"I think we need to talk," my dad said and nodded for me to take a seat.

My legs collapsed from under me and my butt hit the chair. I handed him the other notes I'd been collecting. As much as I'd wanted to throw them out, something had told me I might need them as evidence. My dad read over them, his expression growing darker by the moment.

"When were you going to tell me about this?" he demanded.

"Now?"

He growled and got up, pacing the room. "Jesus, Hayley. You have a fucking stalker and didn't think someone should know?"

"I didn't think it was a big deal. He seemed

harmless."

My dad pointed at the note on the table. "Does that seem like it's just a prank or love note? Because it's not. Whatever you did, it pissed him off. He posted that to the kitchen window, no doubt knowing either I or your mom would possibly see it. Which means he doesn't care if someone knows about his obsession with you. Fuck!"

"I'm sorry, Dad. I was going to tell you if it ever seemed like something was really wrong. I've felt like someone was watching me several times, and it's why I decided to bring the notes to you now. I'm getting scared." I glanced at the newest addition. *Whore*. He'd seen me with Hawk? But how? I'd been inside the compound, so unless it was someone who hung around the Dixie Reapers, or was one of them… No, I couldn't even tell my dad that. He'd go after them with a vengeance. "I don't know what that note's about tonight. I just went out with Cuddles. It's not like I tried to sneak into a bar or something."

His gaze narrowed on me. "And have you? Snuck into a bar?"

"No. Everyone in town knows I'm your daughter. Do you really think they'd let me into a bar?" I asked.

He sighed and took a seat again. "Guess not. All right. I'm going to call your brother and get a detective on this. Be extra vigilant everywhere you go. If you think for one second you're being followed or you don't feel safe, you call me or your brother. We'll get to the bottom of this, Hayley."

"Thank you, Dad. And I'm sorry I didn't tell you sooner."

He kissed my forehead and sent me back down to my apartment. My hands shook as I crawled into bed. What did it mean? *Whore*. Why would he say such a thing unless he knew exactly what I'd done tonight? And the only way for him to know would be for him to be watching. From *inside* the compound.

My heart thumped in my chest. I wondered if I needed to tell the Dixie Reapers. I could call Mariah. He knew I spoke to her sometimes, but he'd always cautioned me to stay away from the biker's compound. If he knew I'd been inside the gates multiple times, he'd freak the hell out. I had no doubt he'd be watching my every move until the stalker was brought in.

Whatever freedom I'd had was now over.

But at least I'd had one incredible night first, with a man I knew would star in my fantasies for a long time to come.

Chapter Two

Hawk

I scanned the clubhouse, watching the girls work the crowd. Any other night, I'd have already gotten my dick wet, but ever since my night with Hayley I'd felt a little off. Didn't seem to matter how pretty a woman was, or talented I knew her to be with her tongue, my cock wasn't interested. I didn't know if it was because I'd been her first, or something else. I'd felt a pull to her from the moment I'd laid eyes on her. It had been three fucking weeks and I still couldn't get her off my mind.

Beast had known the moment he saw Lyssa that she'd be his. From what I'd heard while I was at the Dixie Reapers' compound, pretty much all of them had fallen the same way. Had I let Hayley slip through my fingers? Was she destined to be mine? For that matter, did I really believe in fate and all that bullshit?

My phone vibrated in my pocket and I yanked it out. Just about everyone who'd call me was already here, but the number flashing across the screen was familiar. I answered the call and pressed the phone to my ear as I made my way outside.

"Who is this?" I asked.

"It's Preacher. Found out something you might want to know. Or maybe not."

"What the fuck is it, asshole? If you think I want to know, just tell me."

I heard a female voice in the background and figured it was his wife. He rumbled something in reply, but I didn't catch it. When he came back on the line, I could hear the tension in his voice.

"It's about Hayley."

My gut tightened. "What about her?"

"She's in trouble. Didn't know if you'd care or not, but she'd got some asshole stalking her. The chief of police has his cops turning this town upside down trying to find the fucker, but he's being elusive. Leaving notes and gifts for her at home and on her car. Creepy ass shit."

I leaned against the wall of the clubhouse. "And you thought I wanted to know about it?"

"Look, man. I don't know what was going on between the two of you that night, but it was clear it was more than looking for her damn raccoon, unless that's suddenly code for something else."

"Can't say the word pussy?" I asked.

"Not with my kids a few feet away," he said. "If you don't care, fine. Just thought I'd give you a heads-up in case you gave a shit."

"Nothing happened between us."

He sighed. "Right. Sorry I wasted your time."

The line went dead, and I glanced at the phone. Yep, he'd hung up on me. Hayley had a stalker? I didn't like the idea of her being in danger, but she'd clearly not wanted anything more from me. I'd let her know I'd be around another day or two and she hadn't come back. The way she'd spoken about her family, I was surprised they hadn't already found the guy. Or that he'd gotten so close to begin with.

I wasn't about to force myself on her. Still... I scrolled through my contacts. I had some friends not too far from the Dixie Reapers' territory. Wouldn't hurt to ask them to keep an eye on Hayley, or at the very least keep an ear out for any news about the man harassing her. If I lived closer, I'd watch from the shadows and make sure she stayed safe.

I paused in the middle of a text message. I couldn't be down there without letting Torch and

Venom know. It wouldn't be right, and I'd have to clear it with Beast. Fuck it. I couldn't just stand by and let someone hurt Hayley. Even if she didn't want anything from me, I wasn't the type of guy to ignore an issue like this. Especially since the woman had me tied in knots.

I got on my bike and drove to the Pres's house. I hadn't even gotten off the Harley before he'd opened the door and stepped outside.

"Don't tell me someone started shit at the clubhouse," he said.

"No, but I did need to ask you about something."

He motioned for me to come inside. I followed him to his office and took a seat after he'd shut the door. I hadn't said a damn thing about Hayley to anyone in my club, and I didn't want to now. At least, not about fucking her.

"When we were at the Dixie Reapers, I ran across a woman chasing after her pet inside the compound. I helped her out and we talked a bit." There. Seemed reasonable enough. I cleared my throat. "I just got word some asshole is stalking her. I'd like permission to head down there and try to help find the guy."

Beast leaned back in his chair. "You *talked*."

I nodded. "Yep. She was a virgin and you know I don't do sweet and innocent. Doesn't meant I like the thought of some guy out there wanting to hurt her."

Beast watched me and I hoped like hell he couldn't tell I was lying through my damn teeth. I'd never hear the end of it. Finally, he reached for the phone on his desk and put the call on speaker. It rang three times before Torch answered.

"What the fuck do you want?" Torch asked when the call connected.

"Heard you've got a girl down there with a

stalker problem," Beast said.

Torch grumbled something I didn't catch and sighed. "Chief of police's kid, so not one of ours. She's a sweet girl, though, so we're trying to keep an eye out. How'd you hear about it?"

"Word spreads fast through the clubs, you know that. Listen, if you need some additional help, I'll send two men down," Beast said.

"I'll take any help I can get. I'm hoping if the club can find this guy before the cops, maybe it will earn us some goodwill with the girl's dad. Things are mostly legit around here these days, but I still don't want cops sniffing around here."

"I get it," Beast said. "I'll send Hawk and Snake down there tomorrow morning. They can stay as long as you need them."

"Appreciated," Torch said. He paused a moment. "How's Lyssa?"

Beast smiled and gave me a nod, dismissing me from his office. He regaled Torch with Lyssa's latest disaster as I made my way out of the house. I went straight home and packed my saddlebags with enough clothes to last several days. I figured I'd find a laundromat somewhere if I needed it, or maybe one of the Reaper ladies would take pity on me.

"I'm coming, Hayley. Just hold on," I muttered as I ran my hand through my hair.

I didn't know why someone had fixated on her, but I'd make sure he left her the fuck alone. As much as I wanted to bury the asshole, I knew I couldn't. Not with the chief of police looking for the guy. But I could hand deliver him to the cops, make sure he spent a lot of time behind bars. I'd keep my distance from Hayley, not let her know I was there. If I thought for one moment she'd be happy to see me, it would be different.

Christ, I'd seriously fucked shit up. I should have made it clearer to her that I was interested in more than one night. If I'd flat out asked her to come back, would she have? Too late now. As my grandmother had always said, I'd made my bed and had to lie in it. Alone.

I stripped off my clothes and started the shower. Better to take one now than in the morning. I wanted to get on the road as soon as possible. If Snake was too fucking hungover, he could follow me later. The second the sun was up I was hitting the road.

Stepping under the spray, I let the hot water beat down on me. Hayley was my only regret. Despite all the shit I'd seen and done in my life, she was the only thing I wished I'd handled differently.

She'd been… amazing. So tight. Sweet. Fuck, I'd never felt anything like I had the night we'd been together. I fisted my cock and stroked, remembering how it had felt to be inside her. The moment I'd sunk into her virgin pussy had been incredible.

I groaned as I tugged harder and faster. The way she'd moaned and clung to me, the feel of her pussy squeezing me tight right before the gush of her release. *Fuck!* My cum sprayed over the shower wall and I sucked in ragged breaths. Not near as good as the real thing, but my memories of her would have to do. No other woman compared. Looked like my hand would continue to get a workout. I'd already jerked off more than I had in years. It was damn embarrassing.

I quickly washed and got out. After I dried off and pulled on some boxer briefs, I crawled into bed and forced myself to get some sleep. My heart pounded at the thought of seeing Hayley again, even if she wouldn't see me. Maybe being close to her again would be all I needed to get my head on straight. There was a chance my memories of her were more amazing than the actual woman.

At least, I could hope that was the case. If not, I was in for a very lonely life.

Even if I couldn't have Hayley, I could at least make sure she was safe.

* * *

Hayley -- One Week Later

Nausea welled up, the back of my throat burning. *Do not throw up! Do not throw up!* I tried to fight it back, knowing my brother wasn't too far away, which meant he was watching. If I puked in the street, I'd have a lot of explaining to do. As it was, I knew I couldn't hide my secret for too much longer. I placed a hand over my stomach. It figured the one time I decided to go wild and do something crazy like lose my virginity with a stranger, I ended up pregnant.

I hadn't told anyone, which meant I hadn't been to the doctor yet either. But I'd missed my period, couldn't keep much down, and I'd taken three home pregnancy tests. All came back positive. It seemed Hawk had left a little something behind after all. A kid. My hands shook when I thought about him. I'd wanted to call and tell him. One, I didn't have his number, and two... I didn't think he'd want me or a baby.

The hair on my nape prickled and I knew I was being followed again. I just didn't know if it was some of my dad's men, the Dixie Reapers, or if my stalker was nearby. For a brief moment two days ago, I'd have sworn I saw Hawk across the street. I'd stopped and looked again, but he'd been gone. It seemed this pregnancy was doing weird things to me, like making me hallucinate seeing the baby's daddy.

I approached my car and froze when I saw something under the windshield wiper. How the hell had he gotten near my car with so many people watching me? The trembling in my hands increased as I reached for the note.

They can't protect you. You're MINE.

I covered my mouth to stifle the sob I couldn't contain. My knees felt like they'd buckle and a strong arm wrapped around my waist. I felt the cool leather of a cut against my cheek, but my vision had blurred, and everything was spinning.

"I've got you, Hayley."

"P-Preacher?" I asked.

"Yeah, it's me. Hang on, pretty girl. I'll get you to your brother's cruiser. He'll take you somewhere safe while we hunt this asshole down. You've dealt with this long enough."

I cried against his chest and finally released him when he eased me onto the seat of my brother's patrol car. Grant buckled me, then pulled away from the curb, speeding down the street. I cried until I didn't think I had another tear to shed. It wasn't just me I needed to worry about now. I had someone else to consider. The life growing inside me. And I knew I couldn't keep my secret.

"Grant, I need to tell you something." I wiped the moisture from my cheeks and sniffled. "I'm pregnant."

He stomped on the brakes in the middle of the road and stared at me. "Excuse me?"

"I said I'm pregnant. No one else knows, but... if this guy comes after me..." I chewed on my lower lip. "It's not just me now, Grant."

"Fuck!" He slammed his fists into the steering wheel. "Are you fucking serious right now, Hayley?

Who the hell knocked you up? I'm going to rip off his balls and shove them down his throat!"

I flinched at the visual and swallowed hard. "It doesn't matter. He doesn't want a family and I'm not going to force myself, or a baby, on him."

"You need to tell Dad," he said.

"I know. Soon."

He shook his head and made a U-turn, heading for the police station. "No, now. You're telling him right the fuck now, Hayley."

I nodded and folded my hands in my lap, wishing I didn't have to do this. I knew I couldn't hide it forever, but… my dad wasn't going to handle this well. Not even a little bit. I had no doubt he'd go through the roof. I only hoped I could reason with him when it was all said and done. I needed my family now more than ever.

Grant pulled to a stop in front of the police station and I got out, following him inside and down the back hall to our dad's office. He was on the phone when I stepped inside, but motioned for me to take a seat. After his call ended, he glanced at Grant before focusing on me. The look in his eyes said he clearly expected bad news. I rubbed my hands up and down my thighs, knowing it was a tell, and yet I couldn't stop myself.

"What's going on?" Dad asked.

"Hayley has something she needs to say." Grant folded his arms over his chest, his jaw tight.

I licked my lips and looked around the office before holding my dad's gaze. "We need to find the man following me sooner rather than later."

Grant snorted and gave my shoulder a shove. Yeah, I knew that wasn't that I'd needed to say, but I was admittedly stalling. I wasn't ready to tell my dad I was pregnant. Especially since he'd demand to know who had gotten me this way. Never mind it took two people to make a baby. My dad wouldn't care. He'd just think some guy had taken advantage of me.

"I'm pregnant," I said.

The room was so silent I wasn't sure either of them were breathing. I knew I was holding my breath, waiting to see what he'd do or say. I didn't have to wait long. My dad stood, roaring as he knocked everything off his desk onto the floor. I flinched. I'd seen him pissed before, and I'd known he wouldn't be happy. Still, some part of me had hoped he would be calm and rational about it.

"Who the fuck touched you?" Dad demanded, his chest heaving as his hands clenched and unclenched at his sides. I knew he was seconds from coming completely unglued.

"Dad, it doesn't matter. I made the decision to be with him. It's not his fault."

He slammed his fist onto the desk, making me jump. The fierce expression on his face dropped at my reaction and he heaved a sigh. "I'm sorry. I shouldn't have done that. You know I'd never hurt you, baby girl."

"I know." No matter how much my dad might yell, or punch things, I'd always known he'd never hurt me. It just wasn't the type of man he was. My dad was a protector through and through. Always had been, always would be.

"Let's back up," Dad said, taking a seat again. "You not only have a stalker, but you're pregnant."

I nodded and he ran his hands down his face. I hadn't wanted to add to his stress level. It's part of why I'd kept it to myself. Well, both things. I knew my mom worried about my dad all the time, saying he was one step away from a heart attack with as hard as he worked.

"All right," he said. "Any chance the stalker and the father of your baby could be the same guy?"

"No. The notes started before then."

He narrowed his eyes. "The one calling you a whore. He saw the two of you, didn't he?"

My cheeks burned. "I think so."

"We'll talk about the pregnancy more when I get home. For now, I'll double our efforts to find this guy. Maybe I can call in some favors. My department can't be one hundred percent focused on this."

I twisted my hands in my lap. "About that…"

"What the hell did you do now?" Dad asked.

"I might have called Mariah and gone to the compound to talk to her about the stalker thing, and her dad was there. It's why they've been more visible lately, especially when I'm in town." I tightened my hands until my knuckles turned white, knowing the Dixie Reapers weren't my dad's favorite people. "The club has been keeping an eye on me. They want to help."

My dad tipped his head back and I saw his jaw go tight. Yeah, I'd screwed up. Again. I was getting exceptionally good at it.

"Take her home, Grant. And Hayley, stay the fuck there! Lock the doors and wait until I get home. I think we need to have a family discussion about your predicament."

I got up, my legs feeling all wobbly as I left his office. Grant wasn't far behind me as we exited the building and went back to his police cruiser. I got in and buckled up. I hadn't told Mom about the pregnancy either. There was no telling how she'd react, but I hoped it was better than my dad had. Or Grant for that matter. I needed at least one of them to be supportive.

When we got home, I hurried into the house and went straight to the kitchen for something to settle my stomach. I munched on a handful of crackers as I walked through the house, checking all the windows and doors before sitting at the kitchen table. I hadn't seen Mom's car outside, which meant she was likely out shopping or visiting friends.

"Well, Hayley, when you screw up, you do it big," I muttered to myself. Not that I would ever let my child feel unloved or unwanted. Unplanned as this pregnancy might be, I knew I'd love my baby with all my heart.

I placed a hand over my belly and wondered where Hawk was right then. What he was doing... I'd thought about asking Preacher if he knew how to contact him, but I always chickened out. He'd made it clear he didn't want a kid with me. I didn't imagine that would change just because he'd knocked me up. I'd been a one-night stand and nothing more.

I'd have to content myself with the memory of our one night together.

* * *

Hawk

I'd been in town two weeks and hadn't found the fucker who was after my woman. And yeah, I considered Hayley mine, even if she didn't want anything to do with me. Just seeing her again, even from a distance, made my chest ache. I wanted her more than anything, but not enough to force her to see me. She'd made her choice and I'd have to live with it.

Hayley hadn't left her house much, not since the day I'd watched her brother drive her home in a police car. I didn't know what was going on, but her dad had looked pissed as hell when he'd come home that night. I'd heard a lot of shouting and had nearly broken into the house to make sure Hayley was safe. I'd held back, but just barely.

The upside to her not leaving the house was that her stalker had to come to her there. He couldn't find her around town anymore. Which was possibly the only reason I saw him lurking in the wooded area next to the house. In the dark, I'd nearly missed the shadow leaning against a tree. I motioned with my head, making sure Snake, Grimm, and Warden spotted the asshole. Since I knew Chief Daniels and his family were all home, I knew it wasn't any of them. No, this had to be the fucker scaring my woman.

The four of us fanned out, approaching the man from all sides, but clinging to the darkness so he wouldn't spot us. It wouldn't be the first time we'd had to sneak up on someone, and I doubted it would be the last. I knew Snake had at least one weapon ready, Grimm had a 9mm in his hand, and Warden was armed to the teeth. I pulled out the knife I kept sheathed in my boot and crept up behind the man.

He didn't even hear me as I stepped up and placed the blade against his throat. He tensed and cursed, but didn't move.

"What do you want with Hayley?" I asked.

"You're the one who got her dirty." The man's voice sounded like he'd been swallowing gravel. He was wire thin and smelled like cigarettes and alcohol. How the hell had this man ever found her?

"How do you know Hayley?" I demanded, pressing the blade a little tighter.

Snake approached from the front, with Grimm and Warden coming in from either side. The man tensed further when he realized we had him surrounded. I had a feeling we wouldn't get much out of him, and since the cops were looking for him, I couldn't exactly make the fucker bleed.

I dug the knife in a little deeper. "Tell me!"

He gave a wheezing laugh and turned his head, looking at me over his shoulder. I'd seen men with eyes like his. Dead. Soulless. Whoever this bastard was, he hadn't had good intentions for my woman.

"Pretty thing," he said then licked his lips. "She'd have been my good girl, until she spread her legs for the likes of you."

My stomach twisted. *Fuck*. He'd seen us? How the hell had he watched me and Hayley? We'd been too far from the property line at the compound. Had he gotten inside somehow? I glanced at Grimm and knew he was wondering the same thing with the way his eyes had narrowed and his lips had thinned.

"You were inside the gates?" Grimm asked. "Because you couldn't have seen them otherwise."

"Easy enough," the man said.

"Who are you?" Warden asked.

"Don't matter. Do what you have to," he said.

I glanced at Snake and gave a nod. He backed off and turned for the house. I knew he'd bring the chief, and then I'd have to hand the man over. As much as I wanted to gut the fucker right here and now, I couldn't. I'd have to let the wheels of justice turn and put this asshole behind bars. But if he got away, if they didn't lock him up, then he'd be mine.

I leaned in closer and dropped my voice to a low growl. "You show your face around here again, you manage to get away with a slap on the wrist, and I will be waiting. You understand? Next time, you don't walk away."

"You'd have to find me first." He smiled. "And your girl because I'll be coming for her. Now that you've broken her in, no reason I can't treat her like the little whore she is."

My hand tightened on the handle of my knife and I nearly slit his damn throat. Instead, I slammed the end of the butt of it into his head. He dropped to his knees, coughing and trying to shake it off. A well-placed kick to his temple knocked him the fuck out, right as the chief of police walked up.

"Didn't think I might want to question him?" Chief Daniels asked, his eyes flashing with anger.

"He pissed me off. Called your daughter a whore. I decided I'd heard enough from the likes of him." I sheathed my knife. "Could have been worse. I wanted to slice him open. World would be better off without him around."

The chief nodded and gazed down at the man on the ground. He nudged him with the toe of his boot, but the asshole was out cold.

"Want us to dump him in your cruiser?" Grimm asked.

"Just as soon as I get some cuffs on him." He pulled a set from his back pocket and knelt, securing the man on the ground. "He give you anything?"

I shook my head. "Other than spouting off shit about Hayley, no. He wouldn't give up his name or say why he was following her."

Chief Daniels watched Grimm haul the man off. "I appreciate the help apprehending him. And I know my daughter will feel safer now that he's in custody. She doesn't need the stress right now."

I wanted to ask if she was all right, if there was anything I could do, but it was clear she hadn't told her dad about me. Which meant I needed to keep my mouth shut. Even if her dad was the chief of police, and she'd said he was overprotective, I didn't think she'd let them stand in her way of being happy. Would she? It didn't seem likely and just solidified the fact she hadn't wanted more than one night with me. I'd known going into it that she deserved better than someone like me. Some part of me had still hoped she'd want more.

Chief Daniels eyed me. "You know, I typically don't let Hayley hang out with bikers, but since you're responsible for keeping her safe, would you like to meet her? She'd probably like to thank you in person."

I knew I should say no. Didn't mean I had the ability. "I'd love to meet her."

Snake raised his eyebrows with a *what the fuck* expression on his face. Yeah, I wouldn't be able to explain away this one. I only hoped no one figured out I was all messed up over this woman. Only Preacher had seen us together, and he wasn't here. I figured I was safe, unless he'd blabbed to his brothers.

I followed the chief to his back door, and he motioned for me to follow him inside. Hayley sat at the kitchen table with a cup of tea in her hands, and I noticed they slightly trembled. Her eyes went wide when she saw me.

"Hayley, this is..." He glanced my way. "Sorry. I didn't catch your name."

"Hawk."

"Hayley, this is Hawk. He caught the man who's been stalking you. The guy is in my cruiser right now and I'm about to take him in. Thought you might want to say thank you in person." The chief shoved his hands into his pockets and stared his daughter down.

Hayley cleared her throat. "It's nice to meet you, Hawk. Thanks for helping find the guy who's been..."

I gave her a nod. "No problem. Long as you're safe, that's all that matters."

She sank her teeth into her bottom lip. I wished she'd say something else. Ask me to stay. Anything. Instead, she sat quietly while the chief ushered me back out the door. I looked over my shoulder one last time, holding her gaze before the door shut.

At least I now knew there would never be anything between us. She'd have done something other than sit there, right? There was a chance she was in shock because of all that had been going on in her life, but I didn't think that was it.

No, whatever I felt for Hayley was obviously one-sided. I just had to figure out how I was going to move on. Even now, I wanted her.

The chief pulled off in his car and I climbed onto my bike, following Grimm and the others back to the Dixie Reapers' compound. Now that the guy had been caught, I'd be heading home. Probably first thing in the morning. There was nothing here, no reason to stay. If Hayley had given me any hint she wanted me here, then I'd have stuck around another day or two. But she hadn't.

Chapter Three

Hayley

I'd lasted two months. Or maybe my dad had lasted that long. Either way, I'd known this day would come. I hadn't expected it to hurt as much, though. I'd thought I'd prepared myself, but I'd been wrong.

"Give me a name, Hayley," my dad said, his voice getting harsher every time he asked.

"No, Dad. I can do this without him. He didn't ask for a baby."

Dad clenched his fists. "And you did?"

I hesitated. "Well, no. But... I lied to him. By omission. I implied I was on birth control. I'm not showing up on his doorstep, pregnant, because I wasn't honest with him. It wouldn't be right."

My dad's face turned purple and he looked like a cartoon character about to explode. I took a step back. It wasn't that I thought he'd hit me. I just wasn't sure if he'd end up doing something extreme like flipping the table over. I couldn't remember ever seeing him this mad, not even the day I'd confessed I was pregnant.

"You will tell me who knocked you up, or you can get the fuck out. Maybe I've coddled you too much, been too lenient. You have a life growing inside you, Hayley. It's time to grow up. The adult thing to do is tell the guy you're pregnant and make him take responsibility."

My eyes went wide. "You're kicking me out?"

"Yes, unless you tell me who the father is. I don't know why you're protecting him! He sure the hell didn't protect *you*! If he had, you wouldn't be in this predicament."

My mother hovered behind my dad, reaching out to place her hand on his shoulder. I saw some of the tension drain from him. She always had a calming influence on him. The look she gave me didn't bode well. It made me think she'd already tried to talk him out of this and had failed, which meant I was about to be on my own.

"Then I guess I'm leaving," I said.

I turned and walked out, heading down to my little apartment. I packed as much as I could, made sure I had Cuddles' things, and loaded it all into my car. My dad stood in the living room window watching me. If he thought I wouldn't go through with this, he was wrong. I wouldn't let him bully me, even if he did think it was for my own good. He was being unreasonable, and I refused to cave and give him what he wanted.

He thought he was stubborn? Well, I'd inherited it from him and a bit from my mom too, which meant we were at a stalemate and it wouldn't be changing anytime soon. I had no idea where I would go, or how I'd pay for anything. My mom rushed out to hug me.

"I'm so sorry, Hayley. I'll keep talking to him." I felt her shove something into my pocket, out of the view of my dad. "Call me and let me know you're okay."

I hugged her tighter, then got into my car. My dad didn't budge, didn't wave. For a brief moment, I thought I saw him waver, but it happened so quick I could have imagined it. Where the hell was I going to go? It wasn't like I had a ton of friends.

With no direction in mind, I drove aimlessly, only stopping when I pulled up to the gates at the Dixie Reapers. I didn't know why I was here, except it was where all this started. Will was on duty at the gate and he approached my window. I rolled it down, but didn't know what the hell to tell him. He looked into my car, frowning when he saw it was loaded down.

"What's going on, Hayley?" he asked.

"I, um... my dad kicked me out."

He opened and shut his mouth before shaking his head. "The chief threw you out? What the hell did you do? Rob a bank?"

"Uh, no. I'm pregnant."

His expression blanked and he stood up straight. I saw him tug his phone from his pocket and heard the low murmur of his voice. I didn't know what he was saying, or who he'd called, but if it gave me a place to sit for an hour or two while I tried to figure things out, I didn't much care. When he leaned down by my window again, there was compassion in his eyes.

"The VP said to stop by his house. Mariah is fixing you some tea." He eyed Cuddles in the back seat. "I didn't mention your pet, so we'll just let that be a surprise. Pretend I didn't see him."

I smiled and nodded. "I can do that, and thanks, Will."

He let me through, and I followed the road to Mariah's house. I pulled to a stop in the driveway and shut off the engine. Cuddles chittered in the back seat and I grabbed his harness and leash. I got out of the car and opened the back door, opening Cuddles' crate and putting the harness on him before letting him out. He waddled around the yard, and I made sure he used the bathroom before I knocked on Mariah's door.

Her dad, Venom, answered, his eyebrows shooting up when he saw Cuddles.

"My dad threw me out," I said. "And Cuddles too."

He stepped back and waved for me to enter the house, his gaze narrowing on Cuddles. "That thing better be housebroken."

"He is." Mostly. I wasn't sure what he'd do without a litter box available. I'd just have to watch him and make sure he went outside if I was still here in an hour. The last thing I needed was him using the VP's floor as a toilet. I certainly wouldn't be allowed back if that happened.

I found Mariah in the kitchen and I sat at the table. She handed me a cup of hot tea and knelt to pet Cuddles.

"So, the chief is being a jerk," she said.

"Yeah. Although, to be fair, I don't think he believed I'd actually leave."

She took the seat next to me. "What happened, Hayley?"

I sighed and started at the beginning. Well, sort of. I skipped over my night with Hawk and started with telling my dad I was pregnant. When I mentioned my dad knocking everything off his desk that day, or what he'd said today, Venom growled from where he was leaning against the doorway. He'd stayed to listen, but he'd remained quiet so far. Mariah had too, just listening to everything I had to say.

"And so now I don't have a job, or a place to live. I have no idea what I'm going to do, but I refuse to give in to him."

Venom came closer, yanking out a chair by hooking it with his booted foot, and took a seat. "As a father, I understand where your dad is coming from. We don't always realize just how headstrong our daughters are, but I think his heart was in the right place. He wanted to protect you, but you won't let him. By withholding the name of the guy responsible, he feels like you're giving this guy your loyalty."

"Why won't you just tell him?" Mariah asked.

Venom leaned forward, bracing his elbows on

the table. "It's someone he wouldn't approve of, right?"

I nodded. It was a little odd to have this conversation with the feared VP of the Dixie Reapers. Even though his hair and beard were going silver, he still had an air of authority. He definitely hadn't gone soft around the middle either. I'd heard women from my age to senior citizens giggle whenever he was walking around Main Street. Then again, they did that with pretty much all the bikers, even if the town didn't necessarily trust them.

Mariah's eyes narrowed, making her look a little like her dad. She shifted her gaze to Cuddles, staring a moment before looking at me again. There was a question in her eyes, one I wasn't about to answer. She knew my raccoon had a tendency to wander into the compound when we went for walks, if he got off his leash. For that matter, he sometimes managed to yank the leash from my hands, and Cuddles moved pretty fast for a fat raccoon. If anyone put two and two together, they'd realize the father of my baby was a biker. He just wasn't part of this club.

Since I knew he'd been here at least twice, it meant he was possibly well-known. If I said the name Hawk, would Venom know who I meant? I didn't think I wanted to take the chance. I didn't know if Venom would tell him, or if he'd care either way. Worst case, he'd be pissed I lied to the man.

"I don't know what to do. I should have planned for something like this. It wasn't like I could live at home forever, especially now that I'll be a mom. But with the stalker situation, I didn't really have time to hunt for a job, and who's going to hire me when I'll be having a baby before too long? Some of my parents' friends have let me do odd jobs for them, like clean their house or run errands, but that isn't going to support a baby."

Venom drummed his fingers on the table. "What skills do you have?"

"I know how to use a computer. I'm good with social media. If I needed to, I could file stuff or maybe greet customers. I don't have any experience waitressing or anything like that. Do you know of a job opening?" I asked.

"Maybe. Enjoy your tea with Mariah. I'll make some calls and come back in a bit." Venom reached over to pat my shoulder. "Try not to stress too much, Hayley. It's not good for the baby."

Mariah's lips twisted as she watched him walk away. "Wish he'd been that supportive of his own kids."

My mouth dropped open. "What the hell, Mariah? Your dad is awesome."

"I know. It's just that there's this guy who likes me and my dad would freak if I tried to date him." She cut her eyes my way. "It's a cop. Tyson Clarke."

"You like Officer Clarke?" I asked. I couldn't help but smile. I could see the two of them together. The guy was protective to a fault, and from what I'd seen of his interactions with people, he seemed really kind. Mariah could do worse.

"I see him at the coffee shop sometimes," she admitted. "He always flirts with me. But I know my dad wouldn't like me dating someone like him."

She meant someone in law enforcement. It seemed we were on opposite sides of the fence, but we had the same problem. We both liked someone our dads wouldn't tolerate. What a mess. If only I could have fallen for Officer Clarke and she could have been with Hawk. Things would be different then.

Mariah leaned in closer and lowered her voice. "The guy... he didn't hurt you, did he? It was... consensual?"

"He didn't do anything I didn't want him to," I said. "But I lied to him, Mariah. I told him he didn't have to worry about a baby. I made it seem like I was on birth control, except I wasn't."

"We'll figure everything out," she promised. "And I'm sure my dad would let you stay here a few days if you need to."

I heard Venom's booted steps before he entered the room again. "Won't be necessary. I think I've got a place for you, if you agree to work for James Gilbert. He needs some office help at the garage and said he'd include a studio apartment as part of your wages."

I got up and hugged Venom. "Thank you!"

He patted my back before putting some distance between us. Mariah giggled as she eyed her dad, and I realized I'd made the big man uncomfortable. I'd heard he'd been something of a ladies' man back before meeting Mariah's mom. It seemed she'd reformed him. It made me wonder if Hawk would ever find the woman who'd make him want to settle down and have a family. My heart ached, knowing it wouldn't be me.

I still couldn't believe he'd helped catch the man who'd been stalking me. I'd never gotten the courage to ask anyone why he'd been in town. The last thing I needed to do was draw attention to the fact I'd known him. They would think it odd I wanted to know so much about a man I'd just met, and Preacher might remember I'd been with Hawk before.

"I'll give you the address," Venom said. "He wants to see you as soon as possible. You can leave your pet here while you meet with him."

"Thank you. I really appreciate you helping me."

He gave a nod. "No problem."

At least things were looking up a little. Just because Venom arranged for an interview of sorts for me, it didn't mean I had the job. The guy still wanted to meet with me first. If I totally blew it, I'd still be homeless and jobless.

No pressure, Hayley. Not at all.

* * *

Hawk

I hadn't been able to stop thinking about Hayley. Seeing her again had been bittersweet. I'd hoped for some sort of reaction from her. A welcoming smile? Some acknowledgment she knew me? I couldn't blame her for not wanting her dad to know she'd been with a biker. He was the chief of police and not exactly best friends with the Dixie Reapers, much less any clubs from out of state. I'd still held out the hope she'd seek me out that night. But she hadn't.

I'd left at first light, needing to put as much distance between us as possible. I'd always gone through women, used them and tossed them aside, but I'd never had one use me before. Or if they had, it had been mutual. With Hayley, it was different. I wanted more. Maybe it was payback. The one woman I wanted didn't want me back. Was that how all the women had felt? The ones who'd tried to cling to me? Made me feel a little like an asshole.

Forge came into the backroom, slamming the door behind him. I set down the tool and wire in my hand, giving him my attention.

"Something going on?" I asked.

He snorted and looked at all the items in front of me. "Think I should be asking you that, VP."

I rubbed the back of my neck. "Just working

through some personal shit. Nothing related to the club."

"I'll make room in the shop for this batch, unless you're keeping any of it."

I eyed the pieces on the table. There wasn't a rhyme or reason to any of it. I'd been preoccupied with thoughts of Hayley, but I hadn't made any of it for her specifically. Even though I'd found myself sketching out an engagement ring last week, which was fucking insane since I'd never see the woman again. I was so fucked in the head right now.

"You can sell it."

He nodded. "I'll get it polished and packaged."

I gathered the bracelets, ring, and necklaces before handing them over to him. No one knew I made jewelry. At least, no one except Forge. He kept my secret. I liked working with my hands, but I didn't want to advertise it. I made a little bit of money off the things he sold. Not enough to call it a career. More of a profitable hobby.

My brothers would give me shit if they saw the dainty stuff I made. Except Forge. He got it since he worked with metals too. Although, he tended to do larger things like cups, knives, and even swords. I'd seen him make jewelry, but he didn't do it as often as I did.

"You've been in a strange mood for months now," Forge said. "Want to talk about it?"

"Not really."

He nodded. "All right. If you change your mind, you know I won't judge. Whatever is going on, I'll just listen if that's what you need."

I snorted and punched him in the arm. "You're such a girl sometimes."

He waved a bracelet under my nose. "Says the

man who made this delicate thing."

"Asshole."

He smirked and started polishing the items. He held each up, to make sure he'd gotten all the smudges, then started packaging the jewelry in the boxes we kept stocked. A customer had once asked if we'd ever think of offering handmade wooden boxes for the items I made. They didn't know I was the one making the jewelry, but the question had been posed to me. It wasn't a terrible idea, except none of us did that sort of woodwork. Or if a brother did, they hadn't said anything.

"If I didn't know better, I'd say you're hung up on a woman," Forge said.

"What would you know about it? Last I checked, you didn't let any of them stick around long enough to get attached."

"I think Beast has proven it only takes one look. The second Lyssa walked into the clubhouse that day, she was his, even if neither of them knew it right then."

I knew he was right. Not just because of Beast, but it's how I felt about Hayley. We'd only had the one night together, but it was enough. I'd kissed her and known I wanted more, wanted tomorrow and the next day. If she'd given me a chance, come back that next day, I'd have given her the world.

I'd started falling for her that night, and I was a little worried it was too late to back up. Apparently, once you started down that road, you couldn't turn around. I hadn't let the club girls touch me. Not lately. I'd tried a few times, but couldn't get hard for them. If anything, the thought of them touching me made me feel disgusted.

My phone rang and I saw it was an Alabama area code. I started to answer, only to hesitate. It had to be the Dixie Reapers, right? It wasn't like Hayley had my number. The thought of her tracking me down, calling now, gave me a small burst of hope. I answered the call, only to bite back a growl when I heard Preacher's voice.

"Hawk?" he asked, when I didn't say anything.

"Why are you calling? And what the fuck number is this?"

"I left mine at home. This is Tex's number. And I'm calling because you came running when Hayley was in trouble before."

I stopped breathing for a moment. "Hayley's in trouble? Did the asshole go free?"

"Nothing like that," Preacher said. "Listen, I don't know if you care one way or another. Maybe you just like rescuing damsels in distress. Do you care anything about her?"

I ground my teeth together. Did these fuckers find it funny I wanted a woman who clearly wanted nothing to do with me? I didn't say a damn word and Preacher eventually got the hint.

"Right. Guess I was mistaken. Don't worry about it. We'll handle it."

He hung up and I stared at the phone.

"Hayley?" Forge asked from behind me.

"Don't go there," I warned. The last thing I wanted to talk about was the woman who'd stomped on my heart. I'd gone this long without falling for anyone. Why did it have to be her?

"At least I know I was right. It's a woman who has you so fucked up." Forge slapped me on the back. "It sucks, brother. Maybe she'll come to her senses. Any woman around here would give her left tit to be yours."

"Seriously, Forge?"

"What? Just sayin'. You know the club whores have been pouting since you stopped giving them any attention."

"Last I checked, you aren't exactly diving into pussy every night," I said.

"Yeah, well, there are more important things in life than getting your dick wet."

I turned to face him. "You stopped fucking random women years ago. Why? Get tired of it?"

He leaned against another worktable and folded his arms. I wasn't sure if he'd answer at first. "That's part of it. Remember when Meg was here and Cinder came for her?"

I scratched at my beard. "You mean when he nearly took a bullet for her and we damn near lost half our brothers?"

He nodded. "That's it. He was willing to die for her. I knew then I wanted what they had. Took him until he was in his sixties to find the right woman, but it seemed like it had been worth it. So I'm waiting. If a woman can put up with Cinder's cranky ass, surely there's someone out there for me."

He wasn't wrong about that. I'd been shocked to hear he had a woman. Of course, she'd thought he hadn't wanted her, and she'd run. They'd both damn near died, but seemed happy now. Yeah, I could see why Forge wanted that. I did too. Except I'd already met the woman I wanted. Hayley.

"Love can be a pain in the ass," Forge said. "I'd still rather experience it once than never at all. She might change her mind, Hawk. Besides, who the hell knows what a woman thinks? What if you're sitting here, all mopey and shit because she doesn't love you back, and really she's at home thinking *you* don't want *her*?"

I thought about it a moment, then dismissed it. No, Hayley wasn't moping around her house like me. She didn't miss me. Didn't need me the way I needed her. Although, I was curious about the trouble Preacher had mentioned. I didn't think it was anything dire or he'd have pressed the issue more.

"So your woman is in trouble again?" Forge asked. "Seemed that way, yet you're still sitting here."

"I can't keep running off to save her," I said.

"Don't see why not. Maybe she'd realize how much you like her."

Or she'd just kick my ass to the curb. Yeah, I was being a pussy. I could admit it.

"The Dixie Reapers have it handled," I said.

Forge held up his hands. "Whatever, brother. But if you lose your chance with her, you'll have no one to blame but yourself. Just remember that."

Why did I feel like he'd just cursed me? I narrowed my eyes at him, but the fucker just grinned.

Chapter Four

Hayley -- Nine Months Later

My back ached and exhaustion tugged at me. Freya had kept me up all night, again. I'd known raising her on my own wouldn't be easy. My family hadn't been thrilled over my pregnancy from the beginning, but I hadn't thought they'd toss me out like unwanted garbage. All right, that wasn't entirely fair. My dad had been making a point. Problem was I was just as stubborn as him.

I'd refused to give up Hawk's name. Especially since Dad had met him. I still couldn't believe he'd been the one to catch the guy. Why had he been in town? Was it a coincidence he'd been around to help the Dixie Reapers? I didn't even want to think about the possibility he'd been here specifically to help me. If that was the case, maybe I'd been wrong about him all along. Had he wanted more than the one night?

No. He'd have said something, surely. Instead, I'd found out he'd taken off early the next morning. That wasn't the action of a man who wanted more time with me. He'd gotten out of here first chance he had. Which meant I'd been right to keep the pregnancy to myself. I'd warred with myself all that night and had finally gotten up the courage to head to the Dixie Reapers the next morning. I'd called Mariah so I'd have a plausible reason for being there, but the moment she'd mentioned their guests had left, I knew there was no point in going.

If I'd had any doubts Hawk would want more from me, I'd known then I'd meant nothing to him. He would have stayed otherwise, right? I honestly hadn't expected more from him, had even assured him it wasn't likely I'd get pregnant from our night together.

I shouldn't have lied and implied I was on birth control. It was irresponsible and I'd paid the price. Not that Freya was a burden. She was the love of my life, even when she was cranky.

But Hawk had clearly not wanted any of that. He'd just wanted a good time, and I'd wanted to not be a virgin anymore. We'd both gotten what we needed at the time. I'd just ended up with a free gift with purchase.

Freya was now three months old. I had a job I hated, but it kept a roof over our heads for the most part. Or it had. I listened to the voicemail again, my stomach knotting in fear.

I'm sorry, Hayley. I have to let you go and I'll need the apartment too.

My boss, James Gilbert, wasn't a hard ass. He'd actually been super nice, but I also knew I hadn't been doing as great a job lately as I could have. Whether I liked it or not, he was running a business and not a charity. His family owned several garages around town, as well as a towing service. James had been nice enough to let me work at the location he managed and had set me up in a studio apartment as part of my pay. The worst part of losing the job was feeling like I'd let down the VP of the Dixie Reapers too. Venom had set up the job for me, and I'd blown it.

But with all the sleepless nights, and Freya being too much for a daycare to handle, I'd missed a lot of work lately. My mom would have gladly kept her, but she'd worried how my dad would react. I loved my parents, but my dad was being an ass. Even my mom said as much. I knew deep down, he was worried about me, and he'd hoped by pushing me, I'd admit who Freya's dad was so my father could pressure him into doing the right thing. He meant well, even if he was fucking it all up. Because I was just as stubborn as him.

What the hell was I going to do?

My hands were shaking when a knock sounded at the door. I went to open it, hoping it wasn't James with a stack of boxes. Although, it seemed I would need them. I seldom received visitors here. Sometimes Mariah would stop by. We both liked a lot of the same things and would talk while we sipped hot chocolate or tea. We'd bonded a little the last few months, especially after her dad's club helped with my stalker issue. I wasn't expecting her, though, so my anxiety shot through the roof as I pulled open the door.

Delilah, James's baby sister, smiled at me. I didn't know her well, so I doubted this was a social call. So why was she here?

"I heard you could use some help packing."

Shit. I rubbed at my temples and nodded. "So it would seem. I just got your brother's message about a half hour ago."

Delilah frowned. "Seriously? He told me a week ago he needed to let you go. It's part of why Titan and I came to visit right now. I thought you could use some help. I figured with a baby, you wouldn't have a lot of time to box stuff up."

I sagged against the wall, sinking down until my knees pressed to my chest. "He called today. I had no idea, and now…"

Freya started crying again, making me wince. I loved my daughter, more than anything, but lately she'd been a difficult baby. I let her cry another moment before forcing myself up off the floor and I went to get her out of the crib against the far wall. I cradled her close, wishing I knew why she wouldn't stop crying all the time.

The doctor at the free clinic had assured me she was perfectly healthy, but I couldn't help feeling they were wrong. Something was the matter with my beautiful girl, and it broke my heart when she cried like this. Without insurance, or money, my options were limited. My parents would probably help if they knew, but at what cost?

"Hayley, where's her father?" Delilah asked softly. "Why are you doing this alone?"

Not her too! Why did everyone want to know who Freya's father was? There were plenty of single moms in the world. Single dads too. Was I doing such a bad job they didn't think I could handle raising my daughter?

"We were only together the one time. I'd assured him he didn't need to worry about there being a baby. I can't... I can't just show up on his doorstep with an infant in my arms." I swallowed the knot in my throat. "He'll hate me."

And that was my greatest fear. I cherished the night we'd had together. The last thing I wanted was to taint the memory with whatever hateful things he'd spew when he found out I'd lied, and we had a baby. I just couldn't do it. Besides, it was better for Freya to not have a dad at all than to have one who didn't want her.

Delilah's expression softened. We hadn't been close in school, since she was a little older than me, but she'd always been kind to everyone.

"He won't hate you," Delilah said. "Tell me who it is. I can go with you, if you want? We can tell him together."

I shook my head. "He doesn't even live around here. I have no idea how to find him."

She sighed and folded her arms, drawing my

attention to the leather vest covering her shoulders. *Hades Abyss MC* was stitched on the front and I knew the back would say *Property of Titan*. I'd been surprised the first time she'd come back to town as a biker's old lady. She hadn't seemed the type. Although, anyone could see the man clearly adored her, and she was head over heels in love with him. I envied them.

"Where did you meet?" she asked. "Let's start there, and before you shake your head at me, you're out of options, Hayley. You need help, and he has a responsibility to the two of you whether he likes it or not. Your dad was right about that. It's bullshit you're doing this alone, and I could kick your family's asses for not helping more."

My mom snuck money to me when she could and visited when she didn't think my dad or brother would notice. She knew this town spread rumors like wildfire, and I had no doubt my dad knew she came to see me. My mom wasn't as sneaky as she thought, but Chief Daniels didn't like the fact his little girl had been knocked up by some stranger and refused to talk, so he'd put his foot down and I was left to my own devices. Mostly. I knew he was waiting on me to come crawling home and beg for forgiveness, but I wouldn't. I'd done nothing wrong. And if he even tried to tell me he'd been a saint at my age, I'd just stand back and wait for the lightning to strike him dead for being such a liar. I'd heard the stories. Until he'd met my mom, he'd been a man whore.

Even after he'd met her, he hadn't exactly been a boy scout. He'd gotten her pregnant without even knowing it. When he'd found out, he'd married her. But Hawk wasn't like my dad. He wasn't an officer of the law but more the type to break it. I didn't think they exactly had the same moral compass.

"Come on, Hayley. I'm trying to help!"

"At the clubhouse," I murmured. "Cuddles ran into the compound and I chased after him. It was just some guy visiting from another club. I didn't even pay attention to which one."

Delilah groaned and pinched the bridge of her nose. "Great. The truce between the Dixie Reapers and your dad is about to blow the fuck up. Do you at least remember the guy's name?"

"He just went by Hawk," I said.

Freya started to quiet down again, having cried herself to sleep in my arms. Tears streaked her cheeks and she took a shuddering breath before settling against me more.

"Hawk?" Delilah asked softly. "How old is Freya?"

"Three months."

Delilah's lips thinned and her cheeks flushed with anger. "Goddamnit! I need to talk to Titan. Forget your dad being pissed at the Reapers, Torch is about to go nuclear."

I didn't understand what any of that meant, or why the President of the Dixie Reapers would give a shit about who I'd slept with. It wasn't like the guy was part of the club here. Unless he was related to Torch? It didn't seem likely, unless he was a nephew or something.

Delilah pulled out her phone and walked out the apartment door. I heard the murmur of her voice in the hall and not much later the sound of motorcycles pulling up outside. She walked in with her husband and four other bikers, crowding my already tiny apartment. I hadn't realized exactly how small the space was until just now. With only me, Cuddles, and Freya, there was enough room.

"Hayley, you've met Titan before. And you're familiar with Torch and Venom. The other man is Kraken. He's the Sergeant-at-Arms for the Hades Abyss, and he's also with Titan's daughter. They're here to help," Delilah said.

Help? Were they going to pack up my apartment? Or create a miracle of some sort? I didn't understand why she'd called them. Just because Freya was the result of a one-night stand with a biker didn't mean they owed me anything. Unless they planned to haul me to wherever Hawk lived.

"Help me how?" I asked. "I'm not showing up on some strange man's doorstep telling him he's a daddy."

"You got pregnant about a year ago, right?" Torch asked.

My cheeks burned as I nodded. "I didn't mean to go through your gates, but Cuddles got away from me."

"Where is he now?" Venom asked, scanning the apartment. I knew he meant my pet raccoon and not the biker I'd slept with.

I pointed to the far corner where I'd put a wooden cat tree. It wasn't the perfect solution, but Cuddles liked going into the cubbies to hide. I knew he'd be in there right now, sleeping through all the chaos.

"And you're sure the man said his name was Hawk?" Titan asked.

"I'm sure."

Torch glowered and pulled the phone from his pocket. He dialed a number and put the call on speaker. When someone answered, the man's deep voice sounded fierce.

"What do you want, old man?"

"I'll show you old," Torch said. "We have an issue here, but it's not my problem, Beast. It's yours. Remember your trip here about a year ago?"

"What of it?" Beast asked.

"Your VP knocked up one of the local girls. A cop's daughter. Actually, her dad is the chief of police. Hawk has a three-month-old little girl," Torch said.

Something crashed on the other end of the line. "What the fuck? Why the hell didn't she say something sooner? Are you sure it's Hawk's?"

Venom glanced at me before focusing on the phone. "She's scared, Beast. Even now she's trembling so damn hard I think her teeth might be rattling."

I clenched my jaw, realizing he was right.

"He's not going to want us," I said softly. "We're fine here. He can keep living his life, and I'll take care of Freya."

"Without a place to live or a job?" Delilah asked.

The man on the phone sighed. "I have no fucking idea how Hawk is going to react. He's been off for a while now, not acting like himself. I never know what to expect of him these days. I'll bring Lyssa for another visit and ask him to come along for the ride. Can someone at your club give her a place to stay in the meantime?"

Venom and Torch shared a look before they smiled. I didn't think that look boded well for me, and I took a step back.

"I'll put her with Viking. He hasn't been patched in all that long, and he's single. He also has a house with some extra space," Torch said.

"And he's a big bastard, so if Hawk loses his shit, Viking can handle him," Venom said.

Wait. What? They wanted me to stay with a stranger? I felt like everything was spiraling out of my control, and I didn't like it. But I also knew I didn't have many options. It was accept their help, or go beg for my dad's forgiveness. I wasn't ready for that just yet. Sooner or later, we'd have to mend things between us. I hated being alienated from my family.

"We'll be there within two or three days. I have a few loose ends to tie up here," Beast said.

Torch disconnected the call and put his phone away. "All right. Let's get some boxes and get the two of you packed up."

I glanced at the cat tree just as Cuddles poked his head out. "What about Cuddles? Will Viking let him come too?"

Venom snickered. "He will if he knows what's good for him."

Freya started crying again, which made tears prick my eyes too. I rocked her, but nothing worked. I checked her diaper, changed her clothes, and even went into the bathroom to breastfeed her. My little girl was angry, or most likely hurting, but I didn't know why.

When I stepped out, Venom was frowning at me. "She like that all the time?"

My defenses went up. It wasn't the first time someone had asked me that. Freya wasn't screaming for the fun of it. She wasn't a bad baby.

"I've taken her to the doctor at the free clinic a few times, but they insist she's healthy. I think something's wrong," I said.

"I'll call Dr. Myron and get an appointment set up. He's an OBGYN, but he might be able to help or at least refer you to a better doctor," Venom said. "My kids are too old for a pediatrician now. I don't know if the one we used is still practicing, but my wife might be able to find out."

"I can't. I don't have a way to pay him," I said, my cheeks burning with the admission. "I've tried to apply for assistance so we could at least have medical coverage, but the lines are always so long and when I tried to call and set an appointment I kept getting disconnected. I even tried going online to take care of it, but the Internet kept dropping or the pages would time out when they tried to load."

"We'll take care of it," Venom said. "Pack whatever essentials you need for the next hour or two. I'll put them in your car and send you ahead to the compound. Viking will be waiting for you. The rest of us can handle packing up your stuff."

"And Cuddles?" I asked.

Venom glanced at the raccoon who'd climbed out of his hidey hole and was busy washing a piece of apple in his dish of water. "Pack his stuff too. Just whatever he needs immediately."

I hurried to put the diaper bag together with a few changes of clothes and a handful of diapers, made sure there were plenty of wipes, and Freya's favorite blanket. Then I gathered a tote of things I might need immediately. When I'd finished, I looked down at Cuddles, who was sitting by my foot.

"I'll get his dishes," Delilah said. "Anything else he needs right now?"

"His kennel, litter box and litter, and his harness and leash," I said.

"Go get Freya into the car. We'll bring down everything you need and load it into the back seat and trunk." She paused to hug me. "You aren't alone, Hayley. Everything is going to work out fine."

I wished I could be as certain of that, but it couldn't be worse than facing homelessness and being jobless. Once the car had been loaded, I pulled away and drove to the Dixie Reapers' compound. My hands shook a little as I gripped the steering wheel. Twice, I nearly turned around. If I'd had anywhere else to go, I would have. The icing on the cake was driving past my brother in his patrol car. The way his eyes had narrowed, I knew I'd be getting a call soon, wondering why I was heading toward the compound at the edge of town. At the gate, Spencer motioned for me to roll down the window.

"I hear you're going to Viking's place," he said, looking into the back seat at Freya. His gaze turned thoughtful as he looked at my little girl. I knew he probably wondered if the baby was Viking's. Did he think I was a horrible mother for keeping my child from her daddy? Everyone in town speculated as to who the father was. It wasn't like we lived in a large place.

"Take a right inside the gate and follow the curve. His place is toward the back end of the houses. It's a gray-and-white clapboard with a carport and gravel drive. He'll be standing outside waiting for you."

"Thanks, Spencer."

I rolled up the window and followed his directions. The man standing outside the gray house had me stepping on the brakes. Holy hell! I now understood why they called him Viking. The blond giant looked like he'd be better suited to swinging a sword than riding a motorcycle. I eased the car forward and pulled into the driveway. He motioned for me to park under the carport next to his bike.

When I shut off the engine, he opened my door and reached for my hand, tugging me out of the car.

"Thank you for helping us," I said.

He squeezed my hand and glanced into the back

seat. "You can stay as long as you need. Heard your daughter is named Freya."

His deep voice sent a shiver through me. He had to have women falling at his feet. I just wouldn't be one of them.

I nodded. "Um, I think... I think Spencer wonders if she's yours, since we're staying here a few days. He didn't ask outright, and I didn't know what to tell him. I'm still sorting through it all in my head. Until today, I just knew her dad was a biker named Hawk."

It also just occurred to me my daughter was named Freya, like the Norse goddess, and this guy was called Viking. No wonder Spencer had stared at her, the questions clearly tumbling through his mind. I wasn't so sure coming here had been the best idea. I just didn't have any other options.

"Let's get your stuff inside and I'll show you around. Don't worry about any rumors. If these fuckers don't have anything better to do with their time, I'm sure Torch will be happy to give them more work."

I unlocked Freya's seat and lifted it from the car while Viking grabbed our bags. Cuddles decided to chitter, making the giant man pause.

"It's my raccoon. He's tame, and I brought everything he needs."

"Raccoon?" His eyebrows went up. "Interesting choice for a pet. You'll have to tell me how you ended up with one. For now, let's get your stuff in the house and get you settled."

"And Cuddles?" I asked.

"I'll come back for him."

I followed Viking inside and set Freya's car seat on the floor of the living room. It wasn't an overly large space, but it felt homey. The neutral colors screamed bachelor, and I didn't see any photos out anywhere. Nothing personal about the space at all, except a large sword in a glass case.

"That's been passed down through my family for generations," he said. "Come on. Your room is this way."

I left Freya, figuring she'd be okay in her seat since there wasn't anyone else in the house. A hallway had two doors then split into a T-shape. He walked to the T and turned right, pushing open a door. The bedroom was just as neutral and plain as the rest of the house, but it had a full-size bed and dresser. It was more than enough for what we needed. There was also enough room for Freya's crib.

Viking set my things down on the bed. "I'll go get your raccoon and the other stuff in your car."

"Freya is going to wake up any minute. I don't know if they warned you, but she's been crying non-stop. Her doctor keeps saying she's fine, but Venom said the club was going to call someone to check on her."

Viking frowned. "She's sick? What kind of asshole doctor does she have?"

My lips twisted in a grimace. "The free kind."

He tugged me against his chest and patted my back. "I'm sorry. That was insensitive of me. We'll get Freya whatever care she needs. A crying baby isn't going to bother me."

I sighed and pulled away. He seemed like a nice guy. I only hoped he didn't regret letting us stay with him. My stomach knotted when I thought about Hawk coming back. The man on the phone had said he'd bring him here in a few days. What happened if Hawk took one look at Freya and didn't want us? What if he was pissed that I'd gotten pregnant and decided to keep the baby?

"I think I'm going to be sick."

Viking swept me into his arms and carried me down the hall, kicking open the door to the bathroom. He set me down and I dropped to my knees, puking in the toilet. My body shook and I fought the urge to cry. Tears had never done me any good. I stood and rinsed my mouth in the sink before bracing my hands on the counter.

"You've been under a lot of stress, haven't you?" Viking asked softly. "You aren't alone anymore, Hayley. You can stay here for however long you need."

"What if he doesn't want us?" I looked at him in the mirror. "What if he comes here and he's angry I had Freya? What if… if…"

Viking placed his hand on my shoulder and gave it a squeeze. "Stop worrying about the things you can't control, and let's focus on what we *can* take care of. Like Freya. I'll touch base with Venom and see if he reached the doctor's office. I'd imagine he's calling Dr. Myron. All the old ladies go to him. Or maybe Ridley will tell him a pediatrician who can look at Freya. One day at a time, Hayley. And if that's too much, focus on one hour at a time."

"You're not what I was expecting."

He smiled. "Don't tell anyone. I'm supposed to be a big, tough biker."

"Your secret is safe with me." I turned and gave him a hug. Even though we'd just met, for the first time in forever, I felt like I had a true friend.

"Check on Freya and I'll get Cuddles. Everything will be okay, Hayley. You'll see."

Chapter Five

Hawk

"Why exactly do I need to go with you?" I asked the Pres. "I understand your woman wanting to go visit her family. Wouldn't it be better for me to stay here and keep an eye on things?"

Beast stared me down. Once he made up his mind, that was usually it. I had my reasons for not wanting to go. Well, just one. It had been a year since I'd taken Hayley's virginity. And roughly nine months since I'd last seen her. I'd gone with the club to the Dixie Reapers once since then, and I'd hoped to run into her. Her dad had introduced us when I'd gone down to help with the stalker situation, not knowing we'd already met. And she'd acted like I was a stranger. It wasn't like I could say anything to anyone. No one had known we'd been together. Preacher had seen us, but we'd been chasing her raccoon at the time. Perfectly harmless and innocent.

What happened later was another matter.

I'd tried being with women since Hayley, but it always felt wrong. Hell, I couldn't even get hard anymore without thinking about her. I knew if I went with Beast, I'd want to track down the woman who'd captured my attention. The last thing I needed to do was make a fool of myself chasing after someone who didn't want me.

"Beast, you don't need me with you."

"You're going, Hawk. I'm not fucking asking."

I threw my hands up in the air and stalked out of his house. It didn't make any damn sense. There wasn't a single reason he needed me to go to Alabama. I went to my house and packed a bag, hoping we wouldn't be gone for too long. Last time, we'd been there three days. I reached into my dresser to pull out a few shirts and my fingers brushed something.

I froze, knowing exactly what it was.

Taking a breath, I pulled out the box and flicked the lid open. I'd made it during a night I'd been too drunk and stupid to know any better a few months back. I'd twisted the silver wire into pretty swirls around the silver nameplate that said *Property of Hawk*. I'd even engraved it myself.

The bracelet had gone into this box and been shoved into my dresser the next morning when I'd woken and realized what I'd done. It wasn't the first time I'd drunk myself stupid while thinking about Hayley. What the fuck had she done to me? I was two decades older than her. It wasn't like I lacked for female companionship. I had my pick of women. And yet I wanted the one who didn't seem to want me back.

Fucking figured.

I shut the box and gripped it in my hand, nearly tossing it back into the drawer. Something stopped me, and I put it into my bag instead. The chances of running into Hayley were slim, and even slimmer she'd want anything to do with me. I finished packing and went out to my bike. I balanced the duffle in front of me while I drove to Beast's house. Even though he'd have his woman and kid in the car with him, I knew they'd have room for my stuff too.

It was the least he could do since he was forcing me to take this trip. I tossed my bag into the back of Lyssa's SUV, then pulled away to wait for them by the gate. I gave a nod to Brick and Ranger who were going too. I wondered why Beast felt the need to have so many of us with him. Was there something going on he hadn't mentioned? We'd had Church three days ago when he'd announced this damn trip, but he hadn't said anything else. No danger heading our way, or issues with any deals. It was weird as shit, but the Pres was being tight-lipped about it.

"You look like you're going to the gallows," Ranger said.

"Maybe I am," I said.

Brick snorted. "He hasn't been right for a while now. Hasn't been with the girls at the clubhouse, or any others that I've noticed. Your dick broken? Or have you discovered you're gay?"

I flipped him off, making him laugh. "Laugh it up. You're not exactly getting younger. How long before you need those little blue pills? And no, I'm not gay. I still like pussy, but I'm more particular."

Brick sobered and glared at me. Served the fucker right. Although the tinge of pink on his cheeks made me wonder if he'd already needed those pills. If so, I felt sorry for the bastard, but at least his dick wasn't refusing to work because of a certain woman. If I didn't find a way to get Hayley out of my system, or into my bed, my life was going to be a never-ending nightmare.

Beast and his family rolled up to the gates in Lyssa's Escalade. The club had given him shit for driving it the first few times, but Casper VanHorne had given it to Lyssa. Since it had sentimental value, it was here to stay. I had a feeling if the damn thing were to die tomorrow, VanHorne would just send her another one. Or something even flashier.

We pulled through the gate and down the winding drive to the street. As much as I didn't want to take this damn trip, I also knew my place. I pulled in front of the SUV with Beast and his family behind me. Brick and Ranger took up the rear. I didn't know how many stops we'd have to make. Last time, Lyssa had been pregnant. Now there was a small baby who'd need diaper changes, feeding, and whatever else tiny humans required.

My bike ate up the miles, and by the time night fell, we'd pulled up to the gates of the Dixie Reapers' compound. A Prospect let us through, but once inside I wasn't sure where to go. I braced my feet and let my bike idle while I waited for instructions.

Torch ambled out of the clubhouse and approached our small group. He went up to Beast's window and waited while my Pres rolled it down. The man winked at his daughter and smiled into the back seat at his granddaughter, Madison.

"There's an apartment set up for you, one for Ranger and Brick, and another for Hawk," Torch said. "You remember where they are. The doors are unlocked. The one on the far left is stocked for your family. The old ladies left some things in there for Madison. Gifts. Hope you have room to take it all home. If not, my woman is going to start bitching I need to take her to Tennessee."

Beast chuckled. "I can see Madison is going to be spoiled."

Torch nodded. "That she is. The apartments for the others have beer and basic shit stocked. After you're settled in, stop by the house. My wife has been baking and cooking all day, and I think she bought out the butcher so there's plenty of steak to go around. Bring your brothers with you."

Beast nodded. "We'll be there."

Great. Just fucking great. Like I wanted to socialize tonight after the long-ass haul here, especially when I hadn't wanted to come. I didn't know of a way to back out without offending Torch, and I damn sure didn't want to hurt Isabella's feelings. She was a sweetheart.

"It's mostly family," Torch said. "But a few of the other Reapers may drop in for a few. Everyone wants to take a peek at Madison, even if it's from a distance."

Torch backed away and we followed Beast through the compound to the apartments. He parked in front of the one on the end, with Ranger and Brick next to him. I took the next one over. They were all one level, but connected to form a line of six. They'd started out putting in duplexes, from what I'd been told, but had given them to the prospects to share. Instead, they'd followed the example of the Devil's Fury and put in small two-bedroom apartments for guests.

I retrieved my duffle from Lyssa's SUV and tossed it into the apartment I'd be using for however long we were here. If I was going to be somewhat presentable for dinner, I needed to shower and put on clothes that weren't covered in road dust. The apartment had one bathroom with a shower/tub combination. I cranked the water and let it heat while I pulled out some clean clothes. The Reapers kept each apartment stocked with travel-size shampoos, soaps, and other necessities. I grabbed what I needed for my shower and stripped out of my clothes.

I scrubbed my hair and beard before soaping my body. Closing my eyes, I let the hot water beat the back of my neck. The last fifty or so miles, tension had slowly crept into my body, and now I ached and was fighting back a headache. I wondered what Hayley was doing, or if she even still lived here. She was young and could have taken off for some other town by now. Especially since her stalker was rotting in prison.

Leaning forward, I pressed my forehead to the tiled wall.

You need to forget her. She's long gone. You're too damn old for her anyway.

Easier said than done.

How did you forget the most perfect woman you'd ever met? I liked her quirkiness, her curves, and her passion. As for her age, I could lie to myself all I wanted. Truth was, Beast and Lyssa had just as many years between them, if not more, and they seemed to have the perfect relationship. Age was a number, but maturity was another matter. I didn't even mind her having a pet raccoon. It just added to her cuteness.

As with nearly every time I thought of Hayley, my dick got hard. I reached down and gave it a stroke. Didn't matter how many times I yanked one out, it wasn't enough. I'd still be unsatisfied when it was over.

I remembered the way Hayley had looked in the moonlight, spread out under me. I stroked harder, thinking of how hot and tight she'd been. I'd never felt anything so perfect in my life. Groaning, I tightened my grip and tugged harder. It was only another moment before I came, my release spraying across the shower wall.

I stared down at my still half-hard dick and gave a humorless laugh. Nothing ever worked. Unless it was Hayley on her knees in front of me, or spread out like a buffet, I'd never feel satisfied again. I knew it in my gut. I needed to find her. Maybe if I saw her again, she wouldn't seem as wonderful as she had before. Perhaps my memory of that night, and the brief encounter later, was faulty.

But first I needed to get through dinner at Torch's place.

I finished cleaning up, then dried off and pulled on fresh clothes. I combed back my hair and smoothed down my beard. Pulling on my cut, I checked over my appearance in the mirror. I looked tired as fuck and felt it too. A glance at the time told me we'd probably need to head to the Pres' house in a moment. Not enough time to take a nap.

I heard a bike start up nearby and cracked my neck, trying to prepare for being pleasant for the next hour or two. I wasn't up for it. Then again, I hadn't been up for it a lot lately. If I wasn't trying to drink myself to sleep, I was trying to keep busy so I didn't think about Hayley. Beast had known the moment he saw Lyssa she was meant to be his. Was the same thing happening with me? Had I gotten so hung up on Hayley because she was mine?

* * *

Hawk

I got on my bike and waited for Ranger and Brick. Lyssa's SUV was already gone, so I figured they'd gone to her parents' house early. When my brothers came out, I started the engine on my Harley Davidson and took the lead. I'd been to Torch's house before, when we'd visited previously. His wife, Isabella, was always welcoming and had a smile for everyone. Seeing the two of them together made me wish I had a woman by my side. Someone sweet like her, but who could handle this way of life.

I saw several bikes out front, which meant the others he'd expected were already here. Or at least some of them were. I hoped this didn't turn into something huge because all I wanted was to crash for a while and wait for the days to pass. Being here, knowing Hayley was possibly within reach, fucking sucked.

I heard the noise out back and walked to the

gate, letting myself through. Brick and Ranger were on my heels. I scanned the large yard, spotting Beast and Lyssa with Torch and Isabella. Their other kids were playing with some of the Reapers' kids. Madison, the baby of the hour, was in her grandfather's arms. The Reckless Kings were my family, but seeing this, all the kids and old ladies, it made me realize that having a club of brothers was awesome, but my life was still missing something.

I heard a baby crying in the back corner of the yard and turned my head in that direction wondering who else had a baby. My gaze landed on one of the newly patched members of the Dixie Reapers, and when I saw the baby in his arms and the woman standing next to him, it felt like someone had punched me in the gut.

Hayley.

She was with Viking? And they had a baby?

I sucked in a lungful of air. Before I realized what I was doing, I'd taken a step closer to them, then another. The baby was turning red in the face as Viking tried to soothe her. Hayley reached for her, placing the baby against her chest, her expression pinched as she rubbed the infant's back.

"Hayley," I said, wondering why my voice sounded so strange even to my own ears.

She jolted and looked at me, her eyes wide and panic flashing in them. Why the hell would she be scared of seeing me? Was she worried I'd lash out because she was with someone? I glanced at Viking. He seemed a little too laid-back considering I'd just walked up to his girl.

"Hawk," she said softly, drawing my attention. "It's been a while."

I nodded, eyeing the little girl in her arms. With

all the pink, I assumed it was a girl. The baby was still crying. No, more like screaming. My brow furrowed, wondering if she was all right.

"Hayley, why don't you take Freya inside?" Viking suggested. "Might be too much going on out here for her."

Hayley nodded, clutching the baby to her. She brushed past me and headed for Torch's house. I wanted to follow, but knew it wasn't my place. I saw Cuddles streak across the yard and chase after her, slipping into the house right on her heels. It seemed the raccoon had even made himself at home here. My chest felt tight as I realized she'd moved on. I'd been thinking about her non-fucking-stop for a damn year, and she had a kid with someone else. What the fuck? Had she gone after this guy the next day? Was that why she'd acted like I was a stranger when her dad had introduced us?

"Freya is special," Viking said. "And so is her mom."

I nodded. Couldn't disagree about Hayley. And since Freya was Hayley's kid, the baby was probably as awesome as her mother. All the screaming aside.

"You're a lucky bastard," I said. "Hayley's one of a kind."

Viking folded his arms over his chest. "Odd thing to say for a man who took her innocence, then left without giving her another thought. You may have caught her stalker, but when she needed help again, where were you? I know Preacher called and told you she was in trouble. I'd think if she were so special, you'd have wanted to spend more time with her. Not fuck and run."

My hands fisted at my sides, and I fought not to take a swing at the prick. I might be the VP of another club, but I was at Torch's house. I wouldn't disrespect a member of his club, no matter how much I wanted to put him in his place.

"She didn't come back before I left," I pointed out. "It wasn't like I knew where to find her, but she damn sure knew where I was. I figured she didn't want more from me. When I did come back and saw her again, she acted like we had never met. It was clear she'd moved on. I'm guessing she'd hooked up with you by then."

Viking shook his head, his lips twisting as he muttered under his breath. "You're both quite the pair. She's scared shitless you didn't want her, terrified what you'll do when you…"

He stopped and stared up at the sky.

"When I what?"

Beast and Torch came over, flanking me. I thought they were here to either put me in my place where Viking was concerned, or back me up. It never occurred to me they wanted to make sure I wouldn't lose my shit, or run away like a little bitch.

"When you find out you have a kid, and your woman is too fucking scared to tell you because she thinks you'll hate her," Torch said.

What. The. Fuck. "I don't understand."

"I think you do," Beast said. "Freya isn't Viking's daughter. She's yours."

My vision tunneled and I heard my heartbeat in my ears. It felt like the world went away for a moment. The words played on repeat in my mind. I had a daughter. With Hayley. And she hadn't told me? She was scared of me?

Fuck! What had I done to make her think I would hurt her? Or our kid? Shit. This was seriously fucked-up, and I didn't know how to fix it. But I now understood why Beast had insisted I come with him. Why hadn't she said something before now? I didn't know how old Freya was, but had she known when I'd been here the last time?

Beast gripped my arm, holding me upright. "Easy, brother. She thought she was doing the right thing. Didn't think you wanted a kid, or her. She didn't want to track you down and saddle you with a responsibility you never asked for."

I ran a hand down my face and shrugged off the Pres. "I'm fine. I just... What the fuck is she doing with Viking?"

"Your girls needed a place to say," the giant blond said. "Hayley lost her job and her apartment. I'm just being a good friend, letting them have someplace safe to stay while your Pres got you here. We were hoping you'd pull your head out of your ass."

I had a kid? With Hayley?

I tried to think back to that night. What had I said or done that made her think I'd throw the two of them away? All I'd thought about since then had been her. I'd wanted her with me, hoped she'd reach out. It wasn't like I'd known how to reach her. And maybe I'd been a chickenshit and hadn't wanted to put myself out there. No one liked being rejected. In hindsight, I could have maybe asked Preacher if he knew how to get in touch with her. But I'd thought she hadn't wanted anything to do with me. It never occurred to me she was keeping her distance because she'd found out she was pregnant and thought I wouldn't want either of them.

"Go talk to her," Torch said. "But don't stress her out. She's been puking her guts up since she found out you were coming. It's not good for her, or for Freya."

"Freya," I murmured, still dazed from the

knowledge I had a kid. One dressed in pink at that.

I tugged my arm free of Beast and turned toward Torch's house. My steps were slow and measured as I crossed the distance and went inside. I didn't want to make Hayley run off, but Torch was right. We needed to talk. I found her in the living room curled into the corner of Torch's couch, our daughter in her arms and Cuddles sitting on her feet. Freya was still screaming, and I worried something was wrong with her.

"Is she all right?" I asked.

Hayley flinched and glanced my way. "The doctor said it's called purple crying and should pass soon."

I sat next to her, staring at our daughter. I hadn't planned to be a father anytime soon, or ever. It seemed life had other ideas. I reached out and ran my finger over Freya's arm, marveling at how soft she felt. The little girl hiccupped and turned her gaze my way, quieting a little.

"Do you want to hold her?" Hayley asked.

I rubbed my hands up and down my thighs. "I don't know. I've never held a baby before. I might drop her."

"Hawk, she's your daughter. You won't break her," she said.

I gave a jerky nod and held out my hands. Hayley handed her to me and showed me the correct way to hold her. Freya had gone quiet and seemed to be content staring at me. Did she know I was her dad? Could she somehow sense it?

Cuddles chittered and scurried into Hayley's lap, watching me carefully. I wondered if he thought of Freya as his, like he'd claimed Hayley.

"I'm sorry I didn't tell you," she said. "I thought I was doing the right thing. You seemed worried when you realized we hadn't used a condom."

"I know nothing is foolproof, Hayley. Not condoms or birth control pills. Not even that shot thing."

She sighed. "Right. Except… we didn't use any of those things."

I managed to pry my gaze off my daughter and looked at Hayley. "What?"

"I lied. Or rather I omitted the full truth?" She licked her lips and turned her face away. "I could tell you were going to freak out, so I lied by omission to keep you from worrying you'd gotten me pregnant. I mean, what were the odds? When I found out we really had made a baby that night, I didn't think you'd want either of us. I was trying to give you your freedom."

I could have kicked my own ass right then. Was I pissed she'd kept my daughter from me and denied me the chance to experience the pregnancy with her? Sure. But I could admit I wasn't totally blameless either. She was right. If she'd said she wasn't on birth control that night, I might have freaked out a little. Until I realized I wanted to keep her around. It wouldn't have mattered then. If anything, I'd have been excited over the idea of having a baby with her.

Hell, if she'd given me a chance, I might have tried to get her pregnant on purpose, just to have a reason to hold onto her.

"Hayley, keeping her from me was wrong. Even if I'd been pissed, don't you think I should have had a chance to decide that for myself?"

She winced and I saw tears gather in her eyes. "I'm sorry. I wasn't trying to be selfish or a bitch."

"I know you weren't, baby. I'm not angry, at least not entirely with you. If I hadn't made you think I didn't want a kid, then you'd have found a way to reach me. At least, I'd like to think you would have." I looked down at my daughter. "Or would have told me the next time I was here."

She smiled faintly. "Would have been easier than doing all this on my own."

"On your own? I thought you had family here." I held her gaze. "Your dad obviously loves you a lot. He didn't help?"

"I do have family. They kicked me out when they realized I was pregnant, and I refused to tell them who the father was. Makes my dad a big hypocrite since he knocked up my mom when they weren't even dating, but it is what it is. He thought threatening to make me leave would make me tell him everything he wanted to know. It didn't work. Now he's too stubborn to back down, and so am I."

I thought about my brief meeting with the chief of police. I could see him doing something like that. He seemed like the sort who required everything to go his way, at least where his kids were concerned.

"Your dad sounds like a dick."

She snickered. "He can be sometimes. Then again, not many people tell him no or don't give him exactly what he wants. Perks of his job, I guess."

I tried not to flinch at her words, but would one of those things be my head on a silver platter? If I'd known she was a cop's kid, I might have kept my distance. Yeah, probably something I should have known before I fucked her. Jesus. No wonder she hadn't told her family who I was. If the man hated me for knocking up his daughter, he'd probably hate me twice as much when he learned I was a biker. The cops and bikers didn't exactly mix.

He'd been thankful for my help when I caught

her stalker. Didn't mean he would welcome me into the family with open arms. More like with a shotgun and a freshly dug grave.

"You ready for some help?" I asked. "Because I'm here, and I'm not walking away from the two of you."

Cuddles chittered again, waving a paw at me.

"Make that three of you."

"I'm ready, Hawk. I just didn't want to saddle you with a baby you hadn't asked for. But if you want to be part of Freya's life, I'm not going to stand in your way."

I nodded. "We need to pack up your stuff. Ready to move to Tennessee?"

She blinked at me. "Tennessee?"

"That's where I live, Hayley. I have plenty of room at my house to set up a nursery for Freya." I reached over and placed my hand on her thigh. "And plenty of room in my bed for her mom. I'm not walking away this time. You're mine and so is she."

"And Cuddles?"

"Cuddles can come too. I'd never make you give him up. Besides, if it weren't for him, we wouldn't have met."

She seemed antsy, her fingers twisting in her lap and her body tensing. What had I said now? She licked her lips and couldn't seem to look me in the eye.

"What exactly does that mean?" she asked. "To be yours. I don't want any misunderstandings between us."

My dick had been had half-mast since I'd seen her tonight. What did it mean to be mine? I wanted her as my old lady, in my bed, a part of my life. I wanted *everything*. That's what it meant.

I blew out a breath and went over the basics with

her, since I didn't think she'd been around the Dixie Reapers enough to understand what it would be like to be part of the club. When I mentioned being my old lady, I waited for her to have a fit at any moment and refuse to leave with me. Surprisingly, she took it all rather well. Now I just needed to let the club know I needed a property cut. I was taking my family home.

Since the Pres had dragged me here, and seemed to already know about Freya, I wouldn't be taking it to a vote. They were mine, and any fucker who said otherwise would be swallowing his teeth.

Chapter Six

Hayley

Tennessee. I was in another state, far from my family, and I was completely alone. All right. Not entirely. I had Hawk. And Cuddles.

He'd traveled surprisingly well and hadn't tried to run off whenever I'd stopped to give him bathroom breaks. I'd worried he'd slip his leash and I'd lose him on the way to our new home. Hawk had been great about helping with both Cuddles and Freya.

Freya had been fussy the entire way here, and I'd had to pull over frequently. Hawk hadn't seemed to mind. At least, he hadn't looked pissed off. He'd led the way, with the understanding I'd flash my lights if I needed to stop. He probably hadn't realized I'd be getting off the highway once an hour. It had taken forever to get here, and I ached from head to toe. Not to mention the headache from hell because of Freya's screaming.

Torch had asked for a volunteer to drive one of their trucks here with the rest of my belongings. I'd fit what I could into my car. Mainly Cuddles, Freya, and anything we'd need immediately. Everything else had gone into the back of a truck and Viking had driven it here for me. I heard him talking to Hawk while they set up Freya's crib in a spare bedroom.

Hawk had already pulled out the bed he'd had in there and moved it to a storage building somewhere on the property. It wasn't his personal one, but something the entire club used. Freya was quiet for the moment, sleeping in her carrier. I'd unhooked it from the base, and it was currently on the living room floor near the couch. I hadn't set Cuddles free since Viking and Hawk had been in and out, bringing in my things.

He'd chittered at me from his kennel, but seemed to be sleeping now too.

"Must be nice," I muttered, rubbing at my eyes, then massaging my temples.

I heard a curse come from Freya's new room and stood, stretching. As long as she was secured in her seat, and Cuddles was locked in his carrier, I didn't see why I couldn't leave the room. I staggered my way to the nursery, rubbing at my back. The crib I'd had at home hadn't passed Hawk's inspection. He'd claimed it wasn't sturdy enough and we'd left it behind, but he'd called ahead and asked one of his brothers to buy one before we got here. It had been in a box in the carport when we'd arrived.

They had the frame together, but seemed to struggle with the piece that held up the mattress, and hadn't put in the storage drawer either. Hawk's hair stood up in disarray, like he'd been running his hands through it. Viking seemed more amused than anything.

"Are the two of you playing nice?" I asked.

Viking winked at me. "Hawk is determined to do most of the work himself. I'm apparently in the way."

"She's *my* kid. I should be doing this," Hawk said.

My heart warmed a little at his words. He'd reacted to having a baby far better than I'd thought. Other than being upset I'd kept the pregnancy from him, he seemed ready to jump in with both feet. If only I'd had the courage to seek him out sooner. He'd missed so much already, and I felt horrible about it.

"None of us have had dinner yet," I said. "Aren't the two of you hungry?"

Hawk froze and dropped the screwdriver. "Shit."

Viking snickered. "Forget to feed your woman on her first night here?"

"Shut it, asshole," Hawk said with a hint of a growl to his voice. He sounded downright savage when he did that. It should probably bother me that it turned me on. A lot.

"I can just order something. Pizza? Chinese?" I winced, remembering I couldn't exactly order *anything* unless Hawk gave me money for it.

"That look right there," Hawk said. "What just crossed your mind? Because I don't like it."

"I can't pay for anything. I'm completely dependent on you, and I just volunteered to spend your money on Chinese, which I know isn't the cheapest thing to order."

Hawk came closer and tugged me into his arms. I clutched at his shirt, burying my face against his chest. "I'm not giving you an allowance like you're a kid, Hayley. If you want to order food, get whatever the hell you want. We'll go to the bank this week so I can add you to the account."

"Hawk, you don't have to do that."

He tipped up my chin so I had no choice but to look at him. "Baby, you don't have to do everything on your own anymore. I have more than enough money to take care of you and Freya. I *want* to. So no arguments."

Before I could utter another word, he placed his lips on mine. The breath stalled in my lungs. I melted against him, transported back to our first night together. Hawk deepened the kiss, his fingers tangling in my hair. I clung to him, my body aching and wanting more. Why did I go up in flames with him and only him?

He drew back and released me. I swayed a

moment, a little dizzy and feeling drugged from his kiss. He pulled his wallet from his jeans. He handed me his bank card and pressed a kiss to my forehead. The gesture was so sweet it made my eyes mist with tears. Great. I'd gone from throwing up to crying at the drop of a hat. What the hell was wrong with me?

"Chinese sounds good, if that's what you want to order," he said. "Okay with you, Viking?"

"Yep. I'm good with whatever. As long as you don't feed me raw fish. I draw the line at sushi."

I wrinkled my nose at the thought, making both men laugh. I went back to the living room and grabbed my phone. I hadn't even thought about losing my service. It was just one of those pay-as-you-go types, but it had been all I could afford at the time. My minutes and data would expire in less than a week. I'd bring it up to Hawk another time. Poor man had to feel like he'd been hit by a bus.

He'd arrived in Alabama a single man with only his club responsibilities and left with a woman and baby. I was so grateful. Not just to be here with him, but also because he hadn't gone into a rage over Freya or the fact I'd not been completely truthful with him.

We hadn't had a chance to really talk. We'd left the party after a bit and gone to Viking's house, since that's where all Freya's things were. Once Freya had gone to bed, I'd been so exhausted I'd fallen asleep. Since I had woken alone in my room at Viking's, I'd thought maybe Hawk had changed his mind about us moving in with him. Then he'd shown up at breakfast and asked how long it would take me to pack.

I looked up the number for a local Chinese restaurant and was thankful to see I could order online. I wanted shrimp fried rice and orange chicken with egg rolls, but I had no idea what the guys wanted.

Walking back to the nursery again, I got their order and submitted everything, then paid online with Hawk's card.

Except his card didn't say Hawk.

Alexander Goff.

He'd never told me call him anything other than Hawk, so I'd keep using his club name -- or whatever the term was. Unless he said otherwise. I ran my fingers over his name and smiled. It seemed like such a normal name for a guy who was anything but. Freya started fussing, so I took her from the carrier and checked her diaper before sitting on the couch to feed her. I used her blanket to cover myself, in case Viking walked through. Hawk had already seen my breasts so I wasn't worried about him seeing me breastfeed, but I'd prefer the blond giant not get a peep. He typically made himself scarce when it was Freya's mealtime, but I didn't like taking chances.

I knew it was society that made me uncomfortable doing something as natural as feeding my daughter, but I honestly didn't want random strangers seeing my breast anyway. Getting naked in the open like I had with Hawk that night was so not the norm for me. I'd never been one for wearing daring clothes. The night I'd met Hawk, I'd been in what I called my *around the house* clothes. Something I usually didn't wear out in public, but Cuddles had wanted to go out and I hadn't taken the time to change. I preferred to have all the important bits covered in public, even for something like breastfeeding. I didn't have a problem with other women who were braver than me, feeding their babies in the open. It just wasn't for me.

When Freya had finished, I burped her, checked her diaper again, and decided to hold her until our food arrived. Except… we were behind a gate. Exactly how was our food getting here? I'd seen someone on the gate, like at the Dixie Reapers. Would they let in someone with a food order? Or did we need to let someone know there would be a delivery? Crap! I buckled her back into her seat since I didn't have anywhere else secure to place her just yet.

I hurried back to the nursery. "Hawk, how will our food get here?"

His brow furrowed. "Didn't you ask for it to be delivered?"

"Well, yeah, but they can't exactly get to the house."

His expression cleared. "Right. Kye was on the gate earlier. I'll call and let him know we have Chinese coming. He'll get the food and have someone bring it to the house."

It seemed I had a lot to learn about living here. I wouldn't even be able to order a pizza without having to take extra steps. It was… odd. On the other hand, they were very careful about who came inside the gates. Which meant I'd be safe, and so would Freya. I hoped I didn't come to regret the decision to move in with Hawk. We didn't know much about each other. What if we fought all the time?

I felt his fingers on my cheek and I jolted. My nipples hardened at the contact, and I hoped he didn't notice. I might have moved in with him, but I didn't think I was ready to jump into his bed. My body, however, had other ideas. Already I felt my panties getting damp just from being so close to him.

"There you are," he said, a slight smile curving his lips. "You disappeared inside your own head for a bit there."

"I think I'm a little overwhelmed," I said.

"I get it. We're both going to have to make a few adjustments to our everyday lives. Until now, I've lived alone. As for you, you'll have to learn the ropes around here. Lyssa is from your hometown. Were you friends back home?" he asked.

"No. I mean, we knew each other, but I wouldn't say we were friends."

"Well, she'll be a good source of information for you. She grew up in this way of life, and she stepped right into the position of Beast's old lady with ease. I'm sure she'd be happy to help you figure things out."

"You said I'd have to wear something that says I'm your property?" I asked, not sure how I felt about being owned by someone.

"A property cut." He ran his fingers down my cheek. "It shows everyone you're mine, and they'll know not only to keep their hands to themselves, but they'll give you the respect you deserve."

"You didn't just land a biker," Viking said. "You got the VP of the Reckless Kings."

VP. Like Mariah's dad, Venom. Did that mean everyone would be watching me closely? What if I screwed up? My stomach started churning again and I pressed a hand to my belly.

"Think we're freaking her out again," Viking said. "She looked like that a few seconds before she puked the first time."

"First time?" Hawk asked.

"She's been a mess since she came to my house. She's spent the last four days throwing up off and on. Too much stress I think. Between not knowing how you'd react, being homeless, Freya crying non-stop... she's on overload," Viking said.

"I'm fine," I said.

"Hawk, you home?" someone yelled out from

the front of the house.

Freya started screaming almost immediately, which set off Cuddles. I hurried to my daughter and unstrapped her from the carrier again. Viking was right about me being a hot mess. I wasn't sure I'd survive Freya's purple crying. I wanted to burst into tears myself because I honestly didn't know if I could make it through another day. The constant crying and all the uncertainty in my life made me want to curl up in a ball and suck my thumb like a baby.

"What the fuck, Nitro?" Hawk demanded as he stomped into the room.

"Sorry. I brought your food." He lifted the sacks of Chinese food. "Didn't mean to scare the shit out of the kid."

"Her name is Freya," Hawk said. "From now on, no one just bursts into my fucking house. Got it? Make sure everyone knows."

Nitro nodded, eyeing Freya like she was a bomb about to go off. Honestly, I felt that way some days too. I loved her, more than anything, but she was exhausting. At least I now understood why she was crying so much. It made me feel a little less like a failure as a mother.

"I'll just put this in the kitchen," Nitro said, scanning me from head to toe before he walked out.

"You should introduce your new family to the club," Viking said. "Or you may get more unexpected guests. Beast is the only one here with a woman and kid, right?"

"Yeah," Hawk said.

"So, everyone is going to be curious about Hayley and Freya. Better to rip off the Band-Aid and let everyone see them." Viking shrugged. "It's what I'd do anyway. But you know your club better than me.

It's just a suggestion."

Hawk nodded. "Not a bad one either. I'll set something up for day after tomorrow. I want Hayley to have time to rest after the trip here."

When he said sweet, thoughtful things like that, it made me want to kiss him. So far, he'd kept everything PG. At least, when it came to hugs and kisses. I'd gained some baby weight that hadn't gone away after I'd had Freya. What if he didn't find me attractive anymore? My hips were bigger, and so was my ass. Granted, my breasts were still on the larger side since I was breastfeeding, but once they were no longer swollen with milk, the doctor said they would probably shrink.

I knew I had dark shadows under my eyes, and enough luggage for a family of twelve. My hair wasn't quite as glossy as before, and I often didn't even remember to brush it. I felt worn down and very unsexy. I knew Hawk had to have women throwing themselves at him. Was he already with someone else?

Oh, God.

Had he been with someone since the night we'd been together? Or several women? I knew it hadn't been his first time. Far from it. And we weren't exactly a couple. There would have been no reason for him to abstain from sex. My heart rate spiked as fear and jealousy swirled inside me. I didn't like the idea of other women touching him. Kissing him. The thought of him being intimate with other women made my stomach churn.

"I'm going to be sick." I thrust Freya into Hawk's arms and ran for the bathroom. I hit my knees and threw up in the toilet, extremely thankful there didn't seem to be pee on the bowl or the floor. Either Hawk had great aim, cleaned up after himself, or didn't use this bathroom. Whatever the case, I was glad it wasn't dirty.

I dry-heaved when I had nothing left in my stomach. Tears streaked my cheeks and snot ran from my nose. I cried and curled up on the floor in front of the sink.

Hawk knelt by my side, pushing my hair back from my face. I didn't know where he'd put Freya, but he wasn't holding her. "Hayley, baby, what's wrong?"

I just shook my head. I couldn't talk to him, not about this. I didn't want to come across as an insecure little girl, even if it *was* how I felt. He was older than me and probably dated more sophisticated women than me. Maybe I really had wrecked his life by telling him about Freya. He said he wanted to be part of our lives, but he could have done that without us living here. He didn't have to "claim" me to be a father to our daughter.

Viking stopped in the doorway. "Your daughter is fastened back in her seat. I'm going to finish unloading the truck, then I'll take my food to go. I think the two of you need some time alone. I won't head out tomorrow without saying bye first. Also, I think Cuddles is ready for a jailbreak."

Hawk ran his fingers through my hair, patiently waiting for me to either say something or get up. I finally pushed myself upright and reached for some tissue to blow my nose. Well, he'd definitely seen me at my worst now and he wasn't running away. That had to mean something, right?

"I'm going to find the bedding for the crib and put Freya to bed. Then you and I are going to eat some dinner and talk," Hawk said.

"All right." My voice came out scratchy from all the crying and throwing up. I winced at how horrible I sounded. Standing up, I rinsed my mouth in the sink and tried to clean myself up a little. I went to get my toothbrush and toothpaste, needing to scrub my mouth clean. Afterward, I felt a little better. Or at least less gross.

I went to the kitchen and pulled the remaining food from the sacks, setting it down on the table. They'd included chopsticks, but I didn't know if Hawk ate with them or not. I decided to get forks for both of us, but it took a few tries to find the right drawer. By the time the table was set, Hawk was walking into the room and Freya was surprisingly quiet.

My hands shook and I fisted them together, hoping he wouldn't notice. I'd thought of him every day since that first night. In my dreams, I'd been back in his arms. Even before I'd known I was pregnant, I'd wanted to be with him again. Even considering he might not feel the same, that he might have another woman, made my emotions fly all over the place. I wanted to hit something and cry. Scream. And it felt like I might break. Hormones were a bitch.

He put two bottles of water on the table before taking a seat, then nudged a chair out with his foot. I took the hint and sat down. I didn't have much of an appetite anymore, but knew I needed to eat. Since I was nursing Freya, I had to make sure I ate three meals a day. I tried to eat something better than junk food. Normally, I'd have cooked something. I was just too tired today, not to mention I didn't know where everything was in Hawk's house. Or if his fridge was even stocked.

"Are you sick?" Hawk asked quietly. "Have you really been throwing up because of stress or is something else going on?"

"It's just stress," I said.

"Are you sure?" he asked. "Did you see a doctor?"

I shook my head. No, I hadn't been to a doctor about it. I'd felt fine until I'd lost my home. Okay, so not *fine*, but I hadn't been throwing up until then. I figured the two were connected, and Viking had seemed to think the same thing. I couldn't afford to be sick. Not just because I didn't have insurance. Freya needed me.

"I'm going to ask the doctor to make a house call. I'd say we'd wait until tomorrow, but I'm worried about you, Hayley."

"I'm fine," I said.

"No, baby. You aren't fine." His brow furrowed and his jaw tightened. "When's the last time you slept all night?"

"Before Freya was born," I said. "The last few months of my pregnancy weren't the most comfortable. I sleep when I can."

He closed his eyes a moment, a flash of pain crossing his face. I didn't understand why. None of this was his fault. I could have asked Preacher about him, but I didn't. For that matter, I could have told my dad Hawk's name when he asked who'd fathered Freya. I could have stayed home with my parents. Instead, I'd been stubborn and determined to make it on my own.

"We're going to change that. I'm not sure how since you're breastfeeding, but we'll figure it out. You look like you're about to drop, baby."

He wasn't wrong. I *felt* like I would drop at any moment.

"What do you think it means for you to be here? I thought I explained everything well enough before we got here, but I'm starting to think we aren't on the same page. Because I don't just open my home up to anyone, Hayley."

I took a small bite of food and chewed while I thought about how to answer. I wanted to be honest, but there was also such a thing as *too* honest. If I said something that pissed him off, there was nothing that would keep him from tossing me out of the house. And since he'd decided to be a father to Freya, he could very well want to keep her and not me.

Crap. My bite of food tried to come back up my throat.

He reached over and squeezed my hand. "Breathe, Hayley! Jesus. Okay. Dinner can wait."

He stood and lifted me into his arms, carrying me past the nursery. He kicked open another door and I looked around at what I assumed was his bedroom. *Ours*, I corrected as I saw my things in the corner. He sat on the bed with me on his lap, his arms banded around me.

Whether I liked it or not, it seemed like we were going to have a discussion about my place in his life. I only hoped I could handle what I found out.

Chapter Seven

Hawk

The thought of something being wrong with Hayley, of possibly losing her after just getting her back, made it feel like someone was driving a knife into my heart. The fact she kept throwing up scared me shitless. I knew from Beast's griping about Lyssa's pregnancy, or rather the lack of sex after Madison was born, Hayley couldn't have had sex for at least six weeks after Freya was born. I supposed there was a chance she'd been with someone since then and could be pregnant, but it didn't seem likely. She'd given me her innocence. If she'd had a boyfriend, she wouldn't have been struggling so much. Of course, she could have been dating an asshole, but she hadn't mentioned another guy, other than Viking. And he'd made it clear they were just friends.

"Hayley, when I said I wanted you to come live here, both you and Freya, I didn't mean as a houseguest. The property cut means I'm claiming you as mine. I don't think you fully understand what that means."

"I guess I don't," she said.

"In some clubs, men still screw around with the club girls even when they have an old lady. Around here, that shit wouldn't fly. Beast would beat the hell out of anyone who even thought of cheating on their woman. So when I say you're mine, it means I'm yours too. I'm *only* going to be with you, just like you'll only be with me."

I watched her face, trying to judge her reaction. There was a haunted look to her eyes that concerned me. What the hell was she stressing about now? Did she think I just made all that shit up and didn't plan to be faithful to her?

And then it hit me. I'd been worried about her finding someone else. Was she thinking I'd been with other women since the night we'd shared?

"Baby, look at me." Her gaze focused on me, and I noticed her eyes were glassy from unshed tears. It fucking gutted me. "I won't lie. I tried to be with other women after I came back home that first time. I'd told you I would be in town another day or two, and you hadn't come back. I figured you weren't interested in more than our one night together."

She sucked in a breath and a tear rolled down her cheek. I quickly wiped it away.

"It didn't work," I said. "Couldn't get hard for any of them. Only woman I wanted was back in Alabama."

"Really?" she asked, her voice nearly a whisper.

"I swear it, Hayley. I've only wanted you since that night. Hell, I've jacked off to thoughts of you so often I'm surprised I don't have blisters on my hand. It fucking killed me when I saw Viking holding Freya and you standing next to him. I thought I'd lost you for sure, that you'd started a family with someone else."

She sniffled and leaned into me. "We're quite a pair, aren't we?"

I gave a humorless laugh. She wasn't wrong. "Sit here for a second. I have something for you."

I eased her off my lap. She sat on the edge of the bed. I dug through the things I'd taken with me to Alabama until I found the box I wanted. Opening the lid, I removed the silver bracelet and carried it over to Hayley. I reached down and took her left hand in mine and slipped the cuff bracelet onto her wrist.

"You already had this?" she asked.

"I made it," I admitted. "A while ago."

"How long is a while?"

I shifted on my feet, suddenly feeling like a nervous teen boy about to ask out his first crush. "In the last few months. Even though it seemed like you didn't want anything to do with me, I guess part of me always hoped you'd end up here in my house. In my bed."

"Hawk..."

"Call me Alex. But only when we're alone. I know you saw the name on my credit card. No one's called me anything other than Hawk in a really long fucking time. You're not just anyone to me, Hayley. You're my woman. My old lady. The mother of my children."

Her eyes went wide. "Children? Plural?"

I smirked. "I figured we'd wait until Freya wasn't keeping you up all night anymore before we start trying for a baby."

"I'll have to see if I can take birth control while I'm breastfeeding," she said.

Shit. I hadn't thought of that. I wasn't about to wear a condom. Wouldn't be a guarantee anyway, and I liked not having a barrier between us. Maybe there were other options open to us. Wouldn't hurt to look into it.

"Looks like we're leaving it up to fate. Again." She opened her mouth, probably to protest, but I held up a hand. "When you're ready. It's not like I'm going to strip right here and now, Hayley. I'm not a monster."

She blinked at me like a sleepy owl for a moment before sighing. "As much as I don't want to get pregnant again so soon after Freya, I already know I wouldn't tell you no. All it would take is you kissing me, and any rational thought would fly out the window. I don't seem to make good choices when it comes to the two of us being naked together."

I knelt at her feet and cupped her cheek. "If you really want to wait, we'll talk to a doctor and figure it out. I'm not about to force you to have another baby right now. Having you here with me, both you and Freya, is enough. We can take things as slow as you want."

The tension seemed to drain from her. "I've been worried about how things would go when we got here. Part of it is that we don't really know each other. The sex was amazing before, but I want more out of a relationship than sex."

"We have the rest of our lives, Hayley. As badly as I want you, I can wait. I meant what I said. I'll let you set the pace." I smiled a little. "As long as my brothers don't know about it. I have a reputation to protect after all. Until then, I can keep using my hand. At least I'll have you here in my arms. It's more than I had before."

She rolled her eyes. "Of course, you'd be worried about your reputation. Heaven forbid they think you're a nice guy and not some womanizing asshole."

"Just part of being who I am, baby." I pressed my lips to hers. I wanted to linger, to deepen the kiss, but I pulled back before the temptation became too great. Now that we were alone, I didn't know if I'd be able to stop. Not entirely true. If she told me to, I would. But having Hayley in my room, on my bed? Yeah, I was semi-hard and would be ready to go if she even hinted she wanted sex right now. "Have you seen the master bathroom yet?"

She shook her head.

"Wait here, baby. I'm going to run you a hot bath. You can soak for a bit and relax. I'll clear out a few drawers for you in the dresser and shift stuff around in the closet. We can worry about putting your things away tomorrow. You need sleep more than anything else right now."

"Thank you, Alex."

Hearing my name on her lips did funny things to me. My chest felt all warm and my stomach felt strange. Yeah, with Hayley, I was definitely turning into a teen boy with his first girlfriend. I hurried into the bathroom and rinsed out the tub before filling it with steaming hot water. I added some foaming bath with Epsom salts and eucalyptus. Lyssa had brought it over when I'd helped Forge rearrange some stuff at the shop and strained my back. Getting old was a bitch.

I'd not had the heart to tell her big, badass bikers didn't take bubble baths. Right now, I was glad to have the stuff. It seemed like the perfect thing to add to Hayley's bath. My woman looked like she was about to collapse and not get up for a long while. She'd been so focused on taking care of Freya, she hadn't taken care of herself, and no one had been around to take up the slack.

After I filled the tub, I shut off the taps and went to get Hayley. She seemed so shaken, I didn't want to leave her. I kept my gaze on her face as I helped her undress. I might have seen her body before, but it didn't give me the right to look now. I'd be a gentleman, or at least try to be. Whatever she needed, I'd give it to her.

It about killed me to not put my hands on her. I wanted to place my hand over her belly. She'd nurtured our daughter inside her, and I'd missed it. I wondered what she'd looked like, swollen with our child. Her breasts seemed bigger than before, and I had a damn hard time not letting my gaze drop to check them out. I remembered how responsive her nipples had been. Were they still?

I helped her into the tub, put a towel within reach, and dimmed the lights. "Relax, Hayley. Soak as long as you want. We can reheat the food when you're ready to eat."

"I shouldn't stay in here a long time," she murmured, closing her eyes.

"You deserve a break, baby. I'll listen for Freya, and I'll work on making room for your things. Take some time for yourself."

She smiled and held her hand up to me. I grasped it and kissed her fingers then backed out of the bathroom before I decided to stay and help with her bath. Making space in the dresser wasn't too difficult. I managed to empty two drawers within a few minutes, but the closet would be a bit harder. I eyed the gun safe in the bottom and knew I needed to move it. Not by myself, and not tonight, but soon. The house only had three bedrooms, and on the off chance we had more kids, I didn't want to take up the third room with my stuff.

I smiled. More kids. Yeah, I could get behind that idea. To think I'd been single, and fucking miserable, two days ago and now I had a woman and daughter. I just needed to get them both settled into their new home, make sure Hayley was healthy, and hope Freya's purple crying ended soon. Whatever the fuck that was. I seriously needed to look it up and see if there was some way to ease Freya's distress. I didn't think Hayley could handle much more. Every time our sweet girl started screaming, my woman looked like she would fall apart.

I made some space for Hayley to hang up her things, with a mental note to figure out a new spot for my weapons. Then I called Dr. Kestral. He patched us up when things went sideways, but I knew he was a legit doctor and would be able to help Hayley. Or at least check her over and make sure she was healthy. He promised to stop by within the hour, which meant I needed to keep Hayley awake a little while longer.

But first, there was another matter to handle.

I called Torch.

"Hawk, do you have any idea what fucking time it is?" he demanded when he picked up the call. I glanced at the clock, realizing it was barely after eight. I doubted he went to bed this damn early.

"Uh, no. I didn't really stop to look. I need Chief Daniels' number, if you have it."

It was quiet a moment. "Do I seem like the type to go golfing with the chief of police, or what the fuck ever guys like him do for fun? Call the damn station during daylight hours. You know, when people aren't trying to get their fucking kids to sleep."

I winced. Now that I had a daughter, I could sympathize. "Sorry, Torch. I just know it's messing Hayley up that her family dumped her the way they did. I was hoping to talk to the chief and smooth things over, maybe make him see reason."

"Good luck," he muttered and ended the call.

Well, that hadn't gone the way I'd hoped, but it could have been worse.

I heard Hayley call out for me and I rushed to her side, not wanting her to get out of the tub on her own. As tired as she was, she could easily slip and fall. I helped her dry off and change into her pajamas.

"The doctor will be here in a little while," I said. "For now, let's warm up our dinner and get some food into your stomach. I don't think you've been eating enough."

She snorted and smacked her hip. "You didn't notice the extra padding?"

My lips twitched. "Oh, I noticed all the changes, baby. And I especially approve of the 'extra padding,' as you put it, on your hips and ass. You're beautiful, Hayley. Having a baby didn't change that. If anything, it just made you even more stunning."

She shook her head. "I look more like Cuddles right now."

Her eyes went wide, and she slapped a hand over her mouth. Shit. We'd forgotten about her raccoon.

"I'll get him. You go sit in the kitchen." I hesitated a moment. "Will he bite me? He seemed friendly enough at the Dixie Reaper's place, but he's in a new environment, and today hasn't been the easiest day for any of us."

She shook her head. "No, he's really sweet, and he already met you once so it's not like you're a stranger. His harness and leash are by the carrier. He probably needs to go to the bathroom. There's a litter box for him, but I haven't set it up yet, and he has a cat tree he likes to hide inside."

"I'll take him outside. Don't worry, Hayley. Just go sit."

Once I knew she would listen, I let the raccoon out of his cage. He chittered and fussed, clearly pissed we'd forgotten about him. I was surprised at how easily I could get the harness on him, and he eagerly walked on a leash. We went out front and I led him away from the house so he wouldn't leave any surprises where someone might step in it. After he'd finished, I took him inside and set him free in the house.

I found his litter box and other necessities and

got everything set up. I opened the folding doors on the tiny hall closet and decided it would be a good spot for his litter box. I made sure Cuddles knew where I'd put it before I put his cat tree in the corner of the living room and his food and water dishes in the kitchen. Hayley put some fruit in his bowl, and he snacked while we ate our dinner.

By the time Dr. Kestral arrived, Hayley had fed Freya once more and looked like she was ready to fall asleep. He examined her in our bedroom, with me present for the entire thing. Hayley gripped my hand while he listened to her heart, checked her eyes, and went through whatever mental checklist doctors seem to have for a routine exam.

"I'd like to take some blood, but I'll need you to come to my office for that. I didn't have the right supplies at home or I'd have brought them with me. I just want to make sure you have enough iron and get a baseline to use for future visits." Dr. Kestral patted her hand. "Mostly, I want you to get some rest. You won't do anyone any good, least of all your daughter, if you collapse from exhaustion."

"I'll see that she gets more sleep," I said.

"Welcome to the Reckless Kings family, Hayley." Dr. Kestral gave her a wink. "I'm glad to see there's someone who can keep this one in check."

I shook my head, but he'd made her smile so I let the ribbing slide. And the wink. The doc was an unofficial member of the club and had been treating all of us for a long while. He knew how to keep his mouth shut, and he was damn good at his job. I trusted him with Hayley, and with Freya.

"Thanks for coming by after hours," I said, shaking his hand. "Usual fee?"

He waved me off. "Not for tonight. Bring her by

in the next day or two for that bloodwork, but don't wait too long. I don't like how weak she seems. I'm hoping it's just from the long trip and recent stress in her life."

"You and me both," I muttered.

"You've got a good one, Hawk."

Yeah, I did.

"By the way, did you know there's a raccoon running around your living room?" he asked.

I laughed and explained it was Hayley's pet. I thanked him again, locked up behind him, then checked on Freya. She still slept soundly, but I didn't know for how long. When I got to the bedroom, Hayley had already fallen asleep. The move had clearly worn her out. I stripped off my boots and clothes, then crawled in next to her, tugging her into my arms. For the first time in my life, I felt completely at peace, and I knew it was because my woman and daughter were where they belonged -- in our home.

***

Hayley

I hated going to the doctor, and I hated being stuck twice as much. I wasn't a pincushion! I'd dragged my feet for three days, but Hawk had threatened to handcuff me and toss me into the back of my car if I didn't go to the doctor willingly. Watching him try to squeeze his tall frame into my small car was almost worth it. I hadn't been able to hold back my laughter, earning me a glare.

I glanced around the room, trying to look anywhere but at Hawk. For some reason, I couldn't seem to keep my eyes off him today. Might have had something to do with the peek I'd gotten this morning. He'd been in the shower and I hadn't been awake enough to realize the water was running. Until I'd gotten an eyeful of a very naked Hawk in the shower.

I'd been tempted to strip naked and join him, but instead, I'd backed out of the room. I'd admittedly leaned against the wall, listening to him wash, and reached into my panties. My cheeks had burned as I rubbed my clit and gotten myself off. It hadn't been anywhere near as satisfying as sex with Hawk would be, but it had taken the edge off. Being near him, sleeping in his arms every night, was making me constantly ache.

Hawk squeezed my hand, on the side not having the life sucked out of me. It snapped me out of my daydreaming. "Nearly done, baby. You can help me pick out a truck or SUV when we're done."

I blinked up at him in surprise. "You're buying a new car?"

"Need something bigger than your clown car. I can't exactly put Freya's baby seat on the back of my bike."

I bit down on the inside of my cheek. His gaze narrowed, not missing the move. Yeah, I still wanted to laugh when I recalled how his knees had practically been scrunched up to this chest when he'd gotten into the car.

The nurse pulled the needle from my arm and put a bandage over it. "All done. The lab is closed today, but we should have results in the next day or two. Someone will call with the results."

She stepped out and I changed back into my clothes. The doctor had already done a second exam, taken a urine sample, and asked his nurse to take several vials of blood. I didn't know what exactly he was looking for. I hoped he found it without me needing to open up another vein.

"Are you really buying a car today?" I asked.

"Yep, and you're going to help me pick it out. I get final say on how it looks and drives, but I need you to make sure it has all the safety requirements for Freya."

He tugged on my hand and led me up front. After he settled the account, we went back out to my car. He eyed me balefully before scanning the street.

"What's wrong? Scared someone will see you get into it?" I asked.

"Yes. That's it exactly." He ran a hand through his hair. "I had planned to check out the dealership in the next town. You hungry?"

"Uh. I think that just gave me whiplash. How did we go from a car lot to food?"

He grinned. "Because there's a great diner down the block where we can eat while I wait for a Prospect to bring one of the club vehicles. He can drive your tin can back. Better yet. How attached are you to that thing?"

"My dad gave it to me when I turned sixteen and got my license, and it was used back then. It's about fifteen years old now."

"Then we'll shop for two vehicles while we're out."

"Don't I need mine to use as a trade?" I asked. "And are you sure you want two car payments?"

"You're cute." He smiled. "I'm not making payments, baby. We're going to make a cash offer. Besides, the place I want to go will cut me a deal. The owner owes the club."

I wasn't sure I wanted to know why he owed the Reckless Kings anything. As a cop's daughter, and sister, the less I knew the better. Even if this wasn't my family's jurisdiction, I'd rather pretend complete ignorance of any illegal dealings. I'd noticed the fancy clubhouse when we'd arrived that first night. There was no way in hell the club ran one hundred percent legit businesses.

"You can pay cash for two new cars?" I asked.

"Come on, baby. We can discuss finances later. Let me feed you."

"I'm not a man-eating plant," I muttered.

His brow furrowed and he looked adorably confused by my remark. He'd clearly never watched *Little Shop of Horrors*. It seemed my guy was in need of a movie-cation. My. Guy. Holy crap! He'd said he was just as much mine as I was his. I still hadn't really wrapped my brain around it.

He pulled out his phone and sent a quick text before we entered the diner.

A harried-looking waitress motioned to the half-full dining room. "Sit anywhere you want."

"Lyssa says Freya is doing just fine," he said as he slid into a booth. I took the spot across from him, fighting back a smile. "And she sent someone by the house to check on Cuddles. He's apparently chewed the corner of his cat tree, but nothing else seems to be disturbed. He may need some toys for when we aren't home."

"You checked on both of them?" I asked.

"Well, yeah. Freya doesn't really know Lyssa and Beast. Plus, they have their own baby. I don't want them to get overwhelmed if Freya starts crying and won't stop. And I knew you'd worry about Cuddles being alone for too long in a strange place. Although he seems to be settling in pretty well."

His phone chimed and his eyes went comically wide before he turned it to face me. A guy in a Reckless Kings cut cradled our daughter against his chest, where she slept peacefully. It certainly wasn't Beast.

"Who is that?" I asked.

"Copper. It seems he has the magic touch," Hawk said. "Now I think I'm jealous. She likes him more than me."

I studied the image again. "I think she likes him more than both of us. But if he can keep her calm and quiet, I might let him move in."

Hawk snorted. "Sorry, baby. We aren't inviting another man to live with us. You'll just have to suck it up."

"Or send her to his house a few hours a day. I love her. I can't begin to tell you how much. And yet…"

He reached for my hand, giving it a squeeze. "Baby, it doesn't make you a bad mother. Freya needs a lot of attention, and with her non-stop crying and screaming, it would rattle anyone. You've only been in my house a few days, and my nerves are a bit frayed. I can only imagine how you feel after months of listening to her and not knowing how to make her stop."

"I felt so horrible. I kept thinking she was hurting, and I was just too stupid to figure out what she needed. The doctor at the free clinic wasn't very helpful. It wasn't until Venom arranged for her to see a doctor the Dixie Reapers use that I finally found out there was a reason why she cried so much."

The waitress who'd told us to sit anywhere came over and took our order before rushing off to the kitchen. She returned a moment later with our drinks and a promise our food would be at the table soon.

A shiny black truck pulled up out front. Hawk grinned when he saw it. "Looks like our ride is here."

The Prospect brought Hawk the keys and took

mine. He eyed them and looked pained at the thought of driving my car. I couldn't blame him. He wasn't quite as big as Hawk, but it would still be a tight squeeze.

"Want me to park it at your place?" he asked.

"No. Empty everything into the carport then see what Beast wants to do with it. He may want to donate it for a tax write-off for the club."

The Prospect nodded and headed out.

I liked the idea of donating the car. It still ran fine, even if it was a bit cramped. It didn't have all the fancy gadgets the newer cars had, but it would be a dependable ride for someone. Maybe give them a chance for a fresh start.

"Hawk, is there a women's shelter in the area?"

He tensed and eyed me. "Why? You thinking of running?"

I rolled my eyes. "Yes, I'm going to run from the best thing that ever happened to me. Don't be an idiot. I was just thinking someone there might really need a car. Your club could still get a tax-deductible donation from it, but I'd prefer to think of it giving a woman or single mom a chance at finding a better job or getting away from a bad situation."

His gaze softened. "You're something else. I'll message Beast and let him know your wishes where the car is concerned."

Speaking of jobs, I had to figure out what I would do with my time. Hawk made it seem like I didn't need to work. Either way, I didn't think I'd like sitting home all day every day. I needed a way to contribute, if not financially, then in other ways. Maybe not right now, since Freya was still young, but in the next few months. I wondered if I could get someone to watch Freya a few hours a week if I could volunteer someplace.

The waitress came back with our food, sliding both plates onto the table. "Can I get you anything else? Need a refill?"

"I wouldn't mind a little more sweet tea," I said.

She went to the counter and picked up a pitcher, coming back to top off my drink. Then she was gone again, helping other customers. I didn't envy her. She looked about ready to fall over and didn't seem to have any help today.

"I can see the wheels turning," Hawk said, tapping my forehead.

I knew what he meant. I'd been deep in thought when our food had arrived at the table. "I think I want to volunteer somewhere. I won't like being stuck at home all the time, and you make it seem like I don't need to work."

He leaned back in the booth and stretched his legs out. I felt the brush of his denim against my feet. He tossed an arm over the back of the booth and looked out the window. Did he not want me to volunteer? I hadn't realized it would be an issue. If he wanted me to stay home, I'd find a way to not go stir-crazy.

"The club likes to do different charitable things throughout the year. A way to show the community we aren't evil bastards out to rape their daughters or murder their husbands."

I flinched because I knew there'd been a time my dad had felt that way about the Dixie Reapers. Until he'd gotten a chance to know Torch and Venom better. They weren't friends by any means, but he respected them. To an extent. He still didn't want them as family. Shit. I hadn't contacted my family. Did they even know I wasn't in Alabama anymore?

I tried to eat while I stressed over whether or not my family had even noticed I was missing. Not *missing* but no longer in town. Even though my brother had seen me driving to the Dixie Reapers the day I'd moved in, temporarily, with Viking, I hadn't heard anything from him or my parents. Either he hadn't said anything to them, or maybe they'd washed their hands of me. Was I really so much trouble? All because I'd wanted to keep Freya and hadn't wanted to tell anyone who her father was?

"We have a club Treasurer who usually sets up most of those events. The Secretary would help, but we don't have one right now. Prospero and Forge take turns keeping notes for us."

"Do all clubs have a Secretary?" I asked.

"Usually. We had one, years ago. He died and Beast never replaced him. I think he has trouble with it because the guy was his friend long before they were part of the club."

"What does all this have to do with me volunteering?" I asked.

"I thought maybe you could get with Prospero and see if he has anything in the works, or an idea for a future event. Maybe you could help him get it set up. I'm sure he wouldn't mind an extra set of hands. With only two old ladies in the club, and now two daughters who aren't even a year old, we're at a slight disadvantage to a lot of clubs. Like the Dixie Reapers for instance. Their women handle a lot of charity work for the club."

"I wouldn't know how to run anything like that," I said. "But I'd love to help."

"Then I'll introduce you to Prospero tomorrow. In fact, you need to meet the entire club. I know a few have stopped by out of curiosity. I'd rather make it official though. Your property cut should be ready soon."

I touched the cuff on my wrist, and he smiled. I didn't know if I'd like wearing a property cut, but I loved the bracelet. It looked like it would be heavy. Instead, it felt light and delicate. Since he'd placed it on my wrist, I hadn't taken it off. Hawk had said it was pure silver, so it was fine to wear it in the shower. As for meeting his club, I knew he'd held off so I'd have more time to adjust to my new home. I appreciated all he'd done for us. And he was so great with Freya.

"Do you make things like this often?" I asked.

His cheeks darkened a little. Too adorable. I'd embarrassed him. He shoved the last bite of food in his mouth then washed it down with his soda.

"Sometimes," he said. "Only you and Forge know about my... hobby."

"This isn't a hobby. Hawk, the bracelet is gorgeous. I'd love to see the other things you've made."

"Soon. I'll take you by the shop Forge runs. The club owns it, but he sells his custom work in there, and some of my pieces are on display too. No one knows they're mine. Not even anyone in the club, except Forge. And now you."

I nodded, understanding. Well, sort of. I didn't know why he didn't want to show the world what he could do. Did he think it made him somehow less manly? I only wished I had the kind of talent he did. I'd love to be able to make beautiful things. If I had any sort of gifts like painting or something, I hadn't discovered it yet. I could sing a little. Not enough to make a living at it, but I didn't make people cringe when I sang along to the radio or music in stores while I shopped.

"I've been wondering… how exactly did you end up with a raccoon for a pet?" he asked.

I'd wondered how long it would take him to ask. Everyone did.

"Cuddles came to me when he was a baby. His mom had been hit by a car, along with his siblings. The driver was drunk, ran over the raccoon family, and crashed into a utility pole. My brother answered the call about the accident. When he saw the baby raccoon all alone, he sent me a picture in a text message. I got in the car and went right to the scene. Cuddles came home with me, and I nursed him with a bottle. He was too tame to set free, so he's been with me ever since."

"Maybe that could be your volunteer work. We could get you a wildlife rehab license, or whatever is needed to nurse orphaned wildlife."

I smiled, liking the idea. I quickly finished my meal and drink. Hawk dropped some money on the table, even though we hadn't received the check yet. I eyed the bills and knew there was no way we'd come anywhere near the fifty dollars he'd left. Which meant he'd also noticed how run down the waitress seemed. It warmed my heart that he wanted to help her by giving her a generous tip.

Even if Hawk was rough around the edges, he was a good man.

"Time to shop for cars," he said, taking my hand. "And we aren't heading home until you've found something you love."

I sighed, looking up at him. I was pretty sure I'd already found something I loved. It just wasn't a car.

Chapter Eight

Hawk

My phone rang for the fifth time and I stepped away from the salesman and Hayley. She'd test driven three different cars and hadn't loved any of them. I had a feeling she needed to look at the SUVs, but she kept saying they were too big.

She'd also gotten a bit red in the face when she'd excused herself to the bathroom, muttering something about leakage. I hadn't known what to make of it until it occurred to me we'd been away from Freya for a while, which meant Hayley's breasts were probably leaking. If she needed anything from me, she hadn't said.

"Pres, what do you need?" I asked as I answered the call.

"It's about fucking time. What the hell is so important you've been ignoring my calls?"

"Shopping for a new truck for me and something for Hayley."

"That's why I'm calling. It's about Hayley's car."

Shit. She'd had her heart set on donating it. Was there something wrong with it? She'd seemed to think it was a sound vehicle, if a bit on the old side.

"What's wrong with it?" I asked.

"Nothing, as long as she knew about the tracking device and drugs."

My body tensed and I scanned the parking area, making sure no one could overhear my conversation. "What the fuck, Beast?"

"That's what I want to know. I gave the tracker to Shield. He's trying to figure out who's been monitoring her. It could very well be her family, but the drugs... that's another matter. There something you need to tell me about your girl?"

"Fuck no! She'd never touch drugs, much less carry them in the car with our daughter. Someone had to have planted them. Where were they?"

"Inside the back bumper, hidden in the wheel wells, and there was more under the spare tire which was hidden under the carpet in the trunk. I figured she didn't know they were there. The question is how did they get there? Is the car new to her?" Beast asked.

"She said her dad gave it to her when she was sixteen, so she's had it two years."

"Then it's been added because I seriously don't see the chief of police giving his kid a car he didn't thoroughly examine. Besides, the bags in the wheel well wouldn't have stayed there that long. They had to have been put there in the last week or two."

If it was in the past week, she'd either been at the Reapers' compound or here with me. I didn't think anyone at either location would have done something like that. I trusted my brothers with my life, and the Reapers were family. Which meant it happened more than a week ago.

"See what you can find out," I said. "Even if we called her dad, I'm not sure he'd admit it if he'd been tracking her. I think we need to up our security just in case."

"I'll get Forge on it. I'm going to reach out to Torch and Venom, see if they've heard anything. It's a fuck ton of drugs for such a small car. Someone is missing this shit, and I'm betting they're pissed as hell," Beast said.

"We'll finish up here and head home. I'd planned to have the dealership deliver one of the cars and take the other to run some errands, but I'm not sure I feel too safe with her out in the open. Not now."

"You at Carlton's place?" Beast asked.

"Yeah."

"I'm sending Wrangler and Nitro your way. They'll tail you if you need to stop anywhere else. I don't think anyone will fuck with your girl while she's out with three Reckless Kings, especially since she's the property of the VP."

"If they do, I'll be happy to send them straight to hell."

"Keep an eye out until they get there. I'll call Torch as soon as I have those two heading your way." Beast disconnected the call and I shoved the phone in my pocket.

I made my way back over to Hayley, who'd finally caved and was checking out an SUV. It wasn't much bigger than the sedans, and knowing someone had been keeping tabs on her, I'd prefer she have something a bit sturdier. I just didn't know how to steer her toward a bigger vehicle without making it too obvious. The last thing she needed was more stress. I caught the salesman's eye and gave a subtle nod toward a blue SUV on the next row. I'd looked at the model a while back, back when Beast had talked about getting another SUV for his family, and knew it had scored well in collision tests.

By the time Hayley agreed to get it, and I'd picked out my new truck, Wrangler and Nitro had arrived. They'd hung back and appeared to be browsing vehicles. Hayley glanced their way a few times, but didn't seem to suspect why they were here. I'd have to tell her, eventually, so she'd be extra careful if she left the compound.

Since I paid for both vehicles in full, the paperwork was a little lighter than if I'd financed them. We were out of there before too much longer.

"Hayley, I'm going to have the dealership deliver your SUV to the house. I thought we'd go buy a few things for Freya's room before we go home, and there's no point taking two cars."

"Shouldn't we go get her?" she asked. She twisted her hands together, and I noticed she trembled a little. "We've been gone for a while. She's never been away from me this long."

I hesitated. "Baby, she's in good hands with Lyssa and Beast. I promise she's okay. The question is how are you holding up?"

She frowned and looked down at her feet. "I don't know. My breasts hurt from not feeding her, but mostly I think I'm just anxious. I know it's good for her to socialize, probably good for both of us, but it's harder than I'd thought it would be."

I hadn't really thought about how she'd feel being away from Freya. I knew Hayley knew Lyssa, even if they weren't great friends. I hoped they would be eventually. For now, Hayley probably felt like strangers were watching our daughter. But Beast and Lyssa were family. My family.

"You gave them some formula you'd been using to supplement your breastmilk, right?" I asked.

"Yes. I gave them enough for two bottles." She dropped her voice. "And I packed some pads for my bra so I wouldn't leak through my clothes."

"I'll message Lyssa. If they need us to get her sooner, or if she seems hungry and they're out of formula, we'll go home." I paused. "Or if you just really want to go back to her, or get too uncomfortable we can leave."

After she agreed, I sent a text to Lyssa and one to Beast. I helped Hayley into the lifted truck, reaching over to buckle her. Reaching up to cup her cheek, I turned her face to mine and lightly brush my lips over hers.

"Our girl is fine, baby. She's in good hands. You know I wouldn't put either of you in danger, right?" I asked.

"Is that why those two men are here?"

I sighed, wishing I'd had more time. "There's some things we need to discuss. I'd rather do it at home. To answer your question, Nitro and Wrangler are here as extra security for you. They'll follow us to the baby store and tail us on the way home. It's just a precaution."

"Because there's something to worry about." Her shoulders sagged. "I don't like this, Hawk. I hate not knowing what's going on, and yet, I'm not sure I want to know either. One of those damned if you do and damned if you don't situations."

"Trust me to take care of you, Hayley. You and Freya are my priority. I'm not letting anything happen to my girls, okay?"

She gave me a smile, then leaned forward to kiss me. I threaded my fingers into her hair, holding her close as her lips lingered on mine. As much as I wanted to continue, the parking lot wasn't the place for it.

I pulled away and shut her door. Before I got into the truck, I let Nitro and Wrangler know exactly where I was heading next. When I pulled out of the parking lot, they were right behind me. I reached over and placed my hand on Hayley's thigh. I could feel the tension in her body and wished she didn't have a reason to worry. As soon as we found out who'd targeted her, I'd make sure the asshole paid.

The baby store wasn't as much fun as I'd hoped. While I did pick out a few things for Freya and encouraged Hayley to get more clothes for our daughter, I could tell Hayley was too worried to enjoy the shopping trip.

"Baby, nothing is going to happen to you, okay? Let's get whatever you think Freya needs, or some toys she'd enjoy. Let me spoil the two of you a little."

I got a faint smile and nod before she threw her arms around me. I hugged her to me and pressed a kiss to the top of her head.

"I'm sorry, Hawk. You're right. This should be fun, and we're getting to spend time together without our daughter crying non-stop."

"Get a package of diapers for her and more formula, then we'll get the fun stuff."

I paid attention when she placed the necessities in the basket so I'd know what to get next time. While Hayley added frilly dresses to the basket, I tossed in tiny shirts and leggings. My daughter might be cute as hell, but I didn't know what the fuck to do with a girly-girl. I'd teach her how to change the oil in her car, fix a flat tire, and how to ride a Harley. I'd leave the other stuff to her mom.

I picked up a toy that lit up and played music, showing it to Hayley.

"Hawk, it says it for six months and up. Our daughter isn't old enough for that one yet."

"But we can put it aside for when she's older, right? The months will fly by. Better to be prepared."

She rolled her eyes at me, something I noticed she did frequently. Good thing I found it endearing. "Fine. Go wild! Buy whatever you want."

I grinned. "You're learning."

I swatted her ass when I walked past her, making her squeak in surprise. If I'd known how much I'd like having an old lady, I might have gone looking for one sooner. Then again, it wouldn't have been Hayley, and

I was starting to think we were meant for each other. Why else would she have gotten pregnant our one and only night together?

By the time we checked out, we'd filled two carts and even Nitro and Wrangler had tossed in some items. Yeah, my little princess was going to be spoiled. And I'd spoil her mother too. I'd touched Hayley every chance I had. Innocent touches, but they were enough to heat my blood. A slide of my fingers against her waist as I leaned past her to grab something off a shelf. The brush of my hand against hers. I hoped no one noticed I was sporting wood in the baby store. Definitely not the time or place. Although, the way her cheeks pinked told me she was just as affected.

I loaded everything into the back seat, except the larger things like the baby swing. I put that in the bed. Nitro said he'd help unload everything when we got to my house. Once we had Freya home, and got her new things put away, I'd sit Hayley down and tell her what was going on, even though I still didn't know a damn thing other than she seemed to be in trouble again.

The last thing I expected was to see Chief Daniels leaning against his truck at the gate to the compound when I got there. To anyone passing by, he would seem relaxed. He'd folded his arms and crossed his booted feet, almost looking bored. I knew the moment Hayley spotted him. She let out a gasp and gripped my hand tight.

"I didn't think he even knew I left," she said.

"Wait. What the fuck, Hayley? You didn't tell your family you were moving?"

Jesus fucking Christ.

Something told me I was about to get my ass chewed by her dad, and I couldn't blame the guy. If our roles were reversed, I'd want to stomp the fucker into the ground. It didn't even occur to me to make sure she'd told her family goodbye. I'd just packed her up and moved her here. I'd known they'd thrown her out, but I should have clarified that she'd had no contact with them. That was on me.

I rolled down my window and yelled out to Iggy. "Let him through. He can follow me to the house."

"You know him, VP?" Iggy asked.

"He's Hayley's father."

Iggy got an *oh shit* look on his face that I seconded. The chief followed us down the road to the house and he pulled to a stop at the edge of the grass out front. Hayley's new SUV was already under the carport next to my bike. I stopped the truck in the driveway and heard Nitro pull up.

I got out and went around to Hayley's door, opening it for her and helping her down. Nitro stood next to me, eyeing the chief.

"Problem, Hawk?" he asked.

"Yeah, but it's a family issue. Unload this stuff into the house for me? I need to see if he's going to take a swing before we go inside. Don't need him breaking anything."

Hayley grabbed my hand. "I'm more worried about him breaking *you*. He looks pissed."

I approached the man with his daughter in tow. He took off his sunglasses and hung them from the collar of his tee. He looked Hayley over then craned his neck to watch the truck.

"Freya isn't here," I said.

"And where the fuck is my granddaughter?" he asked.

"Safe. The Pres is watching over her while we ran some errands."

Chief Daniels narrowed his eyes and scanned the

house, stopping on the new SUV under the carport. "Something wrong with the car I gave Hayley?"

I rubbed my ear. "About that... I think we need to talk. I haven't told your daughter yet, but I was going to as soon as we put Freya's new things away."

He moved closer, stopping in front of Hayley. "What the fuck were you thinking? Do you have any idea how freaked out your mother is? You just vanished! Someone spotted you leaving town, but we didn't know where you were going right then, or if you were coming back. The guy didn't think anything of it until I started doing my best to track you down the next day."

"Dad, you kicked me out. When I lost my job, and my apartment, I didn't think you'd let me come home. Delilah and Titan forced me to tell Hawk." She looked up at me. "He's Freya's father."

"I figured that much out already," the chief muttered. "Really? A biker?"

I straightened to my full height. I'd known a cop wouldn't be thrilled his daughter was with a biker, but it wasn't like we were low-life scum. He had to know that since I'd heard he'd worked with the Dixie Reapers before. I didn't know what his problem was. Didn't matter. He'd have to get over it. Hayley and Freya were mine, and fuck if I was letting them go.

"You want a beer?" I asked.

"I could use one. Or a dozen," he said.

I nodded, knowing exactly how he felt. We went into the house just as Nitro was leaving.

"That was the last of it, VP. I left it all in the nursery. Figured you'd put shit where you needed it."

"Thanks, Nitro. Stop by and let Beast know I have company?"

He gave me a chin lift and headed out.

I motioned for the chief to come to the kitchen, and I pulled Hayley in my wake. I settled her at the table and handed her a glass of sweet tea before taking two beers from the fridge. I gave one to the chief and kept the other for myself.

Cuddles came waddling into the kitchen, eyed his empty dish, then chittered at me. I got up and took an apple from the fridge, sliced it the way I'd seen Hayley do it, and placed the pieces in his dish. I gave him fresh water before I took my seat again.

Hayley's dad shook his head, smiling a little as he watched the raccoon. He might be pissed his daughter was with me, and that she'd left town without notice, but it was clear he adored her and even had a fondness for her strange pet.

"Now about Hayley's car... I'm hoping you were the one who put the tracking device on it," I said.

He leaned forward and braced his arms on the table. "I think you need to start at the beginning. And by that I mean, how the fuck did you meet my daughter? Because she was already pregnant when I introduced the two of you the night you caught her stalker. Why did you leave her to have a baby on her own? Seems like a shitty thing to do."

Figured he'd go right for the jugular.

"I met Hayley when she was chasing after Cuddles. He'd yanked his leash from her hand and taken off. As for the other, I wouldn't have. She never told me she was pregnant. First I heard of it was nearly a week ago. I packed up her shit and brought her home, where she belongs."

Hayley kicked my foot and glared at me.

"I'm not tracking her car," the chief said. "One of my officers saw Hayley leaving town with bikers. Took them a day or two to remember your cut said Reckless

Kings MC. Otherwise, I'd have been here sooner. Now, how'd you find the device?"

"I had someone clear out her car while we shopped for a new one. Got a call they found a tracking device and... someone hid drugs in her car. A lot of them."

The muscle in his cheek tightened and his lips thinned. Yeah, he was pissed. So was I. Whoever put that shit in her car needed to fucking die. Although, I didn't think a cop would let me murder the guy responsible. He'd probably want to lock them up, except a drug charge wouldn't exactly give them life behind bars, so sooner or later, they'd get out. If they blamed Hayley for their arrest, she'd be a target.

"I had drugs in my car?" she asked, turning deathly pale.

"Yeah. Hidden in your trunk under the spare, inside the back bumper, and in the wheel wells. It's a lot. If you'd have gotten pulled over and a cop had seen it, you'd have been booked for possession with intent to distribute," I said.

Chief Daniels arched an eyebrow at me.

"All right, maybe not back in your hometown because of who your dad is, but once you left? All bets were off."

"Who would do that?" she asked. "When would they have done it?"

"Baby girl, you weren't in your car or have it within sight at all times," her dad said. "I need to know where your car was located the times someone might have had access."

"To the trunk?" she asked. "I always kept it locked. The only person who ever had the key to it, other than you, was... the mechanic."

The chief leaned back in his seat. "Lance

Gilbert?"

"No. I mean, yes. He worked on it several times, but once his son James hired me, I let his garage do any maintenance on it. After I started working at the garage, the car needed an oil change. I had a flat tire they patched another day. Then it wouldn't start one time after I'd gotten to work. I don't remember what they had to do to it." She sucked her lips into her mouth and shoved her hands between her thighs, rocking back and forth. "It couldn't be James. Right? He seemed so nice."

"How many people worked for him other than you?" I asked.

She shrugged a shoulder. "I think two or three guys either ran the tow truck or worked in the bays. He had someone leave while I was there. A new guy started about two months before I lost my job."

"I need his name," her dad said.

"I don't know. It started with an S. Sam? Saul? You'd have to ask James."

"I'll do that," her dad said. "And then we're going to discuss you running off without even telling your mother."

He pulled out his phone and made a call. I reached over and tugged Hayley's hands free, lacing our fingers together. Between her dad, the Dixie Reapers, and the Reckless Kings, we'd figure out who'd put the drugs in her car, who was keeping tabs on her location, and we'd put a stop to them. I didn't think we'd be lucky enough it would be the same person, but I could hope.

* * *

Hayley

I'd disappointed my dad and hurt my mom. I felt

horrible about it. I should have called before I left town. Or maybe I should have let them know I was losing my apartment. I'd been stubborn and refused to ask for help. To be fair, if I'd gone crawling home, I never would have seen Hawk again. He still wouldn't know about Freya, and I wouldn't be here with him right now. I'd always thought things happened for a reason, even when we didn't understand them.

Beast came over to talk to my dad and Hawk. He brought Freya home. I cleaned her up and fed her while the men dealt with the issue of the drugs in my car. She yawned and smacked her lips once her belly was full and I'd put a fresh diaper on her. I almost placed her in her crib, but my dad had never held her. He'd seen her around town, and even up close a few times. Not once had he asked to hold her. It had broken my heart.

I carried her to the kitchen and the men lowered their voices so they wouldn't wake her. I paused next to my dad's chair and held Freya out to him. His gaze locked on mine before taking her into his arms. His face softened as he looked down at her. I'd have even sworn it looked like he might cry for a brief moment, but I couldn't remember ever seeing my dad shed a tear.

"She's beautiful, Hayley. You did good."

I smiled and ran my fingers over her hair. "Thanks, Dad."

Hawk held out his hand and I went to him, letting him pull me down onto his lap. He banded an arm around my waist and kissed the side of my neck. I didn't know what to think of our relationship, but I was eager to see where things might go. He said claiming me was forever. If that was the case, we had a lifetime to figure things out.

"We aren't going to solve this today," Beast said. "Chief Daniels, why don't you spend some time with your family. Typically, we'd offer you a guest house, but having a cop around might make everyone here a bit antsy. Your kind doesn't usually like us too much."

"Understandable. But just so we're clear, I'm not here as a cop. I'm here as a father and grandfather. Not to mention I don't have jurisdiction."

Beast smiled. "In that case, you're welcome to the guest house. I'll have someone stock the kitchen, assuming you'll be here a few days."

My dad nodded. "If my daughter is all right with me staying, I'd like to remain here until we figure out who's after her. However long that takes."

"Won't the department miss you?" I asked.

"I put in for a few days off. I can request more. Let the mayor know it's a family emergency. Can't promise your mom won't try to drive here. I damn near had to cuff her just to get her to remain behind."

I laughed and shook my head. It didn't surprise me. My mom let my dad think he was getting his way, but often she did her own thing anyway. Which meant she was probably already on her way here.

"Then it's settled," Beast said. "I'll have the kitchen stocked, and make sure you have anything else you might need. Hawk can show you where it is when you're ready to retire for the night."

My dad shook Beast's hand and thanked him. The big Pres walked out with one last look at Freya. It seemed my daughter was going to wrap everyone around her little finger.

"While I'm sure Hayley would like to cook for you, I say we order something. If it can't be delivered, I can have someone pick it up," Hawk said. "It will give the two of you more time together."

My dad glared at him. "I'll have plenty of time for her, and for you. The asshole who knocked up my baby girl and left her."

"Dad, stop." I placed a hand on his shoulder. "It's not Hawk's fault. Remember what I told you before. It takes two people to make a baby, and he didn't know about Freya. I never told him."

"And why is that?" my dad asked.

"Because she thought I wouldn't want a family," Hawk said. "She was wrong, by the way."

"You clearly already knew her the night you caught her stalker. Is that why you were in town? Because of Hayley?" my dad asked.

Hawk nodded. "I heard she was in trouble and I wanted to help. I'd hoped she might want to see me again, but she acted like she'd never met me. I waited all night, thinking she might come to the clubhouse. She never showed, so I left at first light."

"I tried to go see you the next morning. I was too late," I said.

"The two of you are clearly together now. This isn't a temporary thing, is it?" my dad asked.

"No, sir. She's here to stay," Hawk said.

My dad looked like he might take a swing at Hawk.

"Let's get one thing straight. I'm not a 'sir' to you. You don't look that much younger than me. Exactly how old are you, Hawk?" he asked.

Oh hell. This wasn't going to go over well. Not even a little.

"I'm forty. Before you say anything, I know I'm a lot older than Hayley, but it doesn't matter to me. I care about her. She's beautiful, kind, and absolutely amazing. And our daughter is perfect," Hawk said. "The raccoon is even growing on me."

"I'm fifty-three," my dad said. "I guess you can call me sir if you insist."

"Dad, you know you can't say anything about the age difference between me and Hawk. You and Mom aren't exactly the same age. The two of you have a happy marriage. There's no reason Hawk and I can't be happy together. You always said age was just a number."

"It is," my dad said. "But I have the right to change my mind when it comes to my daughter seeing someone a lot older than her."

I tapped my chin. "What's that called again? Oh yeah, it makes you a *hypocrite*!"

"Keep sassing me. I can still put you over my knee," my dad groused.

"Nope. That would be my job now," Hawk said.

My cheeks burned and I took Freya, rushing from the room. I wasn't about to sit around and discuss Hawk giving me a spanking. Not in front of my dad of all people. What the hell was wrong with the two of them?

Cuddles climbed my dad, begging to be held. Nothing melted my heart quite as much as seeing my tough father holding my raccoon. Even when Cuddles had been small, my dad would walk around the house, cradling him like a baby. He'd never let anyone see that side of him outside our house, so I cherished those memories. The fact he was letting Hawk see him like this told me he'd accepted our relationship, no matter how much huffing and puffing he was doing.

The rest of the night went relatively smoothly. We ate, laughed over something stupid my brother had done, and my dad left for the guest house close to midnight. After such a long day, I wanted a shower before bed. While Hawk showed my dad where he'd be staying, I stripped out of my clothes and stepped under the hot spray.

I washed my hair and soaped my body, letting the water pound my neck and shoulders. I'd been so tense lately. The hot bath Hawk had fixed for me that first night had helped a lot, but today had been too stressful by far.

I'd enjoyed the conversations I'd had with Hawk the last several days. We had completely different taste in music and movies. For every action flick he'd asked me to watch, he'd willingly sat through a musical or romantic comedy. I'd discovered we both liked to read, even though we didn't like the same books. There were times I wasn't sure how things would work between us. I'd always heard opposites attracted, and that seemed to be the case with us. I hoped we weren't heading for a big disaster down the road. Then he'd say or do something that made me laugh or feel all warm inside, and I'd know that we were going to be just fine.

I heard the shower door open. Hawk's scent teased my nose and I smiled as he placed his hands on my waist. He kissed my shoulder, then the side of my neck. Every nerve ending lit up. My nipples pebbled and I knew I wanted his hands on me. The way he'd teased me at the baby store, I'd almost begged him to make me come in the car.

"Couldn't resist. Is this okay?" he asked.

The tension I'd felt slowly ebbed. When he touched me, it was like the world fell away. Even if he only held my hand, it always made me feel better. It was like magic. Or maybe it was something more. Like love. I'd read plenty of books about love at first sight. Until Hawk, I hadn't believed in fairy tales. When he'd come to bring me here, to claim me and our daughter, it was both terrifying and exciting.

"More than. I'm tired of waiting. It's not like we haven't slept together before. We made a baby!" And yeah, Freya was a handful, and it would be better to wait. I knew that. But I wanted to feel closer to him. No, I *needed* to.

I felt him smile against my skin. "Yeah, we did. And she's beautiful like her mom."

I turned to face him, placing my hands on his broad chest. My heart slammed against my ribs and it felt like my clit was pulsing just as hard. I'd more than healed since having Freya. From what I'd read, it wouldn't hurt this time. Even before, it had only been a brief flash of pain and then nothing but pleasure. I'd been sore as hell the next two days, but it had been worth it. If I'd had the guts to seek him out the next day and we'd gone for round two, I think I'd have been begging him for more, regardless of how tender I'd been between my legs.

"Touch me, Alex. Please. I've dreamed of this moment for so long. It feels like it's been forever."

"Because it has."

He backed me against the tiled wall and kissed me long and deep. My knees went weak as I clung to him. His hold tightened on me and I felt the hard length of his cock. I worked my hand between our bodies and wrapped my fingers around him. He groaned and I felt a shudder run through him.

"I wanted to take my time with you. I'd planned to seduce you and spend all night making you come over and over." He placed his forehead against mine. "I didn't count on needing you so damn much. One touch and I'm about ready to come all over your hand."

"I don't need a seduction, Alex. Just you."

He kissed me again, his tongue slipping between my lips. It felt like I was floating on a cloud. He lifted my leg over his hip, and I curled it around him. He placed the head of his cock against me and slowly pushed inside me. I cried out, my fingers digging into his shoulders. He froze, breathing heavy.

"Don't stop, Alex."

He thrust deep, giving me every inch. It burned as I stretched to take him.

"Fuck, Hayley. I can't hold back. If you don't want this, if you've changed your mind, say it now."

"I won't break."

It was all he needed to hear. He sounded like a savage beast as he fucked me. My ass slapped against the wall with every thrust of his cock and pleasure rolled over me in waves. He somehow managed to brush my clit with every stroke, and I knew I wouldn't last. He thought he couldn't hold back? I was seconds from coming and he'd barely gotten inside me. I screamed out his name as I came so hard I nearly blacked out. I felt the heat of his release, and then we were suddenly on the floor of the shower. Hawk leaned against the wall and placed me on his lap.

"That was…"

"Wonderful?"

"I was going to say too short." He moved my hair off my face and kissed me softly. "Let me catch my breath and maybe we can try again. In a bed this time."

"If you make it any better, I may not survive."

He smiled and hugged me tight. "You're good for my ego, baby."

"I don't think you need your ego stroked."

"Maybe not." He winked. "But you can stroke my cock anytime you want."

I giggled and smacked him on the shoulder. He

was terrible, but in the best way.

"Can you come for me again?" he asked.

My breath caught and I nodded. Hawk slid his hand down my belly and between my legs. He parted the lips of my pussy and rubbed my clit. His strokes were so achingly slow and light I thought I might lose my mind. I arched my back, silently asking for more.

He curved his other arm around me more and reached up to cup my breast. He brushed his thumb over my nipples, and I couldn't hold back my whimper. It felt good. Almost too good. He gave the hard tip a slight tug as he pressed his fingers tighter against my clit and it felt like fireworks went off. I came, bucking against his hand. I never wanted the sensations to end and I babbled incoherently. Hawk didn't stop. He played with me until I'd come twice more. Only when I knew nothing other than his cock would satisfy me did I tell him I'd had enough.

Being in his arms felt so right. It was like I was finally where I belonged. Now that Hawk was mine, and I was his, I refused to let anything come between us. I hoped they found the person who'd tampered with my car and put an end to it all. I was tired of people doing stupid things, tired of feeling like I needed to have eyes in the back of my head. All I wanted was to have my happily-ever-after. That wasn't too much to ask, was it? I might not be a princess, but Hawk was still my Prince Charming.

Just with biker boots and a dirty mouth.

And I wouldn't have it any other way.

Chapter Nine

Hawk

Beast had called the officers into Church, along with Chief Daniels. He'd put Torch on speaker so we could all hear what the other club's President had discovered so far. Shield hadn't had much luck with the tracking device. It seemed to be the sort anyone could purchase if they knew where to go and was too common to trace it back to a shop. Which left us with trying to figure out why the drugs had been placed in Hayley's car, and who had done it.

"I talked to James Gilbert," Torch said. "The man Hayley tried to remember is Seb Martin."

"What the fuck kind of name is Seb?" I asked.

"A made-up one," Torch said. "From what Wire and Lavender have dug up, the man was on the run and changed his name four times. We think the drugs in Hayley's car are from a batch that was stolen from the Bartinelli Family about a year ago."

"Again I say… what the fuck?" I looked around the table, seeing the same confusion on everyone's face that I was feeling. "So this guy stole the drugs from the Bartinellis and hid them in Hayley's car because…"

"Opportunity," Torch said. "We assume at any rate. We can't find the guy. He's vanished."

"Thought Wire was the best," I said.

Beast shot me a look that clearly said *shut the fuck up*. I shrugged my shoulder.

"He is," Venom said, joining the conversation. "All the officers are present, by the way."

"Same here," Beast said. "As well as Chief Daniels."

"Wire said Seb dropped off the grid. Didn't even clean out his bank account. If he's using another ID, he must have bought a much better one than all the others. Personally, I think it's more likely the Bartinellis caught up to him and he's in a shallow grave somewhere," Tank said.

"Can you see if there's movement in their organization?" Forge asked. "Are they mobilizing or possibly heading this way? If they want their drugs, they'll be coming for Hayley. If Seb was smart, he'd have sent them after her to deflect attention from himself."

"So we give them the drugs," Beast said.

Chief Daniels growled. "You're just going to give drugs to a known crime family? You know they'll end up in the hands of children. People will die. Do you want that on your conscience? Or do you just not have one?"

Ouch. I waited to see what the Pres would do. On the one hand, he didn't need the chief making him look bad. On the other… Well, I knew Beast didn't want kids to get those drugs either, but Hayley was family now and he'd do anything to protect her.

"I didn't say we'd let them *keep* the drugs, fucker." Beast glared at the chief. "We hand them over, and when they're outside our territory, we arrange for a little accident. But we need to wait until they're far enough away they won't tie it back to us. The last thing we need is them coming for Hayley again. The entire point is to make sure she and Freya are off their radar."

The chief's shoulders sagged. "You're right. Sorry. Do whatever you have to. Hayley is what's important right now. If those drugs end up on the streets, we'll just have to work hard to round them up."

"All right, so the plan for now is to let the Bartinellis know we ran across their missing drugs, and they're welcome to them. I want the drop away from the clubhouse," Beast said. "I'm not putting our women and kids in danger."

"I'm sure you've already thought of this, but in regards to the tracker, could it have been that asshole who'd been stalking her?" Tank asked. "If he kept leaving shit on her car, that meant he knew where he could find her at any time. Right?"

Shit. He was right.

"It's possible," the chief said. "He never would give us much of anything. It was a damn miracle he got sentenced at all. I half expected him to end up locked in a psych ward somewhere. Fucker was nuts."

"The tracker was disabled," Forge said. "Whoever was keeping tabs on Hayley can't do it anymore, assuming it's not the guy in prison. Plus she has a new vehicle. I think we need to focus on the drugs. And see if we can figure out what happened to Seb. If he's still alive, he could still come for Hayley, not knowing we don't have the drugs anymore."

"What if we used the car as bait?" I asked. "No one knows we have the drugs. If this Seb person is still around, he could believe the drugs are still stashed in Hayley's car. And he'll want them back."

"You think he noticed the tracking device was disabled?" Forge asked.

"It's possible. Or maybe he thinks it's malfunctioning. We won't know if we don't try," I said. "I'd rather offer up the car as bait than my woman."

"You think he knows she's here?" Beast asked.

"If he put the tracker on her car, yes. Or if he overheard anyone around town say Hayley left with us." I leaned back in my seat. "The guy is going to be desperate, if he's still breathing. Let's make him think he can have what he wants."

"Forge, work with the chief. I want men watching that car so we can nab anyone who comes for the drugs. And, Chief, you're definitely not a cop right now. We get this asshole, he's not going to jail. Not until we get what we need from him. After that, I say we let the Bartinellis have him." Beast slammed his fist on the table. "Church dismissed. Get the fuck out."

He took his phone off speaker and picked it up. I figured he wanted to talk to Torch about Lyssa and Madison. I left the chief with Forge to go home to Hayley and Freya. They'd both been sleeping when I left the house. It might have been my imagination, but I could have sworn Freya had been a lot quieter the last two days. She still had some crying fits. The last few hadn't been too bad, and she'd been easily soothed. From what Hayley had explained, the purple crying only lasted so long. Maybe it was nearly over.

I knew Hayley would be grateful. She'd been able to sleep a decent amount the last few nights. Well, except last night. I grinned thinking about all the times I'd made her beg for more. I hadn't been able to fuck a woman four times in a row in a damn long time, but Hayley made me feel a lot younger. With her, it seemed I could go all night.

And we hadn't used protection.

It was a gamble. She didn't want another baby so soon after Freya, and I could understand why. If she ended up pregnant, I'd take it as a sign we were just meant to have another kid right now. We'd talked after the shower last night and agreed we didn't want to use condoms. Until we heard back from the doctor, we wouldn't know what other options we had.

I left the clubhouse and headed for my bike. A familiar car pulled to a stop next to me and the window rolled down. Lia smiled, tossing her blonde hair over her shoulder.

"Hey, handsome. Haven't seen you around here lately."

"Not now, Lia." Or ever. I'd fucked her once, and she'd relentlessly pursued me ever since. Some women needed warning labels. Hers would read *clingy* or *desperate*. Neither was attractive. Not for me.

"You seem tense." She got out of the car and placed her hand on my arm. "I can help with that. You know I can."

I tried to shake her off, but she held on tight. "Lia, let the fuck go. I didn't say you could touch me."

She stuck her lower lip out, probably think it was cute. It wasn't. "Hawk, we were so good together. I'd be the perfect old lady for you, and you know it."

"Sorry, Lia. I'm a one-woman man, and since I already have an old lady, you'll have to bug the shit out of someone else."

She took a step back and released me. "What?"

"You fucking heard me." I got in her face. "You don't touch me. Don't come on to me. Don't even speak to me. Understood?"

She nodded quickly and took another step away from me. Good. I didn't have time for her bullshit, and the last thing I wanted was Hayley seeing some bitch pawing at me. We were in a good place right now, and I wanted to keep it that way.

I turned to get on my bike and stopped. Shit. A very familiar blue SUV had somehow managed to pull up on the other side of my Harley without me even hearing the damn thing. Hayley got out and stared at me and Lia before opening the back door. She reached in and I knew she was getting Freya. With our daughter clutched in her arms, she walked over to me.

"She wanted to see her daddy," Hayley said. "We didn't think you'd be gone so long. Is my dad here too?"

"He's still inside." I reached for Freya and held her against my chest before tugging Hayley to my side and kissing her. "Missed you, baby. Both of you."

Hayley peered over at Lia and whispered, a little too loudly, "Is that one of those club girls?"

I closed my eyes and shook my head, fighting back a smile. "Yeah, it is. No fucking clue why Lia is here right now. Not my problem."

"Is it okay I came to find you?" Hayley asked softly.

"Baby, look at me." Her gaze clashed with mine and held. "You need me, or just want to give me a hug, you come find me. I don't give a shit where I am. Only place you aren't allowed is in Church. But you could always hang out at the bar and wait for me."

"Jesus, Hawk. That's your old lady? She looks like a child," Lia said.

I turned to face her, handing Freya to Hayley. I'd never struck a woman before, but I was about to. This bitch had overstepped.

I backhanded her, knocking her to the ground. "That was the only warning you'll get from me."

"You hit women often?" the chief said as he came outside.

Great. Of course he'd see me hit the bitch.

"Only ones who disrespect my woman. She came onto me. Touched me. I told her to back the fuck off. Then she decided to verbally attack Hayley. She's crossed a line." I glared at her. "You have thirty seconds to get your ass back in your car and leave. Don't ever come back, you hear me?"

She nodded and scrambled into her car, making

the tires spin as she took off for the gate. After she shot through it, I made sure Kye knew she wasn't welcome back, then sent off a text to the entire damn club so they'd know too. I wasn't putting up with that bullshit.

"Right. So now that the drama is over, Forge and I have a plan," Chief Daniels said. "I'd rather you stay here with the girls. Keep them safe. I promised to go as support and let your club handle everything."

"Does that mean it's almost over?" Hayley asked.

Her dad nodded. "If everything goes according to plan, yes. We should be back in time for lunch."

"Have you talked to Mom?" she asked.

"I did." His lips pressed together. "I also told her to turn her ass around and go right back home or she'd up in the middle of some dangerous shit. Thankfully, she listened. And before you ask, yes, I'm sure. I made her turn on the GPS on her phone. I can see exactly where she is."

Hayley laughed. "Dad, that's horrible."

"No, it's not. I need her to be safe. She understands, but she wants to see you soon."

"I'll bring Hayley for a visit," I said. "You have my word."

The chief shook his head. "Never thought I'd be taking the word of a biker. Of course, I hadn't thought I'd be calling one family either. You take care of my girl, keep her safe, and make sure she knows she's loved. That's all I can ask of you."

Loved? The look in his eyes said he saw far more than I'd have liked. Yeah, I loved her, but I hadn't told her yet. Maybe it was time.

I helped Hayley in the car and put Freya in her infant seat, then I followed them home. I didn't like sitting on the sidelines while there was a threat to my family. It was hard to let everyone else keep Hayley safe. As I watched her lift Freya from the back of the SUV, I realized they were right to have me stay here. My girls needed me.

Waiting to hear back wasn't the easiest thing. Even with Hayley trying to distract me, I kept an eye on the phone, waiting for a text or call. Anything to say they'd caught the guy. When it finally chimed with a text from Forge, my heart kicked in my chest.

He's here. You have ten minutes.

"Baby, stay here and lock the door. I'll be back soon."

I dashed out the door before she could stop me, jumped on my Harley, and headed for the back of the property. I knew it's where they'd have taken him. Far enough, Hayley wouldn't hear the man scream. Or anyone else for that matter.

I didn't know what I'd expected, but the scrawny man tied to a chair wasn't it. He looked strung out and half starved. This was the idiot who'd put Hayley in danger?

"He had the tracker on the car," Forge said. "We reactivated it after we moved the vehicle. He came to it like a fly to honey."

"He say anything?" I asked.

"Claims he stashed the drugs with the intention of getting them when he thought it was safe. He didn't count on Hayley losing her job, much less leaving town. Sent him into a bit of a panic," Forge said.

"The Bartinellis want their drugs," I said. "You put my woman and daughter in danger because you're a fucking coward."

"Don't matter. You're going to kill me anyway," he said, his words slurring.

"No. I won't. I'm going to make you bleed and *wish* you were dead, but I'm going to leave the killing blow to the Bartinellis."

He paled and started pleading. I didn't give a shit. Hayley could have been killed if the Bartinellis discovered she had their drugs. They wouldn't have cared if she knew about them or not.

I pulled the knife from my boot, the same one I'd used to capture the asshole who'd been stalking Hayley. I slammed it into Seb's thigh. He screamed and thrashed. I pulled the blade free before stabbing the other leg. I left shallow cuts along his chest and torso and sliced his cheek all the way down to his jaw. I'd have tortured him for hours if I'd been given the time.

"Hawk, we need to get him to the exchange location," Forge said. "Can't do that if you keep going. He won't be bothering Hayley anymore. Your family is safe."

I sank my knife into both arms and slashed the backs of his hands before I took a step back. With a nod, I let Forge untie him and take him away. I had blood on my hands and splattered on my jeans. I didn't want to go home like this. If Hayley saw me with blood on me…

I went to Beast's house and knocked on the door. Lyssa answered, took one look at me, and waved me inside. "You certainly can't let her see you like that. You look like you've been on a murder spree."

"That's why I didn't go home and came here," I said.

"Beast's clothes won't fit you, but you can't exactly be picky right now."

"I just need to wash the blood off my skin. Then I need you to call Hayley, find a way to lure her to the backyard, so I can slip through the house and get out of these clothes."

Lyssa sighed. "Fine. I'll do it."

I kissed her cheek. "Thanks, Lyssa. You're one in a million."

"Yeah, yeah. Go wash and get out of my house." She smiled to soften her words.

I hadn't gotten the vengeance I wanted for my family, but it would have to do. As long as Seb and the Bartinellis wouldn't be an issue anymore, I'd have to be content with the blood I drew. I hoped giving a bloody and broken Seb to the Bartinellis would send a message. I wouldn't tolerate anyone coming for my family, no matter how well connected they were. Hayley was a no-fly zone and the surest way to end up in an unmarked grave. I wouldn't hesitate to defend my woman and kid, no matter how many bodies started piling up.

* * *

Hayley

I saw Lyssa's name pop up on my phone. Hawk had programmed the entire club in so I could reach someone in the case of an emergency. Except, I didn't want to answer. The doctor's office had placed me on hold three minutes ago and I wasn't about to risk not speaking to them. The phone stopped beeping only for her to call again almost immediately.

I rubbed at my forehead, fighting back a headache.

"Miss Daniels," said a woman when the elevator music finally stopped. "We have your lab results. Are you able to discuss them with the doctor now?"

"Yes! Please."

"Just a moment."

Cuddles chased after a cat toy someone had brought to the house for him. The bell jingled as he rolled the ball across the floor, and I narrowed my gaze at him. Why did he have to choose now to do something so noisy?

They put me on hold again, but Dr. Kestral picked up right away.

"Hayley, I got your bloodwork back. You're anemic, which we can fix with some iron pills and a change in your diet. At least, that's where we're going to start. I have Hawk's email address. I'm going to send over the dosage I want you to take, how often, and the suggested dietary changes. You need to start it as soon as possible, and I want you back in once a week for us to take more blood."

I winced. "Really? Once a week?"

"Until it seems to be improving. Afterward, we won't need to check it so often."

The front door open and I spun to see Hawk come in with blood covering his jeans. I gasped and nearly dropped the phone. He shook his head and held up a hand, motioning for me to stay put as he rushed past me. I hoped like hell he was going to shower, and then explain what had happened to him.

"Dr. Kestral, I needed to ask you about birth control. We don't want to use condoms and haven't used anything so far. There's a chance I could already be pregnant, but I'm hoping not. Is there something safe to take while I'm nursing?"

"There are actually several options. An IUD, the shot, or the mini-pill. The mini-pill would be the safest if you think you could be pregnant. You said your last period was three weeks ago. So we could test you after your first missed period."

"Thank you, Dr. Kestral."

"If you do go on the pill, it doesn't take effect immediately. You'd still need to use something else to prevent pregnancy, like condoms."

Right. The one thing Hawk didn't want to use. I didn't either really. I liked feeling him inside me. I didn't know firsthand what it would be like to have a piece of latex between us, but I'd heard some women could tell the difference. Others didn't seem to care one way or another.

After the call ended, I went to find Hawk. He'd just gotten out of the shower when I walked in. I admired the way the water dripped down his torso, also noting there weren't any cuts. He'd scrubbed the blood off him and looked delicious. I sank my teeth into my bottom lip and leaned closer. I licked off a water droplet, flicking my tongue over his nipple.

He hissed in a breath and threaded his fingers in my hair, holding me in place. I did it again before sucking it into my mouth.

"Fuck! Please tell me Freya is sleeping and the house is otherwise empty," he said.

"We're alone and she's asleep."

He spun me toward the bathroom counter and started yanking off my clothes. He pushed me down over the counter and kicked my feet apart. I watched in the mirror as he gripped my hips and thrust inside me. My breasts bounced as he fucked me, taking what he needed. It was the hottest thing I'd ever seen, or done. My pussy burned and stretched, but the slight tinge of pain only seemed to heighten my pleasure. I might regret it later and need to soak for a bit. Right now, all I could think about was how incredible he made me feel.

He released my right hip and cupped my breast with his hand. My nipples hardened even more. It was almost embarrassing, how quickly my body responded to his touch.

"So fucking beautiful," he said. He pinched and

tugged on my nipple as he drove into me, the force pushing me up onto my toes. I wanted more. Needed... something. I didn't even know what to ask for. "Tell me you want it, Hayley. Beg me for it."

"Please, Alex. I want to come."

"Play with your clit, baby. Come on my cock. Show me how much you love having me inside you."

I moaned as I did what he said. It only took a few swipes of my fingers before I was coming. Hawk growled and took me harder and faster until I felt the hot spurts of his release.

"Well, I guess I learned something new," I said, as I tried to catch my breath.

"And what's that?"

"If I want you to let go and take me like a savage, all I have to do is lick your nipple."

He laughed and pulled out, swatting my ass. "Next time lick my cock and see what happens."

My lips lifted in a smile. "I just might do that."

He pulled me into his arms and kissed me. I could feel him getting hard again. He lifted me onto the counter before sliding inside me again. This time he took me slow, and gentle. He was tender and loving. It brought tears to my eyes when we came at the same time.

"I love you, Alex."

"Love you too, Hayley. I should have told you sooner."

"You told me now." I kissed him. "That's all that matters."

"Let's get cleaned up and you can tell me who you were talking to when I came home."

Crap. So much for birth control.

"Well, it was Dr. Kestral. He's sending you an email. I asked about birth control, and he said there were options… if I wasn't pregnant." I looked down where we were still joined. "If we keep this up, I'll be knocked up again."

He cupped my cheek and kissed me fiercely. "I'd fucking love to see you pregnant."

I'd thought I needed to wait longer. That was before I'd come here with Hawk. Before I'd realized I loved him. Having a second baby didn't seem so scary anymore. I knew Hawk would be here to support me, and so would the club. I wouldn't have to do it on my own.

"Then let's forget the birth control and just see what happens."

"You mean it?" he asked.

"Yeah."

He carried me to the bedroom and laid me out on the bed. His gaze raked over me, making me feel all hot and achy.

"How brave are you, baby?" he asked.

"Why?"

"I want to try something. I think you'll like it, but if you don't I'll stop."

I trusted Hawk with my life. I gave him a nod to let him know it was okay. My body was strung tight as I waited to see what he'd do. He walked to the closet and pulled down a box. It was still taped shut and I remembered it arriving two days after he'd brought me here. I didn't know what was inside, and I strained my neck to try and see as he ripped the tape off the box.

He pulled out a few packages and set them on the bed. My eyes went wide when I realized he'd bought sex toys. I glanced from them to Hawk and saw he was smirking at me.

"God, I love the way you blush, baby. So innocent, yet not. You okay trying any of these?" he asked. Then he picked up something and tossed it aside. "Not those. No nipple clamps until you're finished nursing."

Nipple clamps? What had I gotten myself into? I pressed my thighs together and realized the thought of him using any of this stuff on me had me so turned-on I'd do just about anything he said.

"I trust you, Alex. I know you won't hurt me."

He leaned down to kiss me, then nipped my jaw. When he drew back, he picked up a box and ripped it open. Whatever he'd bought, he carried into the bathroom before I got a good look. I heard the water running and he came back. There was a bottle of something in one hand and the toy in the other. When I saw it, my heart skipped a beat.

"Uh, what exactly is that?" I asked.

"It's a vibrator," he said. He pointed to the smallest part. "This goes over your clit. Constant vibrations to drive you wild."

Okay. I could understand that much. But… it had too many extra parts.

"This one," he said, pointing to the middle protrusion, "goes in your pussy. It's curved to hit your G-spot. And the last one, goes in your ass."

I gasped and bolted upright. "What?"

He ran his hand down my arm. "Easy, Hayley. If you hate it, I'll throw the toy away. Will you at least try it? I want to make you come so hard you see stars."

Somewhat apprehensively, I lay back. Hawk spread my thighs and used the lube to slick the toy. When he'd finished, he added more of the liquid to his finger and rubbed it against my ass. I squeaked and tensed. He turned the toy on and placed one of the ends against my clit and my eyes nearly rolled back in my head. Soon, I didn't care where his finger was. I actually found myself thrusting against him, needing more.

"That's it, beautiful," he murmured.

He readjusted the toy, letting the other two parts slip inside me. He eased the toy in nice and slow, giving me time to adjust. It was almost too much. My senses were on overload as I squirmed and thrashed on the bed. I came almost immediately, and it seemed like my orgasm wouldn't stop. It was a never-ending wave of pleasure. I lost track of time and of how many times I came. All I knew was that I never wanted it to stop. It felt beyond amazing.

He stroked the toy in and out, making me scream until I went hoarse. My body shuddered and I didn't think I could possibly come anymore. Then Hawk decided to prove me wrong. He pulled the toy from my body before thrusting deep. Settling on his knees, he lifted me so that my ass was in his lap. As he held my hip and thrust, he grabbed the toy and put it against my clit again.

"Oh, God! Oh, God!" All I could do was chant and plead. I was nearly mindless from coming so much. It felt like the world shattered when I came harder than before, and I would have sworn I blacked out for a moment.

Hawk threw the toy across the bed and shifted us so that he lay over me. He powered into me, driving his cock in deep and hard. I felt the heat of his release and his body trembled as he held his weight off me.

We both panted for breath.

"I think you broke me," I said.

He grinned. "Not yet. But we have some time. I'm curious exactly how much you can come in one day."

He was going to kill me with orgasms. But what

a way to go.

Hawk ended up making love to me until Freya woke up. I came multiple times, leaving me boneless and well-sated, before he let me get dressed. I never did find out why he'd had blood on him, but I didn't care so much. I'd seen for myself the blood hadn't been his. There wasn't a scratch on him. Whatever had happened, it probably wasn't something I needed to know. I might accept he didn't always walk on the right side of the law, but I still didn't want to know the details. Probably never would.

"I have something for you," he said.

I tugged my T-shirt down over my hips and pulled my hair up into a ponytail. He took something from the closet and when he showed it to me, tears sprang to my eyes. It was a smaller version of his leather cut, but this one said *Property of Hawk* on it. I hadn't been sure how I'd feel about it. But seeing it now? I loved it and couldn't wait to put it on.

He slipped it over my shoulders and ran his fingers over the back. "Love seeing my name on you. I know you always wear your bracelet, but everyone will see this and know you're mine."

"I've been yours since the night you helped me chase after Cuddles."

He looked around. "Where exactly is your wayward pet?"

"Enjoying the catio you and my dad installed off the kitchen this morning. And I know it was both of you because my dad left a note on the counter, since you took off before I was awake. I opened the pet door you cut into the wall and he waddled right through it and hasn't come back in yet. I think he likes being out in the sun without a leash, but I know he's safe from predators and won't run off. So thank you. It was the perfect solution."

He kissed my cheek. "Anything for you, baby. The hole in the wall was the hard part. The rest was a kit we put together. I admit your dad thought of it."

"When you say anything…"

"I mean absolutely anything. As long as it's not letting you leave me. That I won't do. Not now, not ever."

"I don't want to leave, Alex. You're stuck with me."

"Then what do you want, Hayley? You seem to have something in mind."

"I have this property cut and bracelet that say I'm yours. I want you to have something that says you're mine."

He smiled. "Already ahead of you, baby. I have an appointment next week with a local tattoo shop. I'm getting your name inked on my arm."

"Where?" I asked, eyeing the ink he already had.

He turned his right arm over and showed me the blank space on his forearm. "Here. It's going to take up the entire area. I love you, Hayley, and I want the world to know it. I'm so fucking lucky you're mine. I don't know why you gave me a chance, but it was the best night of my life. One I've thought about every damn day since then."

I threw my arms around his neck and hugged him tight. I'd thought I'd never have a serious boyfriend, never be kissed, much less get to experience sex. Then I'd found Hawk and he'd changed my world. It hadn't been easy. We'd had more rough patches than smooth ones, but it was all worth it. Every tear. Every doubt. I'd do it all again if it meant I'd end up right here. In his arms. It was the only place I ever wanted to be.

I smiled, realizing I'd gotten the fairy-tale ending. I had my prince, the greatest love of all time, and an amazing life ahead of me.

I closed my eyes and sent up a silent thanks to whatever powers had stepped in and sent Hawk to me that night.

Harley Wylde

Harley Wylde is the International Bestselling Author of the Dixie Reapers MC, Devil's Boneyard MC, and Hades Abyss MC series.

When Harley's writing, her motto is the hotter the better -- off-the-charts sex, commanding men, and the women who can't deny them. If you want men who talk dirty, are sexy as hell, and take what they want, then you've come to the right place. She doesn't shy away from the dangers and nastiness in the world, bringing those realities to the pages of her books, but always gives her characters a happily-ever-after and makes sure the bad guys get what they deserve.

The times Harley isn't writing, she's thinking up naughty things to do to her husband, drinking copious amounts of Starbucks, and reading. She loves to read and devours a book a day, sometimes more. She's also fond of TV shows and movies from the 1980s, as well as paranormal shows from the 1990s to today, even though she'd much rather be reading or writing.

Harley at Changeling: changelingpress.com/harley-wylde-a-196

Changeling Press E-Books

More Sci-Fi, Fantasy, Paranormal, and BDSM adventures available in e-book format for immediate download at ChangelingPress.com -- Werewolves, Vampires, Dragons, Shapeshifters and more -- Erotic Tales from the edge of your imagination.

What are E-Books?

E-books, or electronic books, are books designed to be read in digital format -- on your desktop or laptop computer, notebook, tablet, Smart Phone, or any electronic e-book reader.

Where can I get Changeling Press E-Books?

Changeling Press e-books are available at ChangelingPress.com, Amazon, Apple Books, Barnes & Noble, and Kobo/Walmart.

ChangelingPress.com